GOD OF TRAITORS

A novel by Zdravka Evtimova

Published by BooksForABuck.com

ISBN: 1-60215-043-5
ISBN-13: 978-1-60215-043-0

This novel is also available as an eBook. Check with www.booksforabuck.com for pricing and availability.

Chapter 1

LARRY HOFFBURG thought that someone had simply pulled a dirty trick on him. Not very far from the window to the south in his office giving a magnificent view of the surrounding park someone had left a part of a Leila doll -- a little left hand of the exquisite Leila doll, which his factory produced. Larry had good reason to go off the deep end: the tiny left hand of a doll appeared in his office on three consecutive days: always at the same place, in front of the gray screen of the computer. It looked as though the plastic thing was thrown casually there, but no, now that he came to think about it he concluded that the posture of the hand was always the same. The little plastic fingers pointed directly at the body of the Chief Executive Officer and founder of the company that produced the most popular toys in half of the world.

"Who the hell brought that junk here?" Larry muttered under his breath. "Never mind. This time Adrienne Tott will get it in the neck!"

Adrienne Tott was Larry's secretary, a tall breathtaking natural blonde whom the boss trusted completely. She managed the whole administrative team; her vigilant eyes were forever on the alert and neither a living soul nor an inanimate object could wriggle its way to the company without being weighed, analyzed, torn to pieces, and assessed by her. Adrienne had been working for Toys International for eight years; legends and tales were invented in her honor and she well deserved that -- she started as an ordinary typist, unexpectedly moved up the hierarchy reaching unbelievable administrative heights. With time, she became Larry's personal advisor, Larry's secretary and consultant selecting the high ranking staff, personnel policy director, managing director, etc. She was, in short, a person without whose approval the sun simply couldn't rise and shine in the cloudless sky above the plants of Toys International. However, the left hand of the cute Leila doll appeared three times in the Chief Executive Officer's office.

In the beginning, Larry Hoffburg had not paid any attention to it. On the first day, he simply pulled a wry face and chucked it in the waste paper basket. He couldn't be sure when exactly he'd felt the pain in his left arm. Did it happen while he was having lunch with a client when Adrienne came and informed him of an urgent message about the shipments of toy guns to Europe? Or perhaps the painful tightening of the muscles of his wrist started in the late afternoon while he was enjoying a well-earned rest in the easy chair in his study at home. He could not remember. In fact, the pain went almost immediately and Larry instantly forgot all about it. But when on the following day he again caught a glimpse of the plastic hand of the doll at the same place in front of the gray computer screen-- the memory of pain had seized him and together with the memory the annoying spasm in his left wrist made him shudder. Larry's left arm went numb and he could not move it for about a minute. That, however, was not the most unpleasant thing about it. Soon the pain in the wrist turned into an enormous wave that swept over his body leaving him immobile and stiff like a corpse. Then most unexpectedly the numbness was gone simply vanishing without a trace as if it had never been there but the plastic hand of the doll remained pointing its cute pink fingers at the Chief Executive Officer.

"What was that, for God's sake?" Larry moaned in amazement grabbing the cold piece of plastic. His eyes studied carefully the small piece of the toy. There was noting peculiar about it; at first sight everything appeared to be exactly like all the billions of similar pieces that Hoffburg's plants spewed out every single day. Larry, however, had never trusted the impressions he got at first sight.

He didn't take seriously love at first sight, either. Larry was quite skeptical even about his relationship with Adrienne; a series of legends had it had that it had originated "at first sight". Before he invited Adrienne to his bedroom he had hired a detective agency of repute that worked whole-heartedly for a year and a half trying to establish what sort of a rum bird that beautiful blonde Adrienne Tott was. He knew not only the names of the people who had adopted her and the names of their fathers and grandfathers; he had flown hundreds of times over their small estate not far from the Rhine where her adoptive mother still lived. Larry had at hand the results of Adrienne's extensive medical examinations: her blood, skin, urine, fitness, personality and psychological test were carefully studied by experts; he had collected reliable data about all organs of her body and had consulted doctors of medicines on their proper functions. He had detailed information about the price of the medicines that the attractive lady had used in the past to treat some minor indisposition like the flu or ordinary colds. He had familiarized himself painstakingly with her relationships with other men before he met her.

Of course, Adrienne enjoyed great attention on the part of male individuals and that was not hard to explain. It was enough to have a look at her photograph for only a second. Nevertheless, the guys who had worked on the fair lady's CV with respect to her love conquests had not discovered a single long-standing relationship; the most common were the whirlwind romances that lasted no more than three or four months. It was invariably Adrienne who broke with the man, but she had lived with Larry for eight years and so far had shown no signs of intending to leave him.

It was not an accident that Larry, pressing the pink plastic hand of the doll with his fingers, devoted ten minutes of his busy working schedule to ruminations about his attractive secretary. Adrienne Tott was the only person in Toys International who had access to that office with the gray easy chairs, the computer and the two prickly cacti - the only representatives of animate nature, which Larry had admitted into the immediate vicinity of his body. He could not stand animals and plants; they most often carried microbes, viruses and harmful strains of bacteria, but the cactuses They were the only favorites of Larry's, his life turned into a feast whenever tiny rosy-violet blossoms came out on their bumpy stooping backs. Then he was in the best of moods. Now the cactuses had again prepared for their rosy fiesta, but only a foot or two behind them the plastic hand of the Leila doll lay.

The hand of the doll, which he found for the second time on his desk, was subjected to most thorough tests in the laboratories of Toys International plants. Larry himself had watched each separate process of the overall analysis and had studied carefully the results. He held a Ph.D. degree in inorganic synthesis but the lengthy chemical formulas that appeared on the monitors did not arouse the slightest suspicion that something was wrong. The plastic hand he had found in his office was nothing more than a plastic hand -- a piece of one of Leila dolls with funny wide open eyes that made little girls shed passionate tears making their mothers buy them from the local department stores. In fact, Leila dolls turned out to be very lucrative invention for Toys International.

The third time he found a Leila doll hand, the pain exploded in Larry Hoffburg's wrist without its preliminary spasm. It was so excruciating that at the very first instant he lost his balance. Then he attempted to walk and to his amazement made it -- he moved the small of his back slightly, then bent forward to the left, jerked his head in the direction of the door, and stretched out his right hand. Except for his left hand, his body obeyed him. Even his left shoulder carried out his commands. He tried to bend his left arm and was again successful. The pain had dug an agonizing maze in his wrist, in the palm and fingers - exactly the items of the pink plastic piece, which lay in front of his computer.

"It's not only an absurd practical joke!" Larry Hoffburg whispered. "Adrienne must really get it in the neck!"

Now he was absolutely sure. The doors of his office admitted only two persons: Larry Hoffburg and Adrienne Tott. Only they possessed a smart card that opened the series of five consecutive doors. Actually, Larry had always supported the opinion that inaccessibility of this kind was not necessary - his factories produced only toys after all, not nuclear weapons.

"The office of the owner is a matter of prestige the more inaccessible the Chief Executive Officer the greater the probability that the rabble would proclaim him as the next god of success," little Adrienne had said. And you are a god, dearest, didn't you know that?"

Perhaps it was true that his subordinates and most of the thousands of employees earning a living in his factories thought he was a god. He worked his way up from scratch -- a wretched petty troubleshooter repairing dumped electrical appliances; that's what he had been. Years ago he blushed with shame whenever he had to answer how much money he made a year. Larry had always dreamt of much, much money. So much that even the factories he owed and the billions of dollars he made now seemed to be a funny child's play. A man of much money should possess a deluxe personal office. A place in which only the presence of the two cactuses and, from time to time, the sojourn of the blonde fairy Adrienne were allowed; Adrienne who in all probability had smuggled the plastic hand of the doll into his office. Larry himself had never brought a similar piece of plastic there.

Was it possible? Adrienne? This thought was quite unpleasant and he tried to drive it away. Well, if Larry had to be precise, the name of the charming blonde enchantress was not Adrienne. He had chosen it for her because he could not stand her real name Rosalind. The crude clanking sounds of Rosalind did not become the exquisite blue-eyed girl. Whenever Larry heard somebody shout "Rosalind!" he inevitably imagined a fat harridan on the verge of kicking up a row. Adrienne sounded soft and enticing like a whisper of a woman in love at the end of summer; that name reminded him of a Roman empress a golden halo of magic and power around her head. The pain in his left hand began to wear off. Still, it was the flaxen-haired siren for whom Hoffburg fought and transformed into a glamorous business tycoon; it was she that had sneaked the doll's hand into his office. The damned piece of plastic turned the wrist of his left hand into an enormous iceberg of freezing pain. Adrienne but why should she do that? And how, for God's sake, could the darned thing influence him? Wasn't that absolutely absurd

Larry Hoffburg's name had turned into a powerful myth not only for the people who worked in his factories. Young and old mentioned it in almost reverential tones in all European cities where Toys International had subsidiaries. Popular legend had it that the humble troubleshooter scratching a living repairing rusty boilers and electric cookers was a great charmer. He had set his heart on winning a fair lady - Jennifer, the last daughter of an ancient, but impoverished aristocratic family. According to the myth, Larry could not derive substantial benefit from his marriage to the aforesaid gentlewoman, but all the same he tied the nuptial knot because he was a noble young man. The myth invariably underlined Larry's heart of gold but overlooked the fact that gentle Jennifer was a bloated mass of fat, so big that even her blue eyes prone to often shed tears were hardly visible on a flat large face that resembled a piece of jelly and ice-cream cake.

The popular fairy tale abounded in details about how Larry, on the second day of his married life, settled down to business transforming the old castle smelling discreetly of mould into a major tourist attraction. He installed a couple of mechanical vampires in the drowsy uninhabited rooms; electronic reptiles crawled in the interminable vaulted cellars; irresistible beauties with firm shapely breasts were rescued on every alternate Sunday by noble knights provided the tourist paid a reasonable $250 fee. Adrienne, Adrienne, the woman he had admitted to his office and his bed, the fairy who had always been the brains of their relationship, he had to give her that. He stated explicitly from the very beginning: the former typist Rosalind should cherish no hopes that she would ever become Mrs. Hoffburg. Larry would never divorce his wedded wife. He had simply given Adrienne chances to profit by living with him, she had unlimited funds at her disposal, people shuddered at the thought of her fragile flitting shadow.

At a later stage, she could ensnare another big shot, hopefully as big as the famous producer of toys Larry Hoffburg. At present he wanted her only for himself and isolated her meticulously from his influential friends, all of them respected gentlemen belonging to the world of high finance. Was that the reason, which had enraged her? Did his behavior goad beautiful Adrienne into planting the doll's hand in his office?

For a split second, Larry Hoffburg froze in his tracks. The fingers of his left hand had fumbled by chance in his jacket pocket where he usually kept his handkerchief. He needed it at that very moment; the thought of Adrienne had embarrassed him and his forehead was clammy with perspiration. His fingers pressed an exquisite leg of a Leila doll wearing a cute gray jack-boot.

Larry Hoffburg knew subconsciously what would come next. An avalanche of fear clogged his throat and grew uncontrollable turning into panic. The familiar spasm bit his right ankle. A minute after that the sharp pain stabbed him, relentless, dispassionate like death itself. Somebody had slipped the doll's leg into his jacket pocket. He had to remember whom he had met in the morning, he simply had to by all means! He thought hard: it was Wednesday - the only day of the week when he had breakfast with his wife Jennifer. But that day he had not visited Jennifer - of late her enormous fat face made him feel too irritable. He could imagine his wife spreading the dramatic news that Larry had neglected her on the only day he had agreed to dedicate an hour of his precious time to her. Well, he preferred the wry faces of all the other relatives to Jennifer's enormous cheeks, which reminded him of a gammon steak. So, he had met no one in the morning. No one approached him because this morning Larry did not feel like having breakfast. What should his conclusion be then?

He suddenly remembered: on his way to the office, he had stopped for a minute to kiss Adrienne. Again Adrienne She was the only person that could plant the doll's leg in his pocket. He had to summon her right away.

He tried to remember what, in Adrienne, had attracted him so much.

He was again startled by memory of how rapidly the young woman appeared before his eyes. He had forbidden himself many times to steal admiring glances at her slim body. He had ordered himself to avoid, at least during the first minute of their meetings, her quaint eyes - greenish-blue, with deceitful golden spots around the pupil that began to burn every time when Adrienne was pleased with something. He had never succeeded in making her admire him.

The only person Larry fully trusted, his old butler Theodore, had not liked the blonde fairy.

"Bitch," was the brief comment about her he passed. Theodore was 75. In the past, he used to work as a guard of a parking lot and spoke with such a genuine admiration for the cars Larry possessed that the Chief Executive Officer of Toys International found a job for Theodore at his enormous home.

The butler had made a lasting friendship with his boss; for many years now he had been responsible for the rooms in which Adrienne had chosen to leave her things.

"The little one has turned your head," old Theodore had expressed his dissatisfaction with a groan of contempt. "Be careful with her!"

Theodore wondered how Adrienne managed to ensnare the hardheaded businessman. The other women Larry had been infatuated with were neither uglier nor dumber than Adrienne. When Theodore saw the slim blonde at Larry's formal reception for the first time he gave her a month and a half at most in his boss's bed. Unlike all the other smashing women Larry was attracted to Adrienne Tott enraged fat Jennifer in the very beginning asking her if she was Mr. Hoffburg's mother. Theodore did not approve of her flashing eyes that made his employer fall into ecstasies over the prospect of spending the night with her. Jennifer gave the old butler a hundred-dollar bill to throw out the brazen hussy. Adrienne gave him five hundred dollars, so Theodore brought her to Mr. Hoffburg's bedroom on the stroke of midnight though the party was not over yet.

Ten days after that event, fat Jennifer received a brief letter from the typist. Theodore remembered every word of it.

"Dear Jennifer," it said. "I would like to inform you I do not regret that I have stolen your husband. He is so sweet. I suggest you accept the situation calmly and reasonably, so in return I'll be able to let him have breakfast with you on Wednesdays. You are free to spend the time with Larry as you please. I would strongly advise you against telling him how much you love him.
Sincerely,
Rosalind   T."

Old Theodore still kept that letter. Directly after he read it he expressed his opinion that the typist Rosalind would be arrested and detained for disruptive behavior. He predicted that on the very next day, Larry would make all necessary arrangement for the pert intruder to be fired and kicked out of Toys International with worst possible reference from her current employer. Something most unexpected happened - the pert intruder's name was changed and she was given a name of an empress: Adrienne. Gossips and malicious rumors dwelt extensively on all phases of her vigorous forward march but Theodore did not believe "that bitch.". He had received many presents from her but his suspicions lingered and Adrienne's presence in Larry's sumptuous home gave rise to cold lurking hostility between them.

"She has turned your head," Theodore grumbled from time to time. "Some day the little bitch will get you into big trouble."

It was obvious that some day had come and Theodore's dark prognosis was coming true.

Still, Larry Hoffburg trembled against his will, struck with admiration as Adrienne's quick light steps approached him. The memory of Theodore's gloomy eyebrows, of his figure that stiffened with aversion whenever Adrienne handed the butler her coat and hat brought Larry Hoffburg to his senses. Yet he could not get rid of the desire that her quiet caressing steps aroused. He imagined Adrienne's shoes, her feet in them, her breasts that a poet had compared to little hillocks of snow in the beginning of winter. Larry had paid a fat bundle to the poet who composed the lyric for her. The poem was worth the money he spent; its lines mirrored real Adrienne, tender, enticing and inscrutable. To hell with her! This time he would not allow her charm to have the better of him.

Adrienne Tott, the woman who with almost one hundred percent certainty had left Leila's plastic hand in the office of the CEO of Toys International. Adrienne Tott, the only person Larry had met in the morning that could slip the plastic leg in gray jack-boot into his pocket. Then the pain came deadening the corresponding part of his body. Larry Hoffburg had never thought how he was to get into conversation with Adrienne. It was she that always started talking first her words relaxing magically his tired senses, her caresses warming the indifferent blood of his body. But this time

"What will you tell me about that?" Larry said panting, stretching out his hand to her.

He held a little leg and a hand belonging to Leila the doll in his palm. Hoffburg shuddered when he caught a glimpse of the young woman's face. The familiar calm ironic expression was gone, there was no trace of Adrienne's haughtiness that usually imparted cold superiority to her whole being. The skin of her cheeks and chin appeared ashen and wet with sweat. The make-up on her eyelids was smudged and for a split second Larry had the impression that the eerily painted eyelids covered two icy black cavities. He felt horrible.

"Are you OK, Adrienne?"

The young woman did not answer. She looked at him her hands clasped tightly together. Then suddenly the doll's tiny face was in Adrienne's palm beaming its fatuous smile at them. Larry studied it carefully. Actually the blonde held a little plastic ball -- Leila's head - without its usual thatch of beautiful auburn hair, a head without a neck and ears, only a face with lips and eyes that appeared somehow silly.

"I found that for three consecutive days in my office," Adrienne whispered. "Look!"

Her fingers tapped carefully at the plastic ball. The line of the eyebrows appeared slightly distorted, the plastic ball rolled in the palm of the pretty woman and split into two halves. A tiny piece of plastic resembling a hazelnut fell out of them.

"It reminds me of a human brain," Larry muttered. "O, my God!"

"It is the third day," the young woman whispered. "I can't stand it any more. It feels as if somebody's broken my skull and is burning the living cells inside. I can't stand it"

She delved in her handbag looking desperately for something. After a short hesitation she unclenched her fists nervously and Larry saw two more uneven plastic balls resembling hazelnuts.

"Adrienne!" was all he could utter. Then a thought flashed through his mind: the latest models of Leila dolls produced in the factories of Toys International were really designed in such a way that their heads could split into parts thus allowing the kids to familiarize themselves with the structure of human brain.

"Is she really sick or is she just shamming?" Larry thought. The long years he had lived with her prompted him to be particularly wary of rash conclusions. In fact, he had never known what to expect of this woman.

Chapter 2

No power on earth could make Red Kyle to be slack in his work or relax his concentration in the company of a colleague no matter what his rank -- even if it was much lower than his own. But Ella was the worst. The old hound was notorious for her shrewdness and proverbially sharp tongue. Kyle could not stand women who claimed to be detectives but Ella well. Ella made him bristle with resentment. "An old, gaunt withering tree," inspector Kyle considered her. He was an agent of Z class - highest confidentiality - working for the International Investigation Agency and of course his strict upbringing prevented him from giving vent to his heretical thoughts that had tortured his mind for a long time. He had never spoken about them out loud, but on the other hand he had not made any special efforts to conceal them. The disapproving glances he gave her, the tone of voice in which he pronounced her name, his habit of avoiding the narrow corridor where Ella's office was situated - all these were facts that had made inspector Kyle quite famous in the Agency. He did not worry about his good reputation: he could afford a discreet, tactful vilification of her. Kyle was a Z class inspector! Only the Chairman of the Agency and he held that rank.

The Chairman, an old man weighed down by the burden of his seventy years, constantly appeared squashed and drowsy. There could be no doubt that the next Chairman would be Red Kyle. Then, in all probability, inspector Ella Boon would be forced to look for a job somewhere else. No, damn it! She was too famous to send her packing just like that! After the Mojave Desert case lots of other institutions tried to attract her but the detestable hound remained in the Agency just to spite him.

"The old withering tree refused to become a Z class inspector of her own free will didn't meet her personal requirements for such a rank. Oh, she simply doesn't have to give me that baloney!" he thought. That was a move to worm herself into the Chairman's favor. Old Bob was a simple-hearted fellow and she exploited that.

Chairman Bob Hendricks opened his drowsy almost colorless eyes only when Ella entered his office. Then his face that resembled an old worn slipper twisted into a wry grimace, which one could, with utmost effort, call a smile. In such cases Red's black mood lifted as he concentrated on the idea that the name of the next Chairman of the Agency would be Red Kyle.

"--in your area, Mr. Kyle." The hound had again started nagging him. Lost in thought he had not bothered to listen to her. Ella was in the dirty habit of keeping mum like a dead fish but if accidentally the vixen happened to wag her tongue she invariably said things that shattered his peace of mind for months to come.

"I would be grateful if you enumerate all the facts and give me the appropriate details," Kyle said dryly. He'd never allow her to catch him unprepared. He'd rather die than appear in her eyes absent-minded or embarrassed like some dolt. "I am interested in the details, Ella," he added his voice giving a particular jerk when he pronounced her name.

"I'll repeat for you, Mr. Kyle," she said unruffled the sounds of the words jarring on his nerves. "The town is peaceful at first sight. I don't know if I can call it strange," Ella went on coldly without looking at him. "Toys International made a generous charitable donation for Christmas, do you remember? Every family that has children received a gift - a wonderful Leila doll. People were happy and--"

"Who told you that? As far as I know you don't have children," Kyle put in loudly enough to be heard by the Chairman of the agency who at that moment seemed to be dropping off to sleep.

"I don't have children," she said showing no visible signs of discontent. She was as cold as a freezer, damn it, and he never learnt what could throw her off balance. "I don't have children, but I, too, received a Leila doll for Christmas. I found it in my mailbox and thought it was a mistake. My neighbor, a single woman of sixty, found in her mailbox a Leila doll exactly like mine. The retired teachers living next door - the wife gives me lessons in German language - discovered a small package in their mailbox. When they opened it guess what they found? Again a doll. Unfortunately they have neither children nor grandchildren. Isn't it wonderful that Toys International made the lonely people happy, I thought. They've been saving money all their lives to buy a little house in our clean and serene town."

"It would have been better if you had become a poetess," Kyle pointed out gloomily. "The common-sense approach got drowned in the sea of metaphors you poured a minute ago."

'Ella's gray eyes shot him a glance she paid no further attention to the inimical remark.

"Colleagues, we are close to the most unpleasant part of our work today. On Christmas Eve virtually everybody in town -- every family, every lonely person, received a Leila doll. And after that ALL PEOPLE in Jacksonville were in for a most unpleasant surprise. According to the information we have so far at least one person in every family had a serious medical complaint. Most people got a splitting headache. We have at our disposal the medical protocols of the day: you can take a copy of them. The emergency and intense care wards were full of patients. There were long lines of sick people in front of the three clinics in town. The headache was so severe that in isolated cases the patients lost consciousness. Others complained of persistent chest pain and general weakness. So many sick people have never been registered in this part of the world. "

"In my case the headache was accompanied by a temporary loss of sight," the Chairman of the agency remarked. His voice was heard so rarely that some younger employees thought old Bob could no longer speak. It was enough, however, his green eyes to flit from face to face and it became clear that his bent senile figure had nothing to do with his cold brilliant mind.

"I hope, Ma'am," Kyle said nodding his head at Ella, "I most sincerely hope that you did not suffer much. Or you simply don't admit it because suffering is incompatible with the myth surrounding your name."

"Actually I did not feel anything," Ella agreed quietly.

"We all know you are an Iron Lady," the inspector commented his voice sending tiny waves of contempt to her.

"The interesting thing about my case was that several days after Christmas something happened, which amazed me," Ella went on. Her eyes searched Bob's, managed to attract his attention and again between them an invisible but tangible tie was established excluding all the rest from their communication.

"I'm itching to learn what was the extraordinary thing that stunned you, inspector Boon," Kyle said morosely. "I can tell by the expression on your face you are interested in that, too, Bob. Oh, stop looking at her so longingly; she'll torture us long enough before she finally tells us what has happened."

"There's an interesting fact," Ella's voice sounded even and businesslike. She appeared not in the least impressed with her high-ranking colleague's behavior. "I've been suffering from some kind of eczema for years now. The skin of my palms peels off."

"That's something new," Kyle observed. "I was convinced you were perfect."

"I avoided humidity, visited a number of cosmetic centers, I was even subjected to plastic surgery but unfortunately all was to no effect. Look at my palms now."

Inspector Ella Boon put out her hands. Kyle made great efforts not to jump up from his chair and run to see what had happened to her palms. She had approached Bob spreading out her fingers wide under his very nose.

"The skin now is smooth and elastic," Ella began to describe it and Kyle found for the thousandth time he could not stand her. "There is no trace of my eczema. I know it sounds strange." She reached for a medical folder. "Here are the results of my medical tests and the medical history of my complaint - I took them an hour ago from the Center of Dermatology. The results show that my skin is perfectly healthy. The doctors even had suspicions that I was not telling the truth and I had never had eczema. They haven't heard so far that eczema could disappear without any medical treatment Especially if you bear in mind the fact I have suffered from it more than fifteen years.

This time even Kyle was incapable of forming any opinion on the issue in question.

"My eczema healed on the second day after Leila doll was brought into my apartment," Ella said thoughtfully. "I put the doll on the bookshelf, next to Truman Capote's books."

On another occasion Red Kyle would remark that the old hound was putting on airs and trying to pass as a remarkably refined intellectual. "We read authors like Truman Capote" Frankly speaking, Kyle had never come upon anything written by that man. We are an inspector, not a man of letters, damn it! This time he didn't voice his opinion, stood up and approached Ella staring at her palms. The skin was even and white and if he didn't know those were Ella's hands he might say the fingers were delicate and beautiful.

"So, people run to hospitals complaining of unbearable pain, but something entirely different happens to you," Kyle pointed out determined to avail himself of the opportunity and reveal the truth in which he believed. "In fact, with you things always turn out quite the opposite to what one expects."

"Maybe that's right," Ella agreed peacefully. "I took the trouble to check exactly how many people passed through the hospitals of our town asking for medical aid. And I established an amazing fact: every single person of our town registered in the citizenship card index of Jacksonville visited a hospital or a clinic."

"And you tell me that you compared the names of all inhabitants registered in the police card-index with the names of the patients listed in the medical protocols?" The whips that usually cracked in Kyle's eyes when he felt strong enough this time this time were about to jump out and hit Ella's hands, which had gotten rid of their eczema. "You are a very conscientious worker, Miss Boon. Congratulations Thirty-five thousand people live in Jacksonville. That's an impressive number. One could suspect the check you conducted was not too precise. You probably made a short work of it."

"Actually, I didn't run the check all by myself, Mr. Kyle. My associates did it. I'd like to inform you that I have attracted some of your subordinates to work for my team as volunteers. They didn't have time to ask for your permission. Please, excuse them."

"I want their names," Kyle said coldly. "I promise you they all will lose their jobs in the nearest future."

"Oh, come off it!" Ella said. "The computers juxtaposed the people who had medical complaints with the lists of Jacksonville inhabitants in the police card index. My associates carefully followed the check. I assure you it was very rigorous."

"There's no need to beat about the bush," Kyle looked at her angrily. "Speak to the point. The facts are: Toys International sends every living soul in Jacksonville a Leila doll. On the next day the whole town is sick with the exception of the ubiquitous inspector Ella Boon. As usually you are--"

"Wait a minute," Ella interrupted him waving her hand not too politely. "Apart from me, there ate three more persons who did not show up in any hospital asking for help. A remarkable thing happened to each of them. Something similar to the case of my eczema"

"Therefore you can calm down, Ella," Kyle said sharply. "The number of people for whom the tide is flowing in the opposite direction -- exactly like with you -- is very small."

"How did this "reverse effect" find expression in the other three people?" Old Bob's voice was cold and quiet and the inspectors attending the meeting felt they could compare it to touching the body of a poisonous reptile.

In the narrow study a fourth person had not spoken a word so far. He was Val Hughes, a young inspector even more tight-lipped than the aged Chairman of the Agency. Val moved noiselessly, his face very white, with smooth marble skin and dark eyes staring persistently at the faces of his colleagues. Red Kyle was convinced that the young fellow detested Ella at least as much as he himself did. Whenever he accidentally met her in the short cold corridors of the agency he only nodded his head by way of greeting, failing to honor her with a glance.

"I know who the "reverse effect" people are," Val said most unexpectedly. "I carried out an independent investigation into the correlation between the dolls and diseases. Let me tell you from the beginning that I am one of the "reverse effect" people. When I was a little boy I broke my collarbone in a car accident and for twenty years it had been very hard for me to move my left arm. That was the reason why I could not become a fighter pilot. But after Christmas I was able again to raise my arm and I can demonstrate it before you now. I will show you a series of X-ray photographs and medical protocols to prove that my collarbone was broken and the agility of my arm was badly impaired. The X-ray examination I underwent after Leila doll appeared in my apartment shows that all the harmful consequences of the car accident had vanished." For a moment, the young inspector looked Red Kyle straight in the eye. "Sir, have you something to tell us?"

"Why should I tell you anything?" Kyle said and his unruly reddish hair seemed to bristle.

"On the very first I started working for the agency I noticed a long ashen scar on your right hand, Inspector Kyle. At that time, I felt a pang of envy saying to myself "That is the man who pulled out the teeth of the thugs committing the horrible robberies on the East Coast." It was a great honor for me to meet you in the corridors on my way to the Chairman's office."

"Well, thank you," Red Kyle nodded pleasantly surprised feeling a surge of respect for the younger man.

"That was off the point," Val Hughes said his dark sharp eyes fixed on Kyle's face. "The important thing at present is that the scar is not on your right hand any more, Sir. After Christmas you dropped in Dr. Patten's clinic but you did not have any medical complaints. You told the doctor that you had miraculously shaken off the constant strain on your right shoulder and arm that you had felt for years. It happened after you received one of these dolls."

Red Kyle stared at the spot on his hand where the scar had been.

"Yes, it's not there," he said. "I haven't noticed that," he paused then spoke looking hot and flustered. "Very well. I still have the doll that Toys International gave me for Christmas. I'll bring it here. They'll analyze it in our laboratory and everything will be clear. There's nothing easier than that."

"Let's not make rush conclusions, Kyle" old Bob spoke for the second time this evening and that was a sure sign all were in store for a long debate.

"Larry Hoffburg, The CEO of the company and widely known favorite of the population in the whole country has already tested his Leila doll. We know that the old ambitious boy holds a Ph.D. in organic synthesis and after he conducted the tests himself his words were, "There is no deviation from the standard requirements in the chemical composition of the plastic pieces I found in my office."

"The chemical tests of Leila doll I received showed no deviations from the approved standards," Val said quietly. "It should mean that the epidemic has nothing to do will Leila dolls. Miss Boon and I checked the medical diary protocols. You had your Leila doll tested as well. After the tests you had written down "No deviations from the approved standards."

For a second, Kyle felt an acute bodily discomfort. Those two, Ella and the greenhorn, were on the scent acting energetically and consistently. His rank was higher than theirs were, he was to become the next Chairman of the agency, but he was lagging behind them. Why should I call it lagging behind? A cheerful thought crossed his mind. They have found nothing just like me. They are even worse - they have destroyed the material evidence while my Leila doll is intact and an authorized body will test it. They rushed things and that might turn out to be very harmful.

"Let's come back to the point," Kyle said. "Ella, Val and I are the three "reverse effect" persons. Our brilliant colleague Miss Boon declared several minutes ago that the number of the odd guys is four. Would Miss Boon be so kind to tell us the name of the fourth one? I am all ears."

"His name is Don Highsmith," Ella said without looking in the direction where Kyle's chair was. "And Don Highsmith is a very interesting young man."

"Oh!" Kyle exclaimed raising a sardonic eyebrow. "You are ubiquitous, Ella, no kidding! You probably know everything about him. Please, forgive me! You've already invited him over to your office, treated him to a cup of coffee and the guy is looking forward to answering all your intelligent questions."

The old Chairman of the agency collected enough strength, opened his colorless eyelids and turned to Kyle.

"We face a very peculiar thing," his voice sounded muffled, powerless. "Thirty-five thousand people were taken ill suddenly. The population of a whole town suffered from agonizing pain - all with the exception of four persons. What if someone spread the dolls throughout the country? Throughout Europe? And you sit here bandying words."

"You are stretching the truth, boss," Kyle could not stand reproof even on the part of the Chairman. If he was alone with Bob he might let it pass, but now the brash hound Ella was here. "Bob, no sooner had the epidemic broken out than everybody was safe sound and healthy again. Perhaps there will never be any medical complaints if Toys International doesn't make a decision to give an Easter present to the town population. And now, dear Miss Boon lets come back to your discovery: Don Highsmith. Tell us something about that remarkable man. I am starting to lose patience."

"There is a possibility we should not overlook," Val Hughes remarked making Kyle stare angrily at him. Anybody in Val's shoes would have shut up for Kyle was proverbial with his rancor and always invented a way to give the junior inspectors 'hot and strong,' but Val didn't seem to feel uneasy at all. "I'd like to point out that somebody used Leila dolls to cause the epidemic and take his revenge on Toys International."

"It's most probably so," Ella agreed. "Somebody bore a grudge against Toys International and wanted to bring it to ruin choosing the cleverest possible way. No one will buy Leila dolls or any other toys produced by the company and it will soon go bankrupt."

"How was it possible to cause an epidemic of this kind - breaking out so suddenly, afflicting virtually everybody? And the complaints were of a different nature - headaches, abdominal and chest pain etc." Bob's voice faded away as if a powerless stream of water had run dry in the desert. Nobody said anything and the Chairman went on slowly, "It is interesting to establish what exactly the complaints were. Did the person suffer from the same disease in the past or the symptoms were exhibited for the first time. We have to check. Let's listen to Ella first. Miss Boon, what will you tell us about Don Highsmith, the fourth 'reverse effect' man?"

"The fact that he did not visit any hospital or clinic does not guarantee that Don's a 'reverse effect' guy," Val Hughes remarked.

"There's no guarantee at all," Ella agreed. "Don Highsmith is 34, single, has clean record," she went on. "Tried to commit suicide twice. His life was saved in the Walnut clinic. After his second attempt to kill himself he was hardly capable of speaking and stayed in mental hospital. They discharged him after six months hardly able to pronounce articulate words. After Christmas Highsmith took his money back from the doctor whom he had paid in advance to help him restore his speech. Don Highsmith declared that he didn't need exercises any more. He spoke fluently and intelligibly. That is all."

"All?" this time Kyle's amazement sounded sincere. "And you didn't contact that remarkable person? I wouldn't believe that, Ella. That's not typical of you."

"Mr. Highsmith has disappeared," Ella said shrugging her shoulders. "His employer says he hasn't shown up for a couple of days now."

"Where does he work?" Kyle asked.

"He's got a job as a porter in a furniture store," Val Hughes said. "Rust and Martin Furniture Store. Don Highsmith has always had difficulty holding down a job; in the past year he changed eight of them. At least that was what I found in his personal dossier in the police card index."

"You delved even in that," Kyle sighed staring inquisitively at his younger colleague. "What a pleasant surprise, Val."

Val Hughes, not even bothering to thank the Z class inspector for the compliment, went calmly on, "After Don Highsmith proved to the doctors in the Walnut clinic that he had restored his ability to speak, he disappeared without a trace."

Val probably didn't care he was no longer in Kyle's good graces; impolite behavior on the part of Kyle's subordinates was duly punished. "I realized inspector Ella Boon had checked Highsmith's dossier before me and I lay great stress on that fact. She has already contacted the doctor who treated Don Highsmith. This is Professor Rupert Bell, if at all his name means something to you."

"Rupert Bell?" The Professor's name seemed to produce a marked effect on the Chairman of the agency. "Rupert Bell is the doctor charging the highest fees for his services in the whole country. He's often asked to provide medical consultations for hospitals in the USA, Japan, Russia, virtually all over the world. Very interesting"

"I thought it was," Ella's eyebrow trembled slightly as she spoke. "I asked myself the question: how was it possible for Don Highsmith who lost six different jobs during the past year to afford a doctor like Professor Bell? Where did he find money to pay the exorbitant fees? He worked only three hours a day in Rust and Martin furniture store and got barely enough to buy his food and pay the rent for his miserable apartment in Barbara street. It might sound unbelievable to you but Professor Bell declared Don Highsmith paid him regularly his fees. The Professor was shocked when the auburn-haired hunk visited him after Christmas and stated in a clear voice without a hint of stammering or spluttering, "Professor, I am not going to pay you any more. You see I can speak perfectly well and I do not need your services." Professor Rupert Bell was the last man who had talked to Don."

"Did you call him "the auburn-haired hunk"? Red Kyle asked smiling. "Now I realize that you are attracted to auburn haired men. Miss Boon. I am even a little bit scared since my own hair sometimes appears auburn. It happens most often a little before sunset, if you come to think of it.

"Your hair is red," old Bob said appearing half-asleep. "There are no reasons to be afraid of your safety. Excuse him, Ella, sometimes Kyle doesn't know what he's speaking about."

"I know," Ella said unemotionally. "However I recommend you take that case seriously. I think that the symptoms of suffering will appear again. Why? Because my palm is still eczema-free, inspector Val Hughes still has no problems with his arm, Kyle's scar has not reappeared yet i.e. the "the reverse effect" has enduring consequences. It is logical the epidemic symptoms might be an enduring, even chronic phenomenon."

"As usual, you know everything," Kyle put in acidly. "Bob, tell me, how's your headache now? You said it was so unbearable that you experienced a temporary loss of sight. You look better now."

"I really feel better," Bob muttered. "Though sometimes in the evenings I get violent headaches. Well, I lived through that in the past. It's nothing new."

"How serious are these headaches of yours, Bob?" Kyle's voice sounded sincerely concerned. In spite of all his eccentricities the old man meant a lot to him.

Bob invited Kyle to work for the agency twenty-four ears ago. At that time Kyle worked as a policeman in a rural backwater town and he could not but notice that a gang of young men gathered together every Friday not far from the mole of the old port. It had not been hard track them, they were not careful at all, it was a provincial settlement where criminality was virtually non-existent. Kyle discovered the one of the major drug routes in the whole continent. An hour after he received the much-vaunted monetary prize from his local boss, Kyle held in his hands Bob Hendricks's invitation to an official dinner. Bob Hendricks's name had already become legendary and was pronounced with awe and much trepidation by every policeman in Europe.

Bob Hendricks himself had written down the invitation filling the sheet of expensive paper with his energetic quite illegible words. "Dear Red Kyle," it read, " I will be honored if you accept my offer to work for the International Investigation Agency in Jacksonville, Europe. A house will be provided for you. The position is rewarded with a generous salary package. Sincerely, Bob Hendricks."

During all these years Kyle grew to like Bob more and more. The robberies on the East Coast, the deals with human organs he thwarted, the abductions of people for the colonies on the artificial satellite "Chase," the blood-curdling slaughter of children in satanic rituals nearby the ruins of the medieval church "Saint Jane the Healer" -- these were but a few cases of Kyle's contribution to the work of the agency. Thanks to Bob, Red's name had become a legend as well.

He liked his office very much. He had chosen it to be dark and narrow attaching great importance to the fact that it was situated exactly at the opposite end of the corridor far from the place where Ella's office was. Kyle had a genuine affection for old Bob though he did not show it. He'd felt emptiness and a nagging anxiety ever since the day of Bob's first heart attack. The more broken down with age the old man looked the more acute the emptiness that tortured Kyle. He wanted with all his heart to postpone the day when Bob would have to say goodbye to the agency.

At the same time he hoped that day would not be in the interminably distant future for he, Red Kyle was going to become Chairman. Red Kyle, the nondescript policeman of Schwabensee, a remote settlement whose name was printed on the map in such smudgy blue ink that if you wanted to read it you should resort to a magnifying glass. Red Kyle who in the past could hardly dream of heading the police headquarters in the dozy Schwabensee. And yet Bob Hendricks

Red Kyle of course remembered his father but had never called him dad. Before Kyle was born, his father left the family, flying away to a young blonde stunner in the village nearby. She gave birth to two chubby tots so Kyle saw his father not more than twice a year. His mother worked as a tourist agent and was constantly busy with tourist groups throughout Europe. Kyle grew up in his grandmother's house. She was a half deaf, silent old woman who right away made efforts to instill love for flowers into poor Kyle making him weed the flower beds in her garden as a result of which he had been unable to stand flowers ever since. In Red's mind, Bob Hendricks had replaced the concept of family and home with the idea of working for the International Investigation Agency. The only person Kyle could thank in his life was Bob.

"Kyle, can't you hear me?" the old man had again raised his voice more than usual. That, evidently, had been very hard for him. "Ella asked you something, Kyle."

"Of course, Bob. I was thinking about your headache. I hate it when you look so bad, Bob. I mean it's unpleasant to see something eating you. I'd do everything. This case will be forgotten like all the rest of them and there is no reason to worry."

Something in Kyle's voice made Ella and the young inspector avert their eyes from his face. Perhaps he had lost control for a minute; perhaps he appeared soft and absurd. Kyle had promised himself to be strong, severe, unyielding, and never allow the others to pity him, especially the old hound Ella Boon.

Chapter 3

"I am sorry I have to take some of your precious time." Ella tried to speak amicably but the contempt spurting from the young woman's eyes who stood by her side put the inspector on alert. "Miss Adrienne Tott, I understand that Toys International suffered a heavy blow. It is logical - the epidemic swept the town immediately after your company gave its Christmas presents to everyone. I speak of the beautiful Leila dolls."

Adrienne Tot waved her hand impatiently. Her slim figure, looking as though it was making love with the wind, curtsied almost invisibly. What rich context that young supple body expressed - every single shade from the tactful reminder that your presence was undesirable to the categorical order, "Go away! I don't want you at my home!"

Ella showed no sign that she intended to go away.

"I am afraid you have not chosen the most appropriate time for a lengthy discussion with me," Adrienne said her cold eyes dwelling on Ella's face.

"I thought so," the inspector agreed readily.

"If you thought so why did you visit me? I admit your visit does not invite pleasant expectations. If you really wish to achieve any results in your mutual work with me I recommend you leave me alone right away, ma'am. I cannot devote a minute of my time to you. The exit is this way, ma'am. There are a lot of taxis in the street. You can hail one. I can see you tomorrow at 6 PM."

"I believe that you will see me tomorrow at 6 PM as well, Miss Tott. Why should we miss the chance to talk today? Bearing in mind"

Adrienne Tot's body shook impatiently, for a moment her face expressed ennui and irritation. Ella even admired the skills of the young lady's facial muscles to reflect different emotional states of mind.

"You could become a consummate actress," Ella remarked.

"I promise I will think about that," Adrienne Tot had approached the door when she said firmly, "Goodbye, ma'am."

"Miss Tott, you signed the order through which your company sent each citizen of Jacksonville a Leila doll as a Christmas present. Mr. Larry Hoffburg did not sign the order, you did. Why?"

"Because I am in charge of the money for charity in Toys International," the blond answered without delay. "I have signed many documents of this type but the scope of the activities have been much smaller."

"For example?" Ella tried to smile but knew she would definitely fail. She had been unable to master the technique of smiling humbly.

"Last year all married women in Jacksonville received a toiletries and soaps for the Mother's Day on behalf of Toys International. Your name, however, was not on the list. I could not miss the name of Ella Boon - everyone shudders at the sound of it."

"Thank you," the compliment hardly deserved such profound gratitude but Ella had grown accustomed to the idea that sometimes people used her name as a bugaboo.

"You are single, aren't you?" The white-capped waves of Adrienne's question crashed against the inspector's self-confidence yet their context was perfectly clear, "Nobody is crazy enough to live with you."

"I am not married," Ella admitted. "However I did not come here to discuss my marital status. I would like to know what exactly happen days before Christmas when the plastic heads of Leila three dolls appeared in your office."

"I have already given testimony to Mr. Red Kyle, your likeable colleague. I hope you read what I have written."

"Yes, I did," Ella said thoughtfully. "Somebody planted a Leila doll's head in your office and you complained of an excruciating headache. Now try to give me a precise answer, please. Was your headache equally intensive during the three days or was there a tendency to become more acute?"

"I'd say it was equally intensive," the blonde fairy answered cleaning invisible specks of dust from her immaculate dress then added, "Thank God my headaches did not come back any more. In fact, inspector Boon, you haven't fulfilled tour task well. You have not interrogated Professor Rupert Bell who examined me and wrote down everything about my medical complains. I told him in details about them. It is an oversight speaking volumes about a cop of your rank."

Ellie didn't like the word 'cop,' but she ignored it. "Why did you decide I hadn't talked to Professor Bell?"

"Because if you had, you'd have been much interested in my stomach ulcer from the very beginning."

"And why should you imagine your stomach ulcer would be a matter of crucial importance to me?" Ella tried hard to sound friendly and failed.

"Because it was the item your likable colleague Red Kyle started with. He was dying to know what had happened to make it heal completely. Professor Bell told him that my stomach looked so clean and healthy as if I had never suffered from such a condition. Your colleague Mr. Kyle was impressed and even started arguing that I had not really been sick, that I was just faking my headaches, which Leila doll allegedly caused."

"Sometimes people have strange ideas," Ella sighed. "I also think that you didn't have splitting headaches. Am I guessing right?"

"Yes you are," the blonde fairy smiled. "But not quite."

"What do you mean by "not quite"?

"Work a little harder and you'll find that yourself," Adrienne Tott wagged her finger at the inspector. "As far as I know your remuneration package is quite generous. Apart from that, I'd like to reveal a little secret to you: I don't quite like you."

"Well, I can congratulate you on the fact you are healthy and cheerful," Ella said. "There is no way I could check if you really told Professor Bell the truth about your headaches. Neither can I check your allegations that you suffered from stomach ulcer, which most unexpectedly healed, Miss Tott."

"That's your problem," Larry Hoffburg's expert concluded calmly. "What sort of suffering did Leila doll bring you? I won't be surprised in the least if you now tell me that you didn't suffer from headaches at all. On the contrary -- the eczema on your palms vanished without a trace."

Ella stared at her managing to suppress the exclamation that was about to wriggle out of her lips. Of course, it was Kyle who told the dainty belle about her eczema. Why had he done that? It was inappropriate, he had weakened the inquest divulging facts intended for the high-ranking inspectors of the agency!

"I haven't mentioned anything about eczema," Ella said after her breathing became steady again. "It is an unpleasant but not fatal skin condition. And to be honest with you, I wonder where you obtained information on that, Miss Tott."

"You can assume that you are so notorious for your professionalism and inhumanity that every indisposition of yours is subject to public debate. Thus many people are satisfied that God has punished you in the long run."

"It was my colleague Kyle, who told you about my eczema, didn't he?" Ella said.

"No, ma'am." Adrienne swayed her hips enticingly a mysterious smile climbing her lips. "If you promise me you'll leave my home right away I'll be so kind to tell you where I learnt about the eczema on your hands," the blonde fairy was suddenly silent her expression changing to a state of inscrutable thoughtfulness. "I admit we don't get on very well together, inspector Boon."

"That makes me particularly unhappy," Ella said. "Let's revert to my basic question - why was it necessary for you to lie to Larry Hoffburg you had headaches?"

"Wait a minute," the young lady smiled. "I've never admitted categorically I didn't have headaches. As for Larry Hoffburg, I am sure he was pulling my leg. I am not a sleuth like you, Miss Boon but I checked carefully the whole matter - I had been hiding the same Leila doll's hand, the one he found the very first day on his desk, under the sheet of his bed for a whole week. I can assure you, ma'am, that the doll's hand did not give him any pain: on the contrary, he was much more energetic in my bed. Would you like me to describe in details how he made love to me, Miss Boon?"

"I'll leave your home right away, Miss Tott," Ella declared. "Please, answer me how did you get to know about my eczema?"

"I learnt about it five years ago in Walnut clinic. I had just recuperated after a horrible road accident which might have cost me my life. I was allowed to take short walks when you were admitted to the clinic. You were shot through, bleeding and Professor Bell said that if you survived he'd eat his old white coat. As you know very well, you survived. He did not eat his coat because he could not discharge you from hospital perfectly healthy -- the nasty eczema on your palms had not healed." Adrienne Tott beamed her irresistible smile. " Is that why all dirty little jokes about you have it that you don't take off your gloves? You have to kiss my slippers in gratitude for my generosity - I sent you a Leila doll, which helped you rid yourself of your skin complaint."

Ella made for the door not uttering a word.

"I am glad you are leaving," the young blond said instead of goodbye. "Don't come back here again."

Ella had talked to Professor Rupert Bell who had been assigned the task of summarizing the results of the medical complaints in Jacksonville after Christmas. The Professor reported that virtually nobody in town had exhibited a reverse effect with respect to suffering with the exception of three persons: Ella, Val Hughes and Red Kyle.

So, what about Adrienne Tott? Judging by her healed stomach ulcer, she must be another reverse effect person. Why hadn't the Professor informed the agency about her? He had sent a note of warning to the World Center of Epidemic Diseases mentioning nothing about Adrienne Tott. Had Adrienne misled   him?

The health institutions in town recommended all Leila dolls that the citizens had received as Christmas presents be handed over to International Investigation Agency.

When Ella arrived in her apartment on the second floor of an ancient house in Lafayette Street, she found an Email message waiting for her on the screen of her computer, "The headache epidemic had broke out again. I have to talk to you immediately! Professor Rupert Bell."

Ella contacted her young colleague Val Hughes before she drove to the Professor's clinic. He let her know that the second outbreak of the epidemic had not affected him and he felt strong and healthy as usual. She contacted Red Kyle as well and listened unwillingly to his voice, which creaked and croaked with the usual resentment that he harbored against her. Kyle declared he had nothing to complain of although he was unpleasantly surprised it was Ella and not a gentle young lady who had rung him up. Ella Boom herself felt as fit as a fiddle.

There we are, she thought. The people fill the clinics again but the three of us, Val Hughes, Kyle and I are OK. What has happened to Don Highsmith, the man who has vanished and whose ability to speak has been miraculously restored? What is Adrienne Tott doing now? As if reading her thoughts the computer monitor started flashing. A very attractive face appeared on it, the blue mocking eyes boring into her. Ella recognized the face instantly - Adrienne Tott.

"You left my home without saying your farewells and I was deeply saddened by that," Adrienne's voice conquered Ella's narrow study and soon after that became its ultimate master. "I heard on the radio that another epidemic broke out. If you switch on the TV you can see that for yourself. Details of people with faces twisted in pain are given in a BBC news broadcast. This time I will not visit Professor Rupert Bell because I don't have a splitting headache; by the way, I didn't have one the first time either. I believe that now no one will have the bright idea of accusing Toys International of crimes the company has never committed. This time Toys International has not given anybody Leila dolls. As I have already mentioned to you I do not like you at all but I have to see you as soon as possible. Please, hurry."

Ella made up her mind to visit Professor Bell first. She had known him for a long time: a tireless man of fifty, not too tall, a black-eyed confirmed bachelor who managed to make his patients burst out laughing even if they knew their days were numbered. Five years ago, the professor saved Ella's life; in all probability, Adrienne really had been in the clinic at the time when Ella had been admitted bleeding, more dead than alive with exhaustion. In the course of the operation continuing more than nine hours Professor Bell extracted two bullets: bullets which he gave her a month later together with an advertising brochure about Walnut Hospital. Walnut Hospital! A thought flashed through Ella's mind but she was incapable of capturing it.

Walnut Hospital She had to remember. What had she related Walnut Hospital to? What was it? Ella and Adrienne Tott had probably met there; Adrienne Tott said Professor Bell had saved her life after a serious road accident. The Professor had saved Ella's life as well. Both Adrienne and Ella were invulnerable to the epidemic. Furthermore, both of them had got rid of chronic diseases they had suffered from for many years.

It suddenly dawned on Ella that Don Highsmith had tried twice to commit suicide; twice had his life hung by a thread but he had survived. Where had that happened? At Walnut Hospital. And it was Professor Bell who had saved his life. According to Professor Bell's statement Don Highsmith's ability to speak was restored after he received his Leila doll. Was he suffering from a headache now? Walnut Hospital was the only link between Ella, Adrienne, and Don Highsmith: not only that: Professor Bell had in the three different cases saved his patients' lives despite the odds being strongly against them.

Ella already knew that Red Kyle had visited Walnut Hospital as well. As far as she remembered that had happened after a large-scale police action as a result of which the dealers in children's internal organs were captured. Red Kyle was hit by a submachine gun burst and his body was virtually cut into two parts. Even old Bob, the Chairman of the agency had given up hope that Kyle would survive. He used to leap out of his chair trudging up and down the long narrow corridors, his lean shadow dragging behind him bent, broken, powerless Well, on the other hand Professor Bell had saved thousands of people wrenching them from the grasp of death, bringing them back to life. Why were they all vulnerable to the epidemic and only three or four citizen of the town few felt healthy?

The hospital was at the end of the enormous park called the Trail of Tears.

"Strange name for a place where people in love go for walks, young mothers take their children to play and loners like me think their weird little thoughts," Ella muttered. She knew there was an old legend of Celtic warriors that had been captured by their foes. The winners gouged the eyes of the captives, leaving only one man with one good eye to lead them back to their wives and children. Many of the Celtic warriors died. When the survivors finally reached their native land, they were human beings no more. They were ghosts that frightened the women and children trying to take them to the world of the dead wailing and crying, always coming back at the dawn, following one and the same long narrow path that many centuries later their descendants called the Trail of tears.

The park was fresh and cool, the lawns were perfectly mown, all ruins of the pre-historic times were turned by the inventive owners of the land into museums in the open not far from which there were cafes, small restaurants and numerous souvenir shops. It was no chance that Professor Rupert Bell had chosen that place to build his clinic here. The local people still believed that the tortured holy souls of the warriors protected the sick in a mysterious way. Ella thought it was absurd to believe in martyrs and saints when one could commute monthly between the earth and the Moon and people mined hundreds of tons of uranium ore from Mars. Well, people would always be people and needed a power to protect them although all knew very well that such a thing simply did not exist.

Walnut Hospital did not at all look like standard health academies with shiny plastic windowpanes and quiet alleys winding between trees and flowerbeds. It resembled an ancient castle that, in spite of its brightly yellow tiles and cheerful pink facade, towered over the whole neighborhood, its menacing contours casting elongated shadows on the thick tangle of branches of the old oak-trees. The advertising brochures pointed out that the medical equipment in that clinic was the only one of its kind. The most famous physicians in Europe were invited here to hold consultations on medical issues of interest. Mentioning before your colleagues that your child was examined at Walnut clinic was a mater of personal prestige.

Ella's car was new and she enjoyed driving it very fast, the green leaves and the sun making an emerald tunnel before her. She looked forward to talking to Professor Bell and some mild, untypical but persistent inquisitiveness warmed her. A surprise waited for her at the very entrance of the hospital: the red van of the agency was parked there and inspector Val Hughes thrusting his hands in the pockets of his immaculately ironed gray trousers stood by it looking at her. She had a premonition that something irreparable had happened, something that a minute before could have been avoided or driven away.

She hated such presentiments of disaster yet their power was irresistible making her heart sink heavy with sadness and irrational fear that she would be absolutely helpless. Val's face cold and perfectly calm as usual, did not dispel her growing sense of panic. The inspector neither looked her in the eye nor said hello to her. He spoke out in a dispassionate clear voice, "Professor Rupert Bell is dead. He has been murdered."

Before she had time to ask anything Val started giving the details of the crime.

"The Professor has been killed in a particularly cruel way - stabbed with five knives which have remained stuck into his body. The knives are produced by Toys International and have turned into the most fashionable weapon, a firm favorite with the unruly crowds of teenagers. They stick them into trees, into special targets, which are sold complete with the knives.

"When did he die?"

"No more than an hour ago, at about 6:00 - 6:15 PM." For a split second, Val's immovable face trembled; he was about to say something but evidently decided against it. "Have a look at that, inspector Boon. These are the duplicates of the two notes, which we found on the desk in the Professor's office. He was most probably writing that one when the murderer entered the office and took his life."

"Did you send the original notes to be examined in the laboratories?" Ella asked in a stifled whisper.

"Of course we did."

The note Professor Rupert Bell had started writing a minute before he was killed consisted of the following words, "The 'Trail of Tears' experiment turned out to be" Apart from that, there were innumerable fives printed all over the sheet of paper. The fives, small and big, indecisively tilted to the left exactly like the Professor's letters, were written legibly and painstakingly. What did the Professor intend to say further? It was evident somebody didn't want that information to come out into the open. Professor Bell had invited death to his office when he started committing to paper what he had to announce.

The second note that Val Hughes had found on his desk read, "Don't try to find the murderer because you'll flop! I committed the murder, I, Don Highsmith. I am 34. I stand 6 feet 2 inches, I weigh 170 pounds and there are bluish wrinkles both on my face and on my whole body. That is the most striking characteristic feature I have. I would like to inform you that the next corpse you'll run into might be Adrienne Tott's. She shacks up with the old fool Larry Hoffburg just for his money. Larry produces my favorite toys, the cute Leila dolls. That's why Larry will be the third corpse. I kiss warmly all of you. Sincerely, Don Highsmith."

There was little free space on the white sheet of paper; it was taken by dozens of fives, the figures written in neat italic calligraphy. Three names were put down at the bottom of the page carefully arranged one below the other: Rupert Bell, Larry Hoffburg and Adrienne Tott. A beautifully printed interrogative sentence under them read, "WHO ELSE?"

Ella studied the duplicates of the notes for a while feeling totally confused.

"We blocked all the exits," for the first time Val Hughes's eyes, piercing and intent, settled on Ella's face. "We checked everywhere in the hospital and could not find anything. Don Highsmith is positively hiding not far from here. It was impossible for him to run away."

"Why don't we consider the possibility that it was not Don Highsmith who committed the crime?" Ella muttered." Someone laid the blame on the poor wretch we are still unable to find. Don Highsmith is not here to protect himself and it is very easy to say he's the guilty party."

"I've though of that, too," Val Hughes said quietly, making Ella think she had probably offended him. She tried to smile but her young colleague did not notice that. "The computer made a comparison between Don Highsmith's handwriting and the handwriting on the note signed with his name. The computer juxtaposition shows unambiguously that Don Highsmith wrote the note in which he admits he has committed the murder. There can be no doubt about that."

"The computer juxtaposition is not convincing evidence," Ella pointed out.

"I agree it is not," Val said. "I issued an order on behalf of the agency so that in about two hours the ten best European experts graphologists will be present here to start working on the case. As you know it is exceptionally." He inspector was going to use the adjective "complicated" but stopped in time feeling the phrase had turned into a worn out cliché. "You know what's happening in the town, don't you, Miss Boon? The clinics are full of sick people; all doctors suffer from severe headaches, which prevent them from helping their patients. The reported symptoms are graver than the ones exhibited the Leila dolls epidemic. Now I'll tell you something very curious - as I mentioned already, the Professor was killed about 6PM. Doctors and nurses from two hospitals telephoned me that directly after 6PM the number of people complaining of headaches rapidly decreased plummeting almost to zero. I have no explanation for that. The doctors can't explain it either."

"Did the paramedics take out the Professor's body?" Ella sincerely hoped that had already happened. She had stood horrified many times rendered speechless and numb at the sight of murdered human beings. Corpses did not scare her but her soul felt empty. She had desperately hoped that after every case she had gone through evil would become weaker and people better. Then she saw another victim murdered with schizophrenic inventiveness and blood-curdling cruelty and she doubted if the lonely hours and her life were worth living.

"The Professor's body was taken out but you can see the video-report if you want. Everything has been filmed. But..." the inspector paused. Val's manners so far had been anything but indecisive so Ella expected another surprise. "Miss Boon, can I ask you why you came here? I have not sent for you. Please, excuse me if my words sound rude but I'd like you to know from the very beginning that I prefer to work with Red Kyle."

"I'll satisfy your desire, inspector Hughes," Ella hoped it had not become apparent how unpleasantly stung she was. The emptiness in her soul tasted of metal; it seemed she herself was a metal container somebody was trying to stick ice into. Ella Boon, a lonely block of ice, which was going to melt sooner or later once it approached the zone of hotter waters. She would leave the world without a trace, or perhaps only a freezing memory of a friendless woman would haunt the house she had lived.

"I don't want to put obstacles in your path, inspector Hughes." Ella's voice sounded firm in spite of the depressing thoughts burdening her mind. She was too well trained to give vent to her feelings. "Professor Bell asked to meet me at his office ten minutes before I telephoned you to learn how you felt. The Professor had sent me an Email message. I had another message - from Adrienne Tott. The young lady was asking me to visit her without delay. I am very much afraid lest Adrienne be transformed into the second corpse of the series that Mr. Don Highsmith has promised us."

"But Miss Adrienne Tott was here, in Walnut clinic several minutes ago," the young inspector's words had not still lost the imprint of rapture that the blonde had positively inspired. "Adrienne Tott was hardly able to walk," he went on. "She could not talk, she's been suffering from a splitting headache much worse than the one during the first attack of the disease."

Ella screwed up her eyes stumbling across another glaring contradiction. Adrienne Tott had told her that she had been affected neither by the first nor by the second attack of the epidemic!

Chapter 4

"You cannot allow Old Theodore to remain in the room while you are interrogating me." Larry Hoffburg had probably planned to pronounce that sentence making it sound like a request, but the owner of Toys International had forgotten how to do that. Why should a president of a world famous company ask anybody to do something for him when he could simply issue an order? "I insist on Theodore's staying with me. He is the only person in the world I trust."

"I would like to interrogate Theodore for half an hour after your own interrogation is over, Mr. Hoffburg." Ella had made up her mind to meet her opponent on his own ground. "Then I'll compare his testimony with yours."

Larry Hoffburg's face almost merged with the yellow color of the wallpapers in his office.

"How dare you! I warn you Inspector that I have filed a complaint against you. I've asked you not to inconvenience my advisor Adrienne Tott but you seem take pleasure in that. You've been pestering her for over a week."

"Perhaps you are not informed that Professor Bell was murdered. The murderer left a short note telling us that the next two corpses will be yours and Adrienne Tott's."

"I know that very well, inspector Boon. I'd like to tell you something else: I transferred 15,000 dollars in the name of your agency on condition that you are excluded from the inquest. I do not like you, your behavior raises doubt about how effectively you can work and I wouldn't like to talk to you."

"Unfortunately you have no say in this arrangements, Mr. Hoffburg. You can have your 15,000 dollars back from the agency. I am sorry I'll have to upset a person like you but I was tasked with being the leading inspector in the case of Professor Bell's murder." Larry tried to object but Ella interrupted him waving her hand imperatively. "That is the final decision, Mr. Hoffburg. You'll have to put up with me and if you do not do that voluntarily, I will force you to. You are one of the suspects and I am in the right to keep you under observation or even arrest you. I do not advice you to go on being obstinate. So tell me how is your hand? Do you have a headache or any other complaints?"

Larry Hoffburg answered staring at the wall in front of him, "It is the pain in my body that prevents me from kicking you out of my office, Miss Boon. I have the feeling that if I take a step to the door I will collapse.'

"I think you are lying to me, Mr. Hoffburg. At present you feel no pain whatsoever. I am right. Aren't I?"

"Out!" he shouted. The brown butler's face, old and powerless like a withered tree, appeared in the room as Larry's shrill voice faded away.

"Please, ma'am, do not alarm him." Old Theodore's voice sounded spent and impotent making Ella expect it was going to become inaudible in the middle of the very next sentence. "He is so exhausted. Last night the Professor warned him I mean Professor Bell."

"Theodore, go out, for God's sake!" Larry Hoffburg shouted again.

"So the professor was here last night," Ella said surprised. He had visited you just before he was killed."

"Yes, he visited me," the president of Toys International answered emphatically. "I was very honest with him and informed him I would be very glad to see him dead. Theodore was there too. He heard me say these words so it doesn't make sense to conceal them from you, does it? You'll learn everything in the long run."

"Why did you want to see him dead?"

"Hasn't Adrienne explained to you the reason for that?"

"Let's assume she has but I'd like to have your version of what had happened."

"Well, you won't have it. Adrienne hasn't told you anything," Hoffburg snapped. "You know very well that Adrienne simply cannot be the next corpse. She cannot."

Ella needed some time to brace herself up. She didn't know how to react. One has to use only facts that have been checked and are indisputable. That's rule number one, she said to herself.

"The Trail of Tears experiment turned out to be -- that was what Professor Bell was writing before he was murdered. Evidently somebody didn't want the information about the experiment to leak out. That was first. Second: Don Highsmith, the alleged murderer, warns the agency that you and Adrienne Tott will be killed as well. Now tell me - do you know Don Highsmith?"

"Are you jeering at me? Few dared do that and they still regret their stupidity, you can take my word for that."

"I asked you if you knew Mr. Don Highsmith,"

"OK, but be careful, Miss Boon. You wanted it that way. Don Highsmith was my wife's fiancé. She's Jennifer Cost-Hoffburg."

"So it is reasonable to assume that you stole Jennifer from Don Highsmith?"

"Assume whatever you please, Miss Boon."

Ella studied attentively the office of the president of Toys International. Her eyes were drawn to two cactuses - two really sumptuous representatives of the thorny plant family. She approached the flowerpots stretching out a hand to stroke them.

"You are not at your home!" Hoffburg jumped enraged. "Don't touch my flowers. Step back! Now!"

"Please, excuse me," Ella said with sincere regret. "I wanted to have a look at them at a closer distance. It seems to me you never take the cacti out of your office, Mr. Hoffburg?"

The question remained hanging in the air, unanswered. Ella decided to try another approach.

"Could you tell me something more about your loyal butler Theodore? What sort of a man is he?"

"Theodore used to be a guard of the parking lot of Walnut Hospital," the president of Toys International spoke in a brusque tone." He had been working there for twenty years. I thought he could be useful to me and offered him to become my butler. He's been working in my house more than ten years now. Are you satisfied with that?"

"Of course, Mr. Hoffburg," Ella answered smiling for the first time then stared inquisitively at his gray expensive suit that had been ironed immaculately.

"Look! Look!" She cried out sharply. "What's that on your shoulder?" She put her hand on the gray fabric enveloping his massive round shoulder and before he had time to react she tapped him several times. "Well, your arm does not hurt at all, Mr. Hoffburg. And I will tell you why: four years ago you had a serious road accident - your skull was fractured. No one believed you would survive. Your wife, Jennifer Cost, ordered expensive wreaths for your forthcoming funeral at Smith's undertaker's office, eminent poets wrote elegies devoted to your honesty, fortitude and uprightness. But you survived. Professor Rupert bell saved your life - the man you wanted to see dead."

"Why do you think my arm doesn't hurt?" Larry asked smiling contemptuously. Ella's hand still lay on his shoulder and he pushed it down gruffly.

"You were operated on in Walnut Hospital. Adrienne Tott, the woman you shared your happy hours with, was in the car by your side when the dreadful road accident happened. Adrienne was in a critical condition, severely wounded, almost dead. All that was reflected in her medical card and I didn't have to perform astonishing feats to find it out -- massive cerebral hemorrhage, ruptured spleen, several broken ribs. In other words death was inevitable. But the incomparable Professor Bell took charge of the situation, made a series of complex surgical operations and Miss Tott survived At Christmas, she informed you that she had an excruciating headache. Somebody had smuggled a head of Leila doll into her office for three consecutive days"

"You are beating about the bush, Miss Boon. What are you driving at? Why don't you speak to the point? Apart from having no time I can hardly stand you so I'd appreciate it if your words were connected with what was being discussed." Larry Hoffburg poured himself a glass of apple juice offering the inspector nothing but the sight of his powerful back -- impoliteness that was deliberately sought after.

"The topic of our discussion today, Mr. Hoffburg, is the Trail of Tears experiment," Ella prompted him amicably. "In my opinion Mr. President, you and your friend and advisor Adrienne Tott participated in it and that is why your arm does not hurt you. The theatrical performance related to Leila doll's hands that appeared on your desk was a trick you had contrived to make Adrienne Tott keep the secret. Am I right? You most probably knew about the outbreak of the first epidemic. Well, well, well, I understand you don't want to speak about it now. Adrienne however is not a silly woman - she has never acted rashly. How could she! She achieved for eight years more than other ordinary people could make for three generations in their families! Let us at last speak out the truth - it was she and not you who managed the company Toys International. She said she had found a Leila doll's head. You say you found a doll's hand, so I presume you might have known beforehand something about the nature of the epidemic. At least you expected it might be connected with inflammations of the joints or splitting headaches."

"Your story is a complete fabrication from start to finish. You've got a sick imagination, Miss Boon," Hoffburg's categorical voice declared icily. "You are crazy."

"Why, maybe I am," Ella conceded too readily, making Hoffburg stare at her in disbelief. "Why are you so sure Adrienne Tott cannot be the next corpse? Because she is one of the leading figures in the experiment and it is too early to be eliminated. In my opinion, dear Mr. Hoffburg, the Trail of Tears experiment is related exactly to resurrecting people who faced inevitable death. In other words men and women that were doomed. That is a beautiful and exalted idea - to bring nearly dead persons back to life. There is nothing more sublime and nobler than being a Messiah, isn't there? Alas, today one has to pay for everything one gets. Your life was saved so please, tell me how much you had paid Walnut hospital and personally Professor Bell for his timely services?"

"Four million pounds," was the president's instantaneous response.

"I didn't mean the exact amount of money, Mr. Hoffburg," Ella took a step towards the owner of Toys International. "Tell me what you have agreed to do for Professor Bell. Were you involved with the Trail of Tears experiment?"

"I've already informed you about my opinion on that, Miss Boon," Larry shook his head firmly. "What you say sounds wild and extravagant. A person less civilized that me could word it in a much more explicit way."

"Mr. Hoffburg, as a child you suffered from asthma. The attacks of the disease were frequent, severe and almost deathly. All this is true, isn't it? I have checked all your medical documents very carefully. You were ill at the time when you worked as an anonymous obscure troubleshooter repairing busted electrical appliances. But something happened two years ago. Please, remember what it was."

Larry Hoffburg's face lost color, his body froze in an intense arc that was about to burst with vibrant tension. It appeared as if another man had stood up in front of Ella, a normal human being having none of the annoying self-confidence, which imparted a halo of grandeur and inaccessibility to Mr. Larry Hoffburg, the president of a flourishing company.

"I see you've delved into my past," he muttered at last. "A good job for a cop in sorry trim like you."

"I assure you the check-up was thorough but it took exactly twenty-four minutes to make. The computers in Walnut hospital that you paid for a year ago are really top quality. They toiled and moiled for me and it was not hard even for a cop in sorry trim like me to read the information they had found out." Ella smiled pleasantly. "Two years ago, Mr. Hoffburg, your asthma disappeared - simply vanished without a trace as if you had never suffered from it. Asthma is a serious chronic disease demanding a lot of efforts to keep it under control. Please, correct me, if I am wrong."

"So what?" Hoffburg whispered the tense uneasy arc of his body trembling slightly. His left hand made a graceful hardly perceptible move. Nothing in Ella's behavior showed she had noticed it but the meaning of the words she uttered was quite different.

"Do not bother to reach inside your bag for your favorite weapon," Ella told him calmly. "I still don't know what exactly it is but my guess is that the two pleasant-looking cactuses are something worth one's while."

Larry Hoffburg's hand gave a jerk. The cacti smiled behind his back their prickles glittering like miniature stilettos in the sun.

"You know too much to go on living," the president of Toys International sighed. "I am sorry, I warned you I could not stand you." He ducked down swiftly leaving Ella face to face with the cactuses, which stood immobile, casting jagged shadows on the wall. Larry Hoffburg's office did not have a good view of the town. Its windows offered a banal sight of a big parking lot for the cars of the white-collar workers of Toys International. That was quite strange Ella thought.

"You know perfectly well that I cannot be the next corpse. The police will very easily come to the conclusion that you murdered me and that that would be quite stupid of you." Ella walked calmly to the refrigerator, took a can of apple juice from it then approached the cactuses and touched gently their thin sharp prickles. "Your favorite plants are wonderful, Mr. Hoffburg," she said shaking carefully one of the green prickly balls. It glided smoothly half an inch to the left. There was no soil in the exquisite flowerpot. A small object-glass protruded a little over the rim of the flowerpot. Ella put her hand on it.

"Now I understand why all your secretaries quitted their jobs so quickly after you hired them, Mr. Hoffburg," she sighed. "All the three girls whose medical documentation I checked had contracted one and the same terminal disease, leukemia. You subjected them to deathly radiation through these cacti, which are in fact object-glasses! You are not a foolish person; why didn't you think at least for a moment that the three young women contracting deathly leukemia a month after they fled from Toys International worked as your secretaries. You didn't think about that. It's a pity! There is something else that looks very strange to me here. No one has ever looked for these young ladies; no one has complained that they have disappeared. Well, I searched for them. Well, it was a stupid occupation very suitable for a cop in sorry trim like me."

Larry sank down into his easy-chair, his face unperturbed.

"I'm listening to you very carefully, Miss Boon," he said. "Your story sounds very interesting and I admit that my curiosity was aroused."

"Mr. Hoffburg, there is another very interesting fact: not only had the three young ladies disappeared from our serene town." Ella pulled up her chair sipping at her apple juice. "Virtually all people suffering from incurable diseases vanished and are no longer available in Jacksonville. One might think that have evaporated somewhere. They have not died. Their names are not registered in the files of deceased citizen in any European country. No one has ever looked for them. Well, no one but me. What have you done to these sick people, Mr. Hoffburg?"

"Why should you ask me?" Larry Hoffburg said almost inaudibly. "You should know better than that. You are a cop and you are paid to learn things that ordinary people like me should be unable to imagine. Adrienne told me that you didn't have any medical complaints after Leila dolls flooded the town. Furthermore, as far as I know, you got rid of your eczema. Exactly the same thing happened to my asthma. It no longer tortures me and I have forgotten virtually all about its attacks."

Larry rose from his chair taking a few steps to the inspector. He bent forward holding up his hands with fingers extended, his lips taut, colorless, trembling menacingly. Hoffburg's gray piercing eyes fastened on the inspector's face his voice croaking harshly, making her instinctively take a step back.

"Ella, you also participated in the Trail of Tears experiment. Don't you remember that?" his voice faded abruptly and the silence reigning in the room turned into tangible paralyzing fear. Larry Hoffburg's gray eyes crept up her face leaving panic in their wake, which slowly seized her whole body. The constricting sticky waves of fear took hold of her. She had to drive them away. She had to fight against the bear hug of horror.

"The fact that I probably took part in the experiment does not prevent me from feeling fine, Mr. Hoffburg" Ella spoke out coldly. "On the contrary, I have nothing to complain of. To be honest with you, your words have just added to the intrigue of our conversation. It turns out we participated in one and the same experiment, we are experiment colleagues, so to say."

"That's the truth experiment colleagues," Larry said. "I don't see why you should put a spoke in my wheel. It would be far better if you gave me a hand to find at which phase of the experiment we made the damned blunder."

"The damned blunder!" the minute the exclamation slid through her clenched teeth she knew she should have kept her mouth tightly shut. She had made a mistake again. "Yes, yes," Ella paused to draw breath. "You probably know more than me, Larry. You don't mind my calling you by your first name, do you? As far as I remember you called me Ella a minute age not even bothering to ask if I agree to that."

"It is not an honor for me to hear my name pronounced by you, inspector Boon," the man explained making a wry face. "Even my wife Jennifer does not call me Larry."

"Is it only Adrienne Tott that calls you by your first name?" Ella asked perfectly aware of the fact how presumptuous and uncivilized her question sounded.

"Adrienne is the only person who is allowed to call me Larry. Oh, yes, old Theodore, too, and nobody else. So I'd appreciate if you don't use that proper name when you address me. You, of all people!"

Ella peered out of the window not listening for a minute to Larry's words. She had noticed something very interesting not far from the parking lot - the blonde fairy Adrienne was talking to an obese woman. It was obvious the two of them were not discussing a pleasant topic. The fat woman's face looked twisted out of its natural shape her hands resembling soft cushions flailed the air making jerky churning motions. Adrienne's profile appeared perfectly calm her figure irradiating cold self-possessed superiority.

"I think we have exhausted the topic of our conversation, Miss Boon. In my opinion, it is high time you went home or to some other gloomy place."

Anxious to send the inspector away, Larry Hoffburg jumped out of his chair opening the door of his office for her in order to facilitate her retreat. Ella, however, had no intention of taking advantage of her host's courtesy.

"Yes, I'll go home or to some other gloomy place," Ella said. "I'd appreciate it if you answered me two more questions. There are only two of them," the inspector lowered her voice soothingly. "The first one is: Mr. Hoffburg, have you noticed that there have been no deaths in our town? Not a single human being has died for more than two years."

"Listen!" The president of Toys International flew into a rage. "At present, I don't intend to set up an undertaker's office. Neither do I desire to visit an establishment of this kind in the near future. If you'd like to obtain accurate information on all undertakers' offices in town turn to Mr. Smith, the mortician. He is the middleman in discussions between the citizens of our nasty world and God."

"It's interesting that Mr. Smith closed his undertaker's office in our town, Mr. Hoffburg. Jacksonville has a population of nearly 35,000 and there is not a single undertaker's office in it. Strange, isn't it? People here simply don't die. Your ex-secretaries, for example, contracted leukemia then were miraculously cured. Lo and behold, another miracle occurred - the three young ladies pursued successful careers becoming prosperous storeowners. It all sounds very curious, doesn't it?" Ella gazed at Hoffburg's face. "There are incredibly many sick people in Jacksonville. I asked the World Health Institute for statistical data and I found out some striking facts. Jacksonville is the town in which the number of people suffering from malignant tumors is highest in Europe. What will you say about that, Mr. Hoffburg?"

"Is that your final question, inspector Boon?" The president of Toys International asked perfectly composed. "I feel an overwhelming desire to provide explanation for the fact you have just stated but I assure you that I am incapable of doing that. Perhaps you should consult the experts working for the European Healthcare Institute. They might have something to offer you."

"Well, let me put it in a different way: according to the statistical data collected and issued by World Health Institute there are five more European towns where the number of people suffering from malignant tumors is extraordinary high. The towns are: Cerrydale, Bellview, Molten Rock, Siracuse, and Serried Springs. Don't the names of these towns remind you of something?"

"I must admit geography has never been my strong point," Larry Hoffburg smiled. "Inspector, I have an idea! I can order my secretary to go and buy a world atlas; maybe the poor maps can make you leave my office as soon as possible. You can use the atlas to eliminate the gaps in your education, Miss Boon."

"The biggest five factories of Toys International are situated in the towns I've just enumerated," Ella said coldly. "You are not a foolish person, Mr. Hoffburg."

"Thank you," the president of Toys International nodded his head smiling.

"You are not a foolish person," Ella repeated watching closely the expression on his face. "I am sure you can realize that sooner or later the medical statistics will find out the connection between your factories and the spread of the killer diseases. Many people will start asking questions like: "How come the terminally sick people never die? What happens to them? So far, there have been no answers to these questions. However, a nice day dawned when you, Mr. Hoffburg, did not want to wait any more. You made a desperate move; you had decided to spur the sluggish healthcare institutions into action. They should start racking their brains they should be asking what's happening, why it is happening. You made another desperate move: you spread Leila dolls as Christmas presents and Oh, my God! An outbreak of headache epidemic seized the town; the clinics and hospitals were flooded by sick, moaning people. Who was to blame for that dreadful chaos? Who caused the upsurge of the severe medical complaints? The answer comes quite naturally: the guilty party is your company "Toys International". It spread the dolls though the chemical analysis pointed out unambiguously that the Leila dolls did not contain any substance capable of producing the epidemics. Well, who would believe that? All citizens had unbearable headaches, suffered from agonizing rheumatic pains and nobody was interested in the assurances that the Leila dolls were perfectly innocuous. The public wanted to lynch Toys International. Mr. Hoffburg, I suspect your most urgent desire now is to make your own company go bankrupt. Why?"

"You are out of your mind, Inspector Boon. There is no grain of truth in what you said."

"You are afraid of Adrienne Tott, aren't you?" Ella said. "You trembled as I pronounced her name."

"Afraid of my own mistress?" Larry Hoffburg made an expressive gesture meaning clearly that Ella Boon's place was in a psychiatric ward.

"You are afraid of Adrienne and at the same time you are unable to control your passion for her. You had to fake pain shooting through your shoulder, arm or leg depending on which part of the doll's body you had planted in your office. You wanted to get rid of Adrienne by accusing her of placing these small plastic parts of Leila doll's body. Or perhaps you wanted to cast suspicion on Adrienne so that we could arrest her and keep her at a safe place in the Agency?

"You are a psycho, Inspector Boon!" Larry Hoffburg shouted.

"No, I am not," Ella whispered. "Don't forget I am one of the 'reverse effect' persons. I am not afraid of the epidemics. You have filmed everything - perhaps using the camera installed under one of these two cactuses. The film shows how your arm goes stiff, the pain becoming sharp and severe. After that you find a plastic leg and your own leg causes you intense suffering. You sent copies of the film to the World Health Institute and to Bob Hendrix, my boss. You made a special request pointing out how necessary it was for Adrienne to undergo a series of extensive medical tests. In fact you wanted to be rid of her."

"Stop living in a fantasy world, Inspector Boon!" Larry said struggling to regain control of the situation. "You are a cop and you should not let your imagination run away with you. You are being absurd."

"Yes, Adrienne is your mistress but you have never trusted her. She's had many chances to ensnare much wealthier men than you, Mr. Hoffburg her charm, her captivating manners. You know all that very well. She never wanted another man and she is so pretty anyone would be proud to have her. Perhaps somebody made her choose you. Why - to follow closely your every move? But why not kill you? She could have done that easily." Ella approached Larry whose face had become ashen and wet with sweat. "I offer you security, Larry. Why don't you tell me about that great experiment that Professor Bell called "The Trail of Tears"? Trust me! How did you cause the epidemics, the two horrible waves of medical complaints? I am in charge of the Trail of Tears case and I promise I'll protect you. Trust me!"

"How could I?" Larry Hoffburg said shrilly wiping the sweat from his forehead. He clenched his big colorless fists to stop himself trembling. "I did fake pain and I did film everything. It is unbearable to be different from the rest to be a 'reverse effect' guy. Nobody will forgive that! I know many things about you, Ella Boon!"

Larry Hoffburg's voice thinned into a scream. The door of the office opened a couple of inches the old butler's brown face taking a quick peek inside.

"Would you like something to drink, my boy?" He said his small voice echoing hollowly in the room.

"No, Theodore, thank you," Larry answered. For the first time that day, Ella saw an expression of profound gratitude on the president's face. So far, nothing had broken Larry Hoffburg's immaculate defense strategy.

The butler entered the office his steps powerless, his breathing labored and hoarse.

"Are you okay, son?" the old man asked sounding concerned.

"Yes, Theodore, I am okay," Larry whispered.

The old man fidgeted uneasily by the door.

"Inspector Ella Boon," he spoke out at last. "With your permission, I'd like to bring him a cup of tea."

His old face expressed his infinite loyalty to his employer, for a split second reminding Ella of something, stirring a chain of vague evasive shadows in her mind. She could not remember anything definite, could not explain the nagging feeling of loneliness sweeping over her, which she tried in vain to banish.

"May I bring him a cup of tea, Ma'am?" the old man asked slowly rousing Ella from her stupor.

"Of course you may," she said.

When the butler left the office the blood had already come back to Larry's face making him appear much calmer than before.

"What do you know about me, Mr. Hoffburg?" Inspector Boon asked. The president of Toys International kept silent. "Trust me, Mr. Hoffburg. I will provide you with effective protection. I swear I will! What do you know about me?"

"How old are you, Ella Boon?"

"Why should you be interested in that?" The inspector evaded answering the question lowering her eyes.

"I know you are 51. I know what happened to you years ago when you were a very young woman."

Ella failed to stifle her small exclamation staring in astonishment at the man. So far she had been sure no one knew about the events that had occurred more than three decades ago. She had not told anybody about that - the worst weeks in her life, her long illness, the faces of doctors and nurses, the nightmares.

"Twenty-eight years ago your house was destroyed in a fire. The police could not find out if it had been started by arsonists or simply someone had knocked over a lantern and the kitchen caught fire," Larry Hoffburg's voice thinned into whisper. "Your parents died. No one paid attention to you, the paramedics thinking you were dead. But you survived! You were cured by - do you remember who cured you, Ella? It was Rupert Bell, at that time a student in medicine. He brought you to Walnut Clinic. You had been recuperating there for three years and after you left it, Bell bought the clinic and the hospital."

"Three years!" Ella whispered.

"You have no memories of that time," Larry Hoffburg said quietly. "Please, concentrate! Can you remember a fair-haired little girl?"

"I don't remember anything," Ella answered tonelessly.

For a whole minute, Larry stood immobile, gazing into her face.

"Then they have achieved even that complete loss of memory. They have erased everything from your mind! But you can't have forgotten everything"

"Who are they?"

"The Trail of Tears experiment Professor Bell. The sick patients subjected to regeneration I objected but, but they were going to kill me."

"Who are they?" Ella whispered. "Who are they? What do they want? Did the experiment involve using the sick patients? What do you mean by "subjected to regeneration"?"

"They pay a lot if you can make a person so ill that he'd prefer death," Larry blurted out. "You get a lot of money for each person who falls terminally ill. Five of my employees had contracted leukemia while they built five toy factories for me. You know the names of the five European towns where my factories have been built, Ella. You have visited them all. Have you noticed by chance how numerous the flowerpots with cactuses are? The small black eyes of the object-glasses... The dim suffering eyes of the sick It is unbearable, Ella... You think constantly of them, you tell yourself - better regenerated than dead. I'd prefer death though"

"Don't be afraid, Larry!" She took a step towards him freezing in her tracks, dumbfounded by his unexpected reaction - the man turned pale recoiling in horror.

"You are going to kill me, aren't you? They've sent you, I knew it the minute I saw you! In fact, what difference would it make if you did it or Adrienne I've thought of committing suicide. They can't regenerate me! But Adrienne was so sweet, I enjoyed inventing new toys for the little fellows."

His eyes smoldered with anger.

"Come on! Shoot! Kill me, Ella Boon!"

"I will protect you!" Ella shouted. "I am not going to kill you!"

"It's all the same to me. One day you will be like me. Do you remember, Ella - paramedics brought you to Walnut clinic years ago. You had been shot at and you were bleeding heavily from many wounds. All doctors thought you'd die after a few hours, a couple of days at most. But you survived; you had been subjected to regeneration. Adrienne was with you, wasn't she?"

"She told me that herself," Ella answered quickly. "Under interrogation, she informed me that she was accidentally in the clinic at the time I was brought choking on my own blood after being shot in the throat."

"Perhaps they sent her there to spy on you," Larry whispered. "Probably they had not decided yet if they were going to kill you or let you live. They had hesitated finally coming to the conclusion that you would cause more deaths if you remained alive. Shoot, Ella!"

"How much do you know about Don Highsmith? He's tried to commit suicide twice," Ella spoke distinctly her voice very calm. "Has be been subjected to regeneration as well?"

"I won't tell you. You must be one of them. You won't get any answers from me! I know a traitor dies a slow and painful death. The fact you are a cop working for the Agency is of no consequence to me. They have their spies in the Agency!"

"I am not one of them, Larry. I will protect you," Ella took a step to the president of Toys International. "Trust me, Larry. You are safe here. Does Don Highsmith play any particular role in the experiment? Is there a connection between him and Adrienne Tot?"

"You have to know who Adrienne Tott is. Think about it, have a good look at her!"

"I have no information what sort of a person she is. I speak the truth, Larry," Ella had spread her palms in a gesture of openness. She knew from the ancient copperplate engravings that worshippers did that before they prayed to their pagan gods. "Is Adrienne one of them? She probably is, high up in their hierarchy Larry! Larry! What are they for God's sake?"

"They are people! Regenerated people, and therefore they're not humans. How shall I explain that to you? They can put an end to their own life whenever they want and no one can regenerate them against their will. Adrienne Tott is"

The door opened and the old butler Theodore entered the office walking slowly, powerlessly, like an animal smelling death nearby. He held an antique tea tray his hands trembling.

"Larry, my boy, that is for you," he said uttering the words slowly making great efforts.

"Thank you so much, Theodore!" A faint smile climbed Larry Hoffburg's lips making his face ruggedly attractive. "But, but Theodore! What are you doing, Theodore!"

For an instant, sharp a swishing sound broke the silence in the room as if the butler had opened a bottle of a fizzy mineral water, the cork popping loudly. He president of Toys International collapsed on the floor. A splodge of blood appeared by the body, then percolating down through the expensive green carpet.

Ella jumped managing to grab the butler's right hand. The old man's colorless fingers clutched at the tray the teacup falling onto the floor. Theodore still held the gun in his left hand. Ella reached out her hand to catch it. At that moment the muted swishing sound was heard again. The old man's body fell on the carpet like a dry dead bough. Ella breathed heavily, trying hard to gather her thoughts unable to control her trembling hands. Two dead bodies lay prostrate on the floor. A happy, childish smile still played across old Theodore's lips. Larry Hoffburg's face looked tortured, contorted in utter surprise. These two men could never speak again carrying the secret of Trail of Tears experiment to their graves. At the moment when the curtain had just begun to rise, letting her take a tiny, quick peek inside the mystery, Ella felt helpless, vulnerable. A painful, unbearable thought dominated her mind. "I shouldn't have allowed Theodore to kill Larry! I shouldn't have allowed the butler to commit suicide! It was my duty to prevent that. My God I have no witnesses now!"

Chapter 5

"Can you explain why you were in Walnut clinic several minutes after Professor Bell was killed?"

Val Hughes, contrary to his habit of standing immobile by the window, paced up and down his dark office in the Investigation Agency. His eyes dwelt on the cheerless landscape outside of the building: a sad April afternoon, a narrow asphalt path crossing the backyard of the Agency and two anemic cypress trees too delicate to stand the severe northern climate in Jacksonville.

He wanted badly to look at the face of the woman he was interrogating and the questions he fancied asking her had nothing to do with the details related to Professor Bell's murder. The most attractive lady the inspector had seen in his life was perfectly quiet, settled leaning back in the only battered armchair in the room her legs crossed demurely. Her eyes looked as deep and mysterious as mountain lakes the minute when the water became murky with the new streams from the melting snowdrifts Mountain lakes in spring Val Hughes had never had the chance of going to the mountains, of breathing in the fresh crisp wind and looking at the sky and letting it enter his body. He thought he'd always miss the feeling of happiness that lakes inspired him with. They were pure and mysterious, under the stars below the mountain top - he had to walk days on end climbing the steep winding paths to catch a glimpse of them, to see his face reflected in their blue, deceptively calm surface.

The woman was Adrienne Tott, known for nine or eight years as Larry Hoffburg's mistress, the brains behind the plans and contracts of the international toy producing company. Val couldn't keep an eye on Adrienne's quiet elusive profile in the dim light. Her defiance inflamed his imagination. Now he could think of a possible explanation for the words Larry Hoffburg had described his mistress with, "I wanted to run away, at least during the first couple of minutes of my meetings with her, away from her blue, gleaming eyes. The passion stalking in them, full of promise and rebellion, the expectation of happiness I thought I saw always distracted me from my work. I inevitably found I did exactly what she had wanted me to - things that I most often would have never done."

At first, Val Hughes had secretly mocked the President of Toys International. Who could distract a young ambitious inspector working for the Investigation Agency from his goal? It appeared practically impossible. But now

Adrienne sat before him - he could smell her perfume, his eyes could follow her magnificent body. No one even started to suspect he did anything wrong. He was interrogating that woman after all.

Val Hughes wanted to prove he had a much stronger will than the poor aging president of Toys Internationals. Now for example, he studied carefully the narrow asphalt path in the backyard then his attention was drawn to the old cypress trees hidden in the dark April rain while Adrienne Tott sat so very close her strange eyes boring into him. What did she think of him? Did she like him at least a little? Then Val Hughes remembered in a flash that this beautiful woman had been Larry Hoffburg's mistress for eight years. She had taken him to her bed, had put on her make-up for him, had kissed that man who as bald as a coot! Damn it! Adrienne Tott refused to talk to inspector Val Hughes. How long would it take her to answer his simple question? Why had she come to Walnut clinic less than half an hour after Professor Bell was murdered? Was it a simple coincidence?

"You seem not to listen to what I tell you, Inspector Hughes," the young lady said quietly. Was there sadness in her voice or did he just think so on account of the cold lonely rain outside?

"I am listening to you, Miss Tott," the inspector answered in the coldest possible tone of voice. "You are trying to concoct some elaborate story to explain your presence in the clinic. Judging by the myths and legends related to your name, that is not your style. Even if you did kill Professor Bell you'd have prepared an alibi and an answer to all possible questions a half a year prior to the crime itself."

"I am afraid the myths and legends involving my name overestimate my abilities," Adrienne sighed. Val Hughes noticed her slender marble-white neck tremble slightly. Her shapely breasts shuddered "as tender as snowdrifts in the beginning of winter": that was a line of the poem Mr. Somebody, an eminent poet, had written in honor of Adrienne after Larry Hoffburg forked out five grand for that unsurpassable work of art. Damn it!

"What is it? Perhaps there is a coffee stain on my blouse?" Adrienne asked. She had followed his eyes mistranslating his meaning. Or was she faking? Anyway, he'd better stare at the thick April fog, straining his eyes to discern the cypress trees that didn't interest him at all. He felt much safer that way.

"Miss Tott, the stains on your blouse do not concern me," Val Hughes said sharply. Why did you come to Walnut hospital on Thursday half an hour after Professor Bell was killed? I'm asking you that question for the third time. I warn you that if you don't answer me now, I will have to detain you for further questioning in the Agency. Then you'll have to speak before Ella Boon, Red Kyle and our director, Mr. Bob Hendricks."

"To be honest with you, I am not afraid of the people you've just enumerated," the young woman said smiling. Out if the corner of his eye, Val saw her neck tremble again, and that, very strangely, moved him. "I'll answer your question, Inspector. I visited Walnut Hospital on Thursday - only forty minutes after the professor was murdered - because I had a violent headache. I wanted to consult Professor Bell because he was the only person among all medics in town capable of relieving my suffering. It would take a miracle to make my headache go and he performed miracles. I couldn't have known that the Professor would be killed on that very day. If I had anything to do with his murder I wouldn't have shown up at crime scene teeming with policemen. Think about that, Inspector!"

Val Hughes was silent for about a minute. It was very quiet in his dimly lit office and he seemed to hear her heart throb softly; apart from that Val felt her blue eyes study carefully his profile. He wanted to prolong this magic spell by several seconds but he had to speak.

"I'll tell you the only answer why you, Miss Tot, were in Walnut Hospital at the time the murder took place and why you were the only person outside the staff that the policemen intercepted as you tried to leave the clinic. The only answer is that you killed Professor Bell!

"I killed Professor Bell?" The young woman jumped up from her chair her unbelievably attractive face turning intensely red. "Why should I kill him? Why should I destroy the only person able to alleviate the sufferings of thousands of people in Jacksonville? Why should I murder the doctor who had saved my life after I was practically dead? It sounds absurd, Inspector!"

"Two years ago you and your, your--" Val's eyes flashed for the first time since the beginning of the conversation. "You and your sweetheart Larry Hoffburg had a serious car accident. You had a ruptured spleen, broken ribs etc. No one believed that you would survive but you did. There is something else, which is hard to believe: you not only survived but most unexpectedly got rid of your stomach ulcer, which had bled very often making you suffer for long, long years. Larry Hoffburg also survived although all doctors who had examined him thought that he had no more than 1%, at most 2% to go on living. He not only lived through the accident but also was rid of his asthma as you know very well."

"So you think that I must necessarily kill the professor on account of the fact he had saved my and my sweetheart's lives and cured us of our dreadful diseases?" Miss Adrienne Tott's indignation was so tangible he could touch it with his hand. "Your understanding of human gratitude is quite strange, Inspector Hughes."

"I still haven't finished," Val found it very difficult to speak in his usual cutting icy voice. "The patients whom the Professor had saved did not have any medical complaints while the rest of the population of Jacksonville, thousands of children suffered severely. The professor made these people different from all the rest. The epidemics did not affect them."

"And you thing that's bad?" Adrienne waved her hand declaring suddenly, "Calm down, Inspector. I also suffered severely you can take my word for that. I had a splitting headache which made me visit Professor Bell last Thursday."

"You told Inspector Boon an entirely different story. You had stated you didn't have a splitting headache. You felt healthy both in the beginning when Leila dolls were spread in town and during the second attack of the epidemic.

Now you give me another version claiming you suffer so much, in fact worse than most people. Would you be so kind to tell me when you were speaking the truth?"

"Now I can hardly see your face," the young woman said quietly. "I am racked with pain, gradually losing sensation in my hands and legs."

"Therefore, you had lied to Inspector Ella Boon," Val spoke firmly but he hated to do that; he'd have gladly redoubled his efforts to make her wonderful blue eyes forget all about suffering but he had to go on attacking her. "Why did you lie to Inspector Ella Boon? You are perfectly aware that lying will not help you. It will only confirm our suspicions."

"I can't stand Ella Boon!" whispered the fair-haired young woman. "Her lack of manners is quite appalling. I hate her supercilious habit of nodding her head so coldly and importantly as if you were a stupid third-grader. I was fed up with her brief, meaningful glances. She behaved as if she knew everything in advance having her finger on the trigger ready to shoot me. I don't admire your favorite Ella Boon, Inspector."

Val felt an overwhelming desire to admit that he, too, was not enchanted with Ella's manners but was wise enough not to voice his criticisms. He killed a couple of minutes watching the melancholic cypress trees, plucking up enough courage to remark, "Perhaps you can't stand me, Miss Tott?"

"You?" The amazement flashing deep down her blue eyes turned into a quiet, gentle smile. ""I wouldn't say that of you, Inspector Hughes.

His name, pronounced so softly by her, suddenly acquired a peculiar musical quality making Val feel dizzy and light-headed. He could hardly suppress the thin smile, which, in his opinion, made his face appear childishly cock-sure. What a pity he had to continue in the old angry attacking vein.

"Miss Tott, for me, you are the prime suspect in the case. The policemen had not intercepted other outsiders in the immediate vicinity of Walnut hospital. You were the only one. Apart from that, we caught you out in a lie - the whole story about your splitting headache was nothing but a pack of lies. I'd like to add something else to that: you wanted to meet with Inspector Ella Boon exactly at the same time when Professor Bell had asked to meet her. It appears as though you intentionally tried to keep Inspector Boon away from the Professor!"

"Well, well, well," the young woman sighed. "Let's assume I wanted to meet with Inspector Boon just at the time when the murder took place. How could I talk to Inspector Boon at my apartment killing the Professor at the same time? I was waiting for your favorite Ella in my sitting room and my servant, Mrs. Edna Hays, can tell you how many times I cursed your haughty, swell-headed colleague."

"But why did you want to talk particularly to Ella Boon? I far as I remember you've just mentioned you can't stand her," Val's misleadingly soft words contained an undertone of warning. "Why didn't you try to contact me, for example?"

"There is a convincing reason for that, Inspector Val Hughes," an avalanche of scorching ambers ran down the inspector's back as he heard her pronounce his name. "On Thursday morning, I found a handwritten note in my mailbox. It promised me that in the evening I would be a barely recognizable corpse. The note recommended that I ask Inspector Boon for additional information on the procedure."

"And, of course, you lost the handwritten note?" Val would bet anybody a hundred dollars that the material evidence in question had been destroyed long time ago if it had been there at all. He was totally convinced that the handwritten note was one among the numerous yarns, which wonderful Miss Tott willingly span.

"I have kept the note," she said and Val again felt the scorching ambers on his back. "I'll show it to you. The long years of working for Mr. Hoffburg have taught me to be very careful with all types of written evidence."

"Has Mr. Hoffburg taught you anything else?" Val Hughes asked bitterly feeling more than ever how much he hated the president of Toys International.

"He taught me to be selflessly in love," the young lady said most unexpectedly.

"Selflessly in love?" Val repeated thoughtfully. "What should that mean I wonder?"

"It meant I had to love only him and no one else. I should not even think of other men. You would have wanted the same thing from me if you had had the possibility to be in his shoes."

"I don't envy him his shoes," Val lied passionately. "I don't like you, Miss Tott."

"It wasn't necessary to say that, I can see it in your eyes," the young woman whispered smiling.

"Where is the note?" Val asked sternly knowing he was on slippery ground. He should have steered the conversation away from any embarrassing subjects, he should have kept it under control. He had to make no more mistakes now. "Will you show me the notorious note reading you'll be the next corpse?"

Adrienne silently gave him a sheet of paper - most ordinary sheet of paper torn from a schoolboy's pad. The whole free space on it was filled with big, angular letters; it was evident the sender had been in a great hurry scribbling the words. The punctuation marks, at least at first sight, appeared to be all right. Val Hughes impatiently read the three lines of the short note.

Chick,

Although you are absolutely magnificent, today, 2 April, Thursday, at about 8 PM you will be a magnificent corpse. For further details do not hesitate to contact the aging chick Ella Boon.

Sincerely,

Don   Highsmith

"It's good you have kept the note," Val Hughes said coldly. "You have probably heard about that remarkable man Don Highsmith."

"Yes, I've heard a lot of things about him," Adrienne Tott answered calmly. "That is the man who had murdered Professor Bell. I learnt that he was the guilty party watching a series of TV reports. Don has promised Larry, too, to transform him into a corpse. The television has been blaring out information about Don every single half hour providing minute details bearing almost no relations to the murder."

"I suppose it really annoyed you," Val said quietly gazing at the exquisite soft outlines of Adrienne's shoulders. Her blond hair fell over her eyes making her tilt her face, pretty, mocking, mysterious, up to his then she settled back into her chair.

"If you really want to know the truth you'll have it in a minute. I carefully watched all the reports on Professor Bell's murder." Adrienne amused herself staring at the shadow that Val's body cast on the floor. "Inspector, I saw on the TV the note, which Don had left on the desk of the murdered professor. A remarkable murderer, a guy fond of leaving instructions everywhere he goes, explaining painstakingly his next step. It seems to me he doesn't want his crimes to be attributed to somebody else. In fact, I am deeply indebted to him for that, Inspector. He has admitted to his crime and I can't understand why you should put the blame on me."

"The police have not intercepted any other outsider but you in Walnut hospital. There were the registered patients, the medical staff and you, Miss Tott. Don Highsmith could not have vanished without a trace; he couldn't have simply evaporated, could he?"

"You found no trace of me either at the crime scene, did you?"

Val looked closely at Adrienne's face. It was as calm as usual gentle mockery playing on her soft lips.

"You always said Don - I was impressed you didn't use his whole name Don Highsmith. Why? Do you know that man?" So far, Val had always been convinced he possessed skill and an eye for detail noticing the slightest changes in the expression of the person he was talking to. Adrienne's face was something entirely different. It was dangerously closed showing no emotion, concealing the slightest shivers of excitement, revealing nothing of the doubts that most probably disturbed that young attractive woman's mind. "You know Don Highsmith personally, don't you, Miss Tott?"

"Of course I know him."

"Can you tell me where you first met him? I'd like to know more about his domestic and financial circumstances."

"It will be my pleasure," the young woman answered smiling. "Don Highsmith had been Jennifer Cost's fiancé and as you know very well Jennifer is Larry Hoffburg's wife. After Larry and I became lovers he got into the habit of dedicating too little of his precious time to his wife. So Don Highsmith started fawning on Jennifer and no one could blame him - her property amounted and still amounts to astronomical figures, Inspector."

"My question was where you first met him," the Inspector reminded her dryly.

"I met him at a party for the New Year's Eve," Adrienne answered without delay. "Jennifer had asked Don and me to celebrate the New Year in the family circle, so to speak. It was only natural Larry was there, too, and was not very happy with Don's presence. I still wonder when Larry was more furious - when Dan held me in a passionate tango or when he was dead on his feet hardly able to stand Jennifer's enormous mass as they danced. It was very amusing. I'm honest with you."

"Is that everything you can tell me about Don? Could you judge him on such a brief acquaintanceship?"

"Yes, that's all, Inspector Hughes."

"You are lying to me again, Miss Tot. You knew Don Highsmith several years earlier before you shacked up with your boyfriend Larry Hoffburg, "Val's disappointment was so huge Adrienne could feel it trembling in the air.

"I had not known that man before I moved into Larry's place," she said insistently.

"All right, then. Go on lying to me!" The young inspector stood up pacing nervously up and down in front of the only window in his office. "Have in mind that your lies raise serious doubts as to your protested innocence. Your odd behavior invites suspicion." The windowpane reflected the woman's figure its lusterless surface imparting intangibility an unreal purity to it. "Only a couple of days ago your boyfriend Hoffburg sent me a copy of his investigation into your very intriguing CV. Your real name was Rosita Tott and you assumed the name Adrienne at his insistence. You are an adopted child. Your adoptive parents had taken you from Walnut Clinic."

"I have never known I am an adopted child," Adrienne whispered. "You are lying to me, aren't you? Don't be counting on me to start whimpering or assaulting you. I won't claw you across the face although you deserve it. Neither will I kneel down admitting Don Highsmith was my lover. That would indirectly mean that I was an accomplice to Professor Bell's murder. That would be a truly amazing achievement - I killed the doctor who had saved my life!"

"You are an adopted child," Val Hughes said firmly. "Your natural parents refused to give their names to the authorities, leaving you at a small municipal child care institution. Your adoptive parents are: father Henry Tott, a florist who owned a little gift store; mother - Sarah Jane Tott, a seamstress. Your adoptive father died ten years ago, committing suicide. To put it plainly and more directly - he hanged himself from a beam. His motives remained unclear. Your adoptive mother thought he was desperately in love with his adopted daughter i.e. with you. She suspected he had even tried to rape you. Your mother, by the way, is still quite active living on her old age pension. I know, however, that you pay her electricity, hot water etc. bills. You even pay for the maintenance of her old house, a fact that surprises me. Your boyfriend Larry Hoffburg has provided you with generous monthly medical insurance covering every single organ of your body. Judging by the document he had turned over to me your teeth that now look splendid were gappy and decayed years ago. You had to wear a brace to correct them; quite a few famous dentists had been laboring away over your dental caries. Larry had paid them more than 85 grand. As I can see it was worth his while."

"Yes, it was," Adrienne whispered. "You sound seriously worried about that and rightly so! Eighty-five grand is eighty-five grand! I wonder how you'd react if you had to pay yourself."

The inspector had turned his back to Adrienne his eyes intent on her reflection in the windowpane.

"Miss Tott, you can have a look at the list of your lovers that Larry Hoffburg points as his predecessors. Would you want me to read that list to you? Oh, no, I won't do that. The list is too long and as Larry himself thinks it's most probably incomplete - sixteen guys altogether. Don Highsmith is seventh on that list. He had been living in your flat for about eight months - at least that is the official statement of the detectives whom Larry had hired to find out what the duration of that relationship of yours was. Why do you persist in denying you knew Don Highsmith before the New Year's Eve party to which Jennifer, your boyfriend's loyal wife, had invited you?"

"You think I remember the names of all guys I met by accident and spent a couple of nights with?" Adrienne asked quietly.

"Eight months is not a couple of nights!" Val said sharply turning to look her in full in the face. It was pure and irresistible. "Adrienne, you are lying again. There is no way I could check if you had had a splitting headache or if you have any medical complaints now. But you knew Don Highsmith before Jennifer's party."

"You know everything about me," the young woman said quietly. "How many times did you read the names of all my lovers on the list? Three times? Five times? You hated me all the while, Val Hughes. You did hate me and all the while you interrogated me you wanted me. Badly. Desperately. You wanted me, Val Hughes, in spite of the list you are still holding in your hand. I am right, aren't I?"

Val Hughes didn't answer. He stared at the cold April rain nodding his head.

"Larry Hoffburg had studied you very carefully before he let you enter his bedroom, Miss Tott. He'd wanted to be convinced of the high quality of the item he intended to invest money in He did not love you and you knew that very well. He didn't care about you except for definite moments when he needed you as a means of recreation. Well, that is your problem not mine," suddenly, Val Hughes pronounced a sentence that sounded like an explosion in the hushed room. "How much do you know about the Trail of Tears experiment?"

"I analyze the information coming from the TV on that issue," the young woman answered calmly. "The police think that Professor Bell was murdered so he could not tell anything about that experiment. In other words he was silenced for good. Most of the interviewed citizens think that the experiment has to do with the epidemic and the waves of medical complaints By the way, Inspector, so far I have not heard you moan and groan - perhaps you are one of the guys who are not liable to diseases, suffering and injury? You are among those lucky ones who always feel good."

Val Hughes felt her blue eyes settle comfortably on his face. He had never imagined it would be so hard to meet her gaze.

"You know very well, Inspector Hughes, that Ella Boon whom you respect so much has had nothing to complain of in the course of the terrible epidemic. I got rid of my ancient ulcer after I visited the Walnut Clinic. The eczema I knew she suffered from, a skin condition making the skin of her hands become red, rough and sore, vanished into thin air after Toys International gave out those notorious Leila dolls. When I saw inspector Boon back at the hospital, her eczema looked appalling. At the time she interrogated me, a day or two ago, her hands appeared to be perfectly healthy, pink and normal. Perhaps Inspector Boon herself can tell you everything about the Trail of Tears experiment!"

"In my opinion, you most probably are Don Highsmith's accomplice. You will be charged with being an accessory to murder but I still haven't proved that and I have no right to detain you."

"All right," the fair-haired beauty said waving a hand vaguely in the air. "If I really was an accomplice to murder why should I lie to you that I didn't know Don Highsmith? It would mean I was tying a noose around my own neck, wouldn't it, Inspector? I am not a brainless person I assure you. I have simply forgotten all about Don Highsmith - perhaps he was not even a passionate lover -- so why should I bother?"

"He had been living with you for eight months," Inspector Hughes reminded her.

"Sometimes I let men hang around with me just because I pity them," she said her eyes flashing defiantly. "That's not a convincing reason for making efforts to remember their names, is it?"

Again, the Inspector started pacing up and down his narrow office looking out of the window. The rain had stopped at last.

"I hope the interrogation is over," the pretty woman said standing up ready to go.

Val Hughes hesitated. Did it make any sense to go on asking her stupid questions? He was not satisfied with what he had achieved, he had not learnt anything new - nothing but some shades of meaning he could analyze but that appeared to most probably lead nowhere. Adrienne Tott had slipped out of his grip and yet

"No, the interrogation is not over," he said approaching the only battered filing cabinet in his office. He thought for a while then took out a pen and a writing pad and gave them to her. "You have plenty of sheet of paper at your disposal, Miss Tott. I'd like you to describe two events or incidents in your life, which have impressed so much that you simply can't forget them. You can describe them briefly writing no more than a dozen of sentences or you can use the whole writing pad I gave you. It's up to you."

"Don't talk nonsense!" Adrienne exclaimed her hands still dancing excitingly in the air caught the writing pad, crumpled several sheets of paper up into a ball and threw them into the wastebasket.

Val Hughes bent over to the old filing cabinet, took out another writing pad and gave it to the fair-haired woman.

"It's not a request. You have to do it," he said firmly. "Start writing now. You have one hour at your disposal."

He had to force himself not to stare at her so intently. Her hand, exquisite like light white foam on the crest of a wave, ran over the sheet of paper. Her face, thoughtful and pure, at times lit up glowing at the memories of the people and places she was describing. Val Hughes tried hard to resist the sneaking admiration for her sweeping over him. He tried in vain to think about the list of her sixteen former lovers. He forced himself to read an article in the newspaper he didn't know he had to keep from imagining Larry Hoffburg's ruddy square face, his big thickset body saying and said himself, That woman had been putting up with him for eight long years! She might have even been in love with him!

In spite of that, Val again and again fastened his gaze on her white hand touching the sheet of paper, on her face that now looked sweet, almost childish. And he suspected she had had a hand in Professor Bell's murder! For the first time since he started to work for the Investigation Agency Val thought he was doing a dead-end job. If he was an ordinary teacher in English or an owner of one of these small and cozy Italian restaurants, then I wouldn't have ever had the chance to meet her. Even if that had happened, she would have passed by me as if I were a poster advertising a film she didn't give a damn about. Well, it was about time he thought of more important and serious issues like, like what? For example, he should delve into Ella Boon's past? His colleague was not affected by the epidemic, apart from that Don Highsmith had scribbled in his note that Adrienne could turn to Ella for additional information on the murder

Val Hughes had collected the note that Adrienne had received in the morning when the Professor was murdered. The crumpled sheet of paper was going to be subjected to a series of extensive and rigorous tests but Val had almost no doubts that it was authentic. The handwriting was Don Highsmith's all right. So far so good! But Adrienne had not explained how she had received the letter from the murderer. Was it posted to her? He had to clarify this; he had missed the most important issue straying from the point, getting drowned in dozens of faulty lines of reasoning.

"Excuse me, Miss Tott," Val wanted to make things clear without delay hoping that if he surprised her he could obtain more relevant information. "Miss Tott, you have not explained to me how you got the note from the alleged murderer."

"You said you wouldn't disturb me while I described the most interesting happenings in my life," she said her voice so quiet and heavy with indignation that Val was sorry he had interrupted her. In fact he regretted not so much ever having intervened, he thought it was a pity her face lost its serene childish ·

expression. Now it again turned into a face of an inaccessible, unbelievably attractive woman.

"Did Don Highsmith post his note to you?"

"No, I found it after I woke in the morning of 2 April. The note lay on my little low table next to the bottles of makeup."

"Do you fully understand the meaning of what you've just said?" Val looked at her in amazement. "Val Hughes had entered your house or perhaps you yourself had let him come in? Are you sure the note had not been on your low table before the Professor was killed?"

"All the time I know perfectly well what I keep on my table, Inspector," Adrienne answered calmly. "There was no note on it before the murder. I had not let Don Highsmith enter my house, but it is not difficult to get in my living room, for example. All one has to do is to pull up the Venetian blinds and walk in. There is an even easier way - one can come to one of my twelve porches and then can very easily jump through the window."

"Aren't you afraid of robberies?"

"Inspector Hughes, in the neighborhood where I live there has been not a single robbery in the last two hundred and thirty years."

Val shook his head in exasperation. The measured tones the fair-haired mermaid spoke in and her air of calm superiority annoyed him intensely. She was being arrogant, too arrogant.

"There is a possibility that you, Miss Tott, had acted in coordination with Don Highsmith; i.e. he had scribbled the note beforehand promising you'd be a corpse. He had even admitted very cleverly that he'd committed the murder while the truth was quite different: the perpetrator of the appalling crime was you. What will you say to that?"

"I'll say, Inspector, that there exist millions of probabilities," the young woman's smile felt icy taking her for a moment miles and miles away from Val's gloomy office. "As the world's philosophers teach us, only one among millions of different probabilities becomes a reality. If I am not mistaken, you receive a very handsome salary, or should I say a top salary, in order to find out which probability has prevailed against all the rest. Well, while you rack your brains trying to set things right, you have no legal right to slander innocent people. Human society has established courts of justice long before you and I were born and I will not let you forget that that simple truth."

"You speak very convincingly about the different probabilities," Val sighed. "I wonder where you heard that from. As far as I know you haven't attended any college."

"You can go on wondering, Inspector. I see you are quite determined to discover the truth about that and I sincerely hope you will get at it in the long run," Adrienne smiled encouragingly. "Would you now let me add a couple of sentences to the description of the two most remarkable events in my life? I will soon be ready, hoping that after that I'll never see you again."

No, Val was in no mood for staring at her light white hand that hardly touched the sheet of paper.

52

"It is very strange," he muttered. "You sound so cheerful and serene two days after you were warned that you will be the next corpse."

"If a lady spends too much time thinking about corpses and crimes she encourages the process of aging in her body," Adrienne said interrupting her work. "Here you are, Inspector Hughes. The most interesting incidents in my life are in your hands. Can I go now?"

For a split second, Val touched her fingers as he took the writing pad from her.

"Could you wait a minute?" Val asked trying not to look at her face.

Then he started reading the lines written on the white sheets of paper.

Adrienne Tott's handwriting was neat and legible, the sentences she had used were short, grammatically correct expressing clearly the meaning she wanted   to   convey.

EVENT 1. I was fourteen living with my parents Henry and Sarah Jane Tott. They might have really adopted me as you, Inspector, said half an hour ago. I lived quite happily and always had enough pocket money. I haven't got on with women and girls since I was five but then I had a friend called Marian. She was the only one among the girls at my school who played with me. The rest constantly egged her on to abandon me. I don't remember why she deserted me - I went to ask her to come over to our place to do the homework in math. When she saw me, she shut the door under my very nose without explanation. I had never been so insulted in my life! That girl refused to talk to me for two long months. Of course, I was very good company - all boys from our class and from the neighborhood did not let me alone, making their best efforts to convince me how much each one of them loved me. The end of the summer term approached, it was the time when the term tests began. Marian was absolutely poor in math. A week before the term test she most unexpectedly rang me up saying she wanted to be friends with me again-- then asked me if we could study together for the test. I agreed. Inspector Hughes, don't think I was a timid, faint-hearted moron readily pocketing insults. No, Sir! I agreed because I had sworn to take my revenge on her. I forgot to tell you in the very beginning that Marian had about a dozen of small red fish. She was madly in love with them - she squandered all her money on food for her pets, reading volumes on their life-styles and mating periods, on fish species, fish farming and hatching etc. What I hated most was her habit of putting on air - her father had bought her a grand aquarium in which her fish swam and flourished. To cut a long story short, I agreed to go to her place and help her with the term test in math, but I had to punish Marion. Nobody could abandon me as if I was a cheap, torn pair of shoes. I had made up my mind to destroy her fish. How was I to do that? If I put some liquid poison in their grandiose glass container while we were doing the problems the teacher had set us, they'd die right away and Marian would guess I had killed them. I had to think and that was what I came up with: at a certain point I told Marian I was very hungry and asked her to make a sandwich for me. There was nothing easier than sending Marian to the kitchen. She had always had an enormous appetite and if she didn't drink gallons of coca-cola it was because she most probably was gorging herself on French fries and cheese. No sooner had she gone out of the room than I pressed ahead with my plan. I had taken from home a pin with a very sharp point. I caught the red fish with the small scoop then stabbed all of them with the pin - one after the other, trying not to miss any of the quick slippery creatures. The fish didn't seem to die while we worked hard preparing for the term test, but on the following day they were quite dead. Marian didn't come to school till the end of the week and when finally she did show up her face was terribly swollen and she still whimpered as she announced to our classmates that her dear pets had all died. She supposed that they had been taken sick and that, alas, all was her fault - she had put them too early in their brand new aquarium. That fat girl never learnt who lay at the bottom of the unfortunate death of her beloved little darlings. She is currently the proud owner of a dolphin-breeding farm in Jacksonville and as far as I know she makes good money.

Once I invited her to a party I was throwing in honor of Larry's fifty-fifth birthday, I just wanted to see how she looked like - she had become obese, enormous, terrible, believe me. She still hadn't got her claws into any potential husband in spite of the legends about big money she was making.

You have no idea how rapidly the news of my invitation swept the town. All papers wrote about it. You have no idea how happy the fat cow was after she kissed me goodbye. That invitation had been her proudest possession ever since. In a letter to me she wrote she had never hoped that she'd be given the rare honor of attending one of my glorious parties. I didn't bother to respond to her   ingratiating   letter.

EVENT 2. I was seventeen. My attachment to my father was exceptionally deep. I knew he felt the same way for me.

Larry Hoffburg's statement that my father had tried to rape me was too exaggerated. I'd rather say it was idiotic, ludicrous. To be honest with you, Inspector, if at that time I had known Henry Tott was not my natural father I would have made my best to seduce him. Perhaps I had behaved too provocatively, who knows? At any rate, when I saw him hanging from a beam in the barn I thought life made no sense any more. Henry Tott was the most wonderful man I had ever seen. The most affectionate, the most good-natured, the most honest and upright human being I had ever known since I was born.

The episode I want to describe has nothing interesting or peculiar about it. I don't know why I remember so distinctly every single detail of it.

Henry had a black straw hat that he almost never took off his head. It was so old, faded and battered that it made me sad to see Henry putting it on his beautiful auburn hair. I made up my mind to find a way to help him. I bought a box of black shoe-cream and painted my father's hat with it. You could not imagine what happened when my family went to church on Sunday! I remember well - the weather was very hot. It was quiet in church and my mother's scream rang out like an explosion her face contorting in agony. She had notices black beads of sweat streaming down my father's whiskers. A number of matrons full of righteous indignation pointed out right away that it was a bad omen. Perhaps they had noticed that Henry and I exchanged glances from time to time. It felt so wonderful as though I had won a two million lottery jackpot!

But when Henry hanged himself, the whole town went mad. They all remembered the black beads of sweat - the bad omen, and, of course, women hated me more than ever but that is beside the point. As you can see, Inspector Hughes, whatever I do, the outcome is invariably blameworthy; I am more often than not sentenced to public censure; a pencil-pusher in disgrace with other law-abiding citizens. Perhaps the incidents I have described reveal a tarnished image of a criminal; an outlaw human society should be ashamed of, a scumbag. Well, what could I do to make you happy about that? You wanted the truth and I provided it for you. In fact I have laid myself wide open to all sorts of attacks but I have been honest with you, believe it or not.

Adrienne   Tott

Val Hughes didn't know what to think. He had not expected to read such imaginative stories. He kept silent for a minute staring at her clear handwriting touching awkwardly the sheets of paper and when their eyes met the expression on his face was strange, wistful, and intense.

"You are looking at me as if you hesitate over whether or not to ask me to dinner," Adrienne said quietly.

"No, I won't ask you to dinner. I wonder if you'd have written the same tales of woe if my colleague, Inspector Ella Boon, had given you that sort of task."

Val Hughes had lied. Just a minute ago he had tried to imagine how the fair-haired lady would react if he invited her to have a drink with him at 'Odille's' but, of course, he'd never do that! She had read his mind. An unbelievable woman in all probability an accomplice to murder, and yet unbelievable!

Suddenly, the telephone Val kept in the inside pocket of his jacket beeped.

"Is that you, Val?" The voice of the Chairman of the Agency, old Bob Hendricks, sounded low and husky. "I'll tell you something very unpleasant. Ella Boon has just called me. As she interrogated Larry Hoffburg, Theodore, his old loyal butler entered the room carrying a tea tray. You know old Theodore, don't you? Yes, yes. The butler shot Larry Hoffburg dead then killed himself shooting a bullet through his own heart. We lost two crucial witnesses, Val."

"But Ella was there all the time!" Val said.

Ella Boon. He had heard several people pronounce her name this afternoon. Don Highsmith, Professor Bell's alleged murderer, had advised Adrienne Tott to turn to Ella Boon for additional information on the murder witnesses. Several minutes before the professor was murdered he had asked Ella Boon to meet her without delay. The butler had killed Larry Hoffburg then had shot himself dead and Ella had been there all the time! Two unimpeachable witnesses were lost. Ella's name had been bandied about too much. She had no medical complaints; the epidemic and diseases had done her no harm whatsoever. All this looked pretty suspicious. But Val Hughes himself was safe and sound unaffected by the raging epidemic. What was he to do?

"As far as I understood as I listened to your telephone dispute, Larry Hoffburg had been murdered!" Adrienne Tott said pronouncing the words firmly and distinctly.

Her eyes were perfectly dry her face remaining impassive. Her hands trembled for an instant and that was the only sign that the new had perhaps disturbed peace of mind. One could never be sure with Adrienne.

"Inspector, I won't be accused of murdering Larry Hoffburg, will I? Well, Don's warning sounds pretty convincing now - all the persons enumerated in his threatening note did turn into corpses. As you can see I am the only exception so far."

Val Hughes didn't say anything. He didn't think that woman needed reassurance from him.

Chapter 6

It was something extraordinary to hold a second convention within one week attended by all inspector of class Z working for the Investigation Agency. In fact, such an unusual event happened for the first time since the institution was founded. Bob Hendricks, the Chairman of the Agency, Red Kyle, Ella Boon and Val Hughes were all the attendees, international celebrities in a world in which the war against crime was substitute for one's private life. In accordance with the established tradition, the Chairman was the first to take the floor but he nodded at the only lady in the room.

"Who could even start imagining that old Theodore should shoot dead his protector and employer?" Ella started quietly. "I have never for a moment assumed that could be possible. I can still see him before my eyes - meek, lifeless old man hardly capable of carrying the tea tray in his hands. An instant after he entered the office, Larry Hoffburg was dead. I have never expected that I could have stopped the old butler from committing suicide. He had a gun in his left hand. I had not even noticed when he left the tray"

"Cut the lamentations and get on with the relevant facts," Kyle interrupted her coldly. "Your regret won't help anybody. We lost two very important witnesses. I am almost certain they were the only ones available - I can feel it in my bones."

Ella didn't say anything so Kyle decided the time had come to give vent ho his anger that he had suppressed for so many years.

"The second wave of the epidemic has died down. But we cannot be sure. There may be another more destructive and virulent one," he remarked his blue eyes blazing with apparent hostility. "Boon's report dedicated to the terminally ill patients and their disappearance into thin air is really very impressive. But I am not happy with the investigation itself. She didn't even bother to check if these ladies had by accident"

"Come off it, Kyle! Tell us what disturbing facts you have unearthed. Your fingers are trembling so eagerly; judging by that you have to say something very important."

"You are not the person who will make me speak," the inspector said his voice thinning almost into whisper. This always happened before he entered a fierce dispute with Ella Boon. "I'd like to remind you there is a hierarchy of structures in the Agency and I, by accident, am higher up than you in it."

"What have you found, Red?" Old Bob Hendricks used the utmost discretion when he talked to Kyle. His presence appeased everybody. He was a tower of strength for all the inspectors inspiring respect for traditions and order and intolerance for long-running disputes. "I am sure what you've discovered is very important and we should discuss it in a relaxed atmosphere. Shouldn't we?"

The last "shouldn't we" was an addition that Bob made to express his appreciation of all Kyle had done for the agency. This phrase, pronounced so softly, worked wonders - the second greatest inspector, legendary Red, felt sure of his power and influence.

"I talked to three girls who worked as Larry Hoffburg's secretaries. All of them suffered from lethal leukemia, "Kyle paused deliberately his eyes holding Ella's. Oppressive silence reigned in the conference room. "One of the girls is the proud owner of a pizza hut, the other two had bought a liquor store a couple of months ago and now they work together there," Kyle paused again his eyes darting from face to face. "I asked the girls to show me their medical records and they kindly provided the necessary information. There were no diseases whatsoever on the records so I checked and checked again. All the three were in the best of health. I would like to draw your attention to the fact that I could not find a diagnosis that read "Leukemia". So I kept asking myself a question "Did Ella Boon think up everything about that dreadful disease killing the three young women?" I would like to make another point: we lost our two crucial witnesses while Ella was interrogating them - curious coincidence reflecting badly on our famous colleague."

"We don't know anything about the Trail of Tears experiment," Val Hughes said thoughtfully from his dark corner. "When Larry Hoffburg tried to let us in on his secret, Theodore killed him. I have underlined two parts in Ella's report on Larry's examination. First - Larry states that that there is a group of individuals carrying out a scientific experiment. He calls them 'the regenerated ones', 'they' or 'them' giving no precise definition what he means by that. They are not human beings yet they are perfectly human, Ella Boon quotes Larry Hoffburg's words in the very beginning her report. We don't know what the basic goal of the experiment is neither do we have evidence what sort of beings the 'regenerated ones' are. Do they intend to cure all ill people? Why did they cause two consecutive waves of mass medical complaints? Why are several people - Ella Boon, Red Kyle, I myself and Don Highsmith, Professor Bell's alleged murder whom we still haven't caught - why aren't we vulnerable to illness? We haven't established if the epidemic affected Adrienne Tott. We have found no unequivocal evidence in this respect. The numerous statements she has made so far are quite contradictory. She told Ella Boon she didn't have any medical complaints and the epidemic had not affected her. As I interrogated her she maintained the very opposite thesis. There is again a serious contradiction involving Ella Boon's name. To cast suspicion on Ella Boon - that is the link to the second major point which I have marked in Boon's report. In the course of the interrogation Larry Hoffburg stated that an inspector working for the Agency was 'one of them' - i.e. one of the guys conducting the experiment.

Therefore, one of us - Val Hughes, I start with me on purpose, Ella Boon, Red Kyle and Bob Hendricks, I have no right to exclude our Chairman - one of us is 'their' agent. Their agent knows what the goal of the experiment is, who has organized it, and how these two waves of medical complaints came to be. Their agent knows also perfectly well what the results of the investigations are and what witnesses the Agency has planned to interrogate. The outcome speaks for itself - Larry Hoffburg was murdered. Their agent blocks every single move we initiate so the investigation makes no progress at all. Thank you for your attention."

"I can make the following conclusion," Ella said standing up and pushing back her chair. "I am 'their' agent amidst the honest inspectors working for the agency. The reasons are obvious and need no further proof or explanation: two vital witnesses died in my presence. There is a high probability that I murdered them myself. Our colleagues Inspector Kyle and Inspector Hughes found contradictory assertions in the testimony Adrienne Tott had given. I could have forged and changed her statements. Why yes, the end justifies the means and I am notorious for my mulishness whenever I pursue my goals. Professor Bell wanted to see me in the evening before he was killed. There's another thing as well: Don Highsmith, the person who most probably murdered the professor, advised Adrienne Tott to turn to me for additional information on the murder case. Apart from that the epidemic did not affect me," Ella sighed, smoothing pedantically her straight hair with her hand. "Inspector Kyle even accused me of having made up stories about the disease the three girls had suffered from. But I can show you copies of their medical records. I have already deposited them in the catalogue of the agency. Each one of you can check that years ago the three young ladies suffered from leukemia. I do not doubt Inspector Kyle's diligence," Ella did not look at anybody. Her face was expressionless, her tall figure, thin, immovable, angular, could hardly tempt a man into asking himself if she had looked beautiful when she was young.

None of the inspectors, with the exception perhaps of Red Kyle, knew her exact age. She was probably in her early fifties. She looked almost as old as Red Kyle, but perhaps on account of her reserved icy behavior or because of her habit of speaking about unpleasant issues abruptly and directly, all thought she was older than him. Once, Kyle had even called her "Grandma Ella". It was well known she had no family. She rented a small apartment not far from the neighborhood with the cozy antique shops. Actually, all the four of them were loners and rented small apartments. It looked as if they had reached an agreement to live as far from each other as possible choosing the four different suburbs of the town. They never talked on the phone on issues outside their professional duties. Once a year, Red and Val Hughes drank a glass of wine together, for Red's birthday. All lived with the murder cases the Agency had to investigate. But now it turned out now that one of them was an agent working for the "regenerated ones".

"Red Kyle is evidently the most exacting and the most pedantic employee of the Agency," Ella Boon went on. "He has not made major mistakes so far. It is possible, however, the young women he found - the owner of the pizza hut and the other two who bought a liquor store - it is possible these three young ladies are not the same girls who contracted leukemia after they worked for Larry Hoffburg." Ella Boon nodded curtly. "That's all I wanted to say. If you think I am their agent I will readily put an end to my participation in the investigation."

"Think! Think!" Old Bob Hendricks said his voice small and cracked with old age. "It was Ella's report that informed the Agency one of us was 'their agent.' If she really had been one 'of them' would she have reported on the traitor among us? She could have easily concealed that fact. Her name has been mentioned very often so far obviously trying to establish a connection between 'them' and Ella Boon. Perhaps someone has made great efforts to remove her from the investigation. Thus 'their' task will become much easier."

"I was thinking about that," Red Kyle's eyes were alight with excitement. "Perhaps 'they' really want Ella away. She's got friends in high places. But who are 'they?' And why should we think 'they' are necessarily evil and pose a major threat to the fabric of our society? Perhaps they have chosen Ella as a point of contact on purpose. Among us all she's the only one that does not resemble a normal human being."

"Red Kyle!" Bob Hendrick's glasses were a flash of lightning scorching the younger inspector. The old man stood up his frail body trembling casting an angular shadow on the wall. "Kyle, we are here to discuss the Trail of Tears case! Please, Kyle!"

"I have been working here for more than twenty years," said Inspector Kyle. "And I have never seen Ella Boon smile. I have never caught her bungling her job either. She is a robot! An automaton! As for the three young women - they are the same! Their names and fingerprints coincide. There could be no doubt that" for a moment, Kyle's voce trembled. He was really excited at the prospect of saying something very important. "Ella said she had the medical records of the three young women their illness diagnosed as leukemia. But I have their medical records, too. I can assure you there is not a single word about leukemia there! Another interesting fact - during the interrogation all the three girls had declared they remembered nothing about contracting a horrible disease. They knew however they had been treated for some indisposition in hospital."

"Somebody has falsified their medical records," Val Hughes said. Have they ever been admitted to Walnut Hospital?"

"Yes, but none of them remembers what the treatment was," Red Kyle answered. "The girls don't have medical records for about a year. Perhaps their treatment took a year," it appeared as though Kyle was talking to himself. From time to time, he scratched his chin, and that was a sign he was agitated. "None of the three girls remembers what exactly she did in the course of that year-- they all have short memories. It seems that period of time has been totally erased from their minds. It is strange."

"Can I say something, please?" although he had been working more than ten years for the Agency, Val Hughes was not yet comfortable when he had to interrupt his colleagues. . There is an interesting passage in Ella Boon's report. I'd like to quote it. 'Ella, I know how old you are,' Larry Hoffburg said. 'You are 51.Thirty-two years ago you had a serious car accident' I (it is Ella Boon who speaks) looked at him in amazement because the facts Larry Hoffburg mentioned were true and undeniable. Larry went on, 'at that time Doctor Rupert Bell has just started his medical career, but he saved your life. Ella Boon. Back then, Walnut clinic was a modest two story building erected not far from the Trail of Tears area. How long did your treatment go on? Don't you remember? Doctor Bell made you stay in Walnut clinic for more than two years. Can't you remember what had happened during that period of time?' I thought and thought. I was aware that these years had passed leaving no trace in my life as if some one else had lived while I was far away. I had no memories of them, nothing but a nightmarish feeling of disaster.' End of the quotation from Ella Boon's report," Val Hughes shook his head. "A nightmarish feeling of disaster," he repeated. "The three young women can't remember anything about that particular year in their lives when they were in Walnut clinic."

"Perhaps all terminally ill people from our town who seem to mysteriously disappear are given long-term treatment It lasts a year or maybe two years," Bob Hendricks, the famous Chairman of the agency, said. "Then these people appear again in the world, perfectly healthy, safe and sound, but they cannot remember anything. They only have a nightmarish feeling of disaster they have gone through."

"The three young women did not mention anything about nightmarish feelings," Red Kyle objected. "They don't remember anything and that is all."

"But if 'they' help people get rid of unbearable suffering why should we be against 'them?'" Val Hughes asked thoughtfully and after a minute answered his own question, "Because let's come back to Ella's report. I quote, 'It is horrible, Ella. It is horrible. You cannot stop living when you want. You die when 'they' want it.' Val Hughes leafed through the pages, paused for a moment and said, "I quote Larry Hoffburg's words, 'I got my new five factories in return for the girls I had exposed to radiation through my cactuses-lenses. They all contracted leukemia. Miss Boon. Have you ever noticed the numerous decorative cactuses placed everywhere in my factories?' End of quotation."

"But Ella Boon might have thought all this up!" Red Kyle pushed back his chair and got to his feet. "Most probably she worked with Professor Bell from the very beginning. The professor had provided her with the falsified medical records of the three girls marking the fatal diagnosis leukemia. After that, Ella lies in her report that Hoffburg has exposed the girls to radiation as a result of which they contracted the terminal illness. Ella is in a strong position: now that both Hoffburg and Professor Bell are dead. No one can dispute the claims she has made in her report or call in question the facts she has chosen to present to us. I think Ella Boon is 'their' agent!"

"But if she is 'their' agent, then why should she work us up against 'them' in her report?" Bob Hendricks objected. "This sounds illogical to me."

"Because she, exactly like Larry Hoffburg, is probably their victim," Val Hughes said quietly from his dark corner. "She cannot stop living when she wants. She will die when and if 'they' want it."

"I have never wanted to commit suicide," Ella assured him coldly. "I assure you I won't die soon."

Val studied her face.

"Ella, 32 years ago you had a road accident and you remember nothing about it. The three young women who miraculously got rid of leukemia do not remember anything either." The young inspector spoke very quietly leaving distinct meaningful pauses between his words. "Doctor Rupert Bell was responsible for your medical treatment. I think that the Trail of Tears experiment started 32 years ago and perhaps your car accident was its beginning. Ella, you have to remember what happened back then. I am convinced that there is a key to the past. I cannot believe that three years of your live can pass leaving no trace."

"I have vague memories of suffering and recurring nightmares," Ella whispered.

"Our young colleague used correctly the phrase "three years of one's life cannot vanish without a trace." Red Kyle said. "But if we believe the late Larry Hoffburg we should accept the fact that 'they are not humans.' And if we assume -- of course I do not encourage you to do that -- I simply ask you to assume that Ella is one of 'them,' then nothing would seem strange enough. Two years of her life vanished without a trace because she is not a human being."

"Ella, you keep an observant eye on everything surrounding you," the young inspector went on ignoring Kyle's remark. "Perhaps you have noticed something peculiar, unnatural or extraordinary after these two years passed? Something in your mind, or something in your surroundings, in the people around you that struck you as odd. Something that makes you feel awkward if you had to share it with another person, but it could be a key to the past revealing at least a part of these two mysterious years."

"I don't remember anything," Ella answered coldly averting her eyes from him.

"I'll help you remember, Boon," Kyle's voice sounded unexpectedly grumpy and querulous. "Thirty-two years ago you started working for the Investigation Agency. The first thing you said when I saw you had something to do with the fact that you could not stand red-haired men. You said you hated their guts. Then you remarked it was very strange because earlier you had not felt such a deep loathing for anybody. Those were the only unofficial words you have ever exchanged with your colleagues in the course of thirty years, Ella Boon. Thirty years is a long period of time."

"I think about you, Val Hughes," Bob Hendricks said in his quiet slightly hoarse voice. "You stayed at Walnut clinic receiving surgical treatment. You were not affected by the outbreak of the epidemic. Can you remember what happened during the time you spent in the clinic or did you suffer a loss of memory?"

"I remember everything very clearly: the injections, the rehabilitation unit, and the walks in the park, my long conversations with Professor Bell and Brahms's music. I suffered no loss of memory, either total or temporary."

"I suffered no loss of memory either with the exception of the days I had spend in the intensive care ward," Red Kyle said firmly. "Professor Bell's round in the mornings and in the evenings, the painful injections he treated me with consideration and kindness. I learnt to appreciate punctuality from him. By the way, that was why my famous colleague Ella Boon has never held me in high esteem. You might hear her brag about precision and priorities, but today she was the only one among us to be late for our council."

"Red Kyle!" Old Bob chided then he uttered his favorite phrase of a peacemaker. "Let's be tolerant to each other, shall we?"

"But Ella Boon was late!" Red Kyle insisted. "We all waited for her. And this particular session of the council is of crucial importance!"

"One of the front tires of my Mazda had punctured. Someone must have done that with a sharp point," Ella muttered, confused. "Please, excuse me for being late."

"Let me make a summary of our conclusions so far," said the Chairman of the Agency making efforts to get up from his chair. They knew how hard it was for him to speak standing, but no one tried to stop him. Perhaps at such moments Bob Hendricks felt he was still alive.

"First, there is a group of individuals carrying out an experiment called Trail of Tears. The only thing we know about 'them' can be extracted from Larry Hoffburg's words that 'they are regenerated therefore they are not human.' Ella Boon was the only witness who heard Larry pronounce that sentence. We doubt that Ella is one of 'them.' There are good reasons to suppose the experiment is related to the disappearance of large groups of terminally ill persons. We have discovered three of them -- the three young women, Larry Hoffburg's secretaries, who had contracted leukemia and had recovered completely. Now they enjoy perfect health. Ella Boon maintains that Larry Hoffburg had exposed the girls to radiation infecting them with leukemia. But mind you, we have a sneaking suspicion that Ella is 'their' agent.

"Second, according to Larry Hoffburg's statement, one of us, the four inspectors attending the council, is positively their agent. We learnt about that from Ella Boon's report! Third, so far we have paid no attention to the fact that Professor Bell had scribbled dozens of fives on the note he'd written before he was killed. The number five painstakingly filling the whole free space on the sheet of paper. Five knives had been stuck into the professor's chest. So far, we know only five persons who have not been affected by the epidemic: Ella Boon, Red Kyle, Val Hughes, the late Larry Hoffburg and most probably Don Highsmith. We stumble again across number five!"

"Fourth, let's concentrate on the mysterious guy, Don Highsmith, with his attempted suicides. Miraculously, Professor Bell saved his life for the second time. Don stayed in a mental institution, he seemed to have lost the power of speech, which he recovered later. All that sounds very interesting. Val's hypothesis was that perhaps Don and Adrienne acted together. They had come to the following agreement in advance: Don was to admit in his note he had murdered Professor Rupert allaying any suspicion that it had been Adrienne Tott who actually did it. We have an indirect proof: Adrienne was the only outsider intercepted by the police in the immediate vicinity of Walnut clinic. Let's not forget that our colleague, inspector Ella Boon, was also intercepted not far from the clinic about an hour later. She claims that Professor Bell wanted to meet with her. Red Kyle and Val Hughes have been officially assigned to conduct the murder investigation. They arrived at the crime scene after an anonymous phone call to the Agency that Professor Bell had been killed. We have to tackle the following tasks now," the chairman's voice faded. His long speech was too much for him. After his trembling hands rested for a minute on the table he made efforts to go on speaking but could not.

"Excuse me," the old man said. "Could I lower myself into my chair? I am afraid I can't remain standing any more"

After a sudden silence fell over the conference room Bob Hendricks went on quietly, "I think Red Kyle should occupy himself with the elusive murderer, Mr. Don Highsmith who seems impossible to catch. Kyle, could you talk to all persons who have known him? You could start with Mrs. Jennifer Cost - Hoffburg, Highsmith's ex-fiancée? You could search for his parents. Yes, Red, you know very well what to do," the chairman used again his favorite phrase acknowledging the power and greatness of the man who occupied the second highest position in the agency. "You'll take on such a thankless task, won't you, Red?"

When the four inspectors thought the session of the council was over Val Hughes unexpectedly got to his feet and started pacing up and down the short narrow space in front of the window. His eyes were drawn to the wet April evening. His face glowed his fine profile a small mat patch of disturbance stirring before the eyes of the three inspectors. Nobody said anything. The young man evidently had some bright idea. The rest, patient, immobile, waited in silence to see what it was. At last, Val Hughes started speaking looking at no one in particular, "I think there is a way to understand if Adrienne Tott had been sick in the course of the two outbreaks of the epidemic."

"Adrienne Tott," Kyle nodded sympathetically smiling. "She is very, very pretty."

Old Bob Hendricks's face twitched his lips trying to smile, too. Ella Boon remained unruffled, distant, ignoring all the fuss around her.

"Don Highsmith wrote in his note that Adrienne would be the next corpse," Vai said trying to catch the chairman's smoldering, dark-ringed eyes. "So we have every reason to detain her. Of course, we'll provide all the comfort and convenience of modern civilization for her. She'll have everything at her disposal but will not be allowed to keep in contact with the outside world."

"That would be an impermissible invasion of privacy!" Ella Boon objected vehemently. "We cannot detain anybody on the grounds that they have been threatened."

"Yet we will detain Adrienne Tott," the young inspector insisted. "She will be allowed to watch TV and listen to the radio. Attention, please. That is my idea: we will reach an agreement with the local TV and radio stations to spread the news that a third, even more virulent wave of the epidemic rages in town. Of course, that will be a lie; there will be no outbreak of disease, but Adrienne Tott will have no idea we are giving her false information. We'll ask her is she has any medical complaints. If she says she has been affected by the epidemic it will be evident she's lying. Perhaps we'll learn whom she's lied to - to me or to Inspector Ella Boon."

"An excellent idea!" Red Kyle was quick to approve of the plan. "But let's not forget that one of us is their agent!" His eyes eloquently turned to Inspector Boon. "Their agent will warn Adrienne about the trap we've laid for her and Val's wonderful idea will go to the dogs."

"We can prevent their guy from warning Adrienne," said the old chairman of the Agency. "All of us, I mean the four inspectors attending the session including me, will not leave the conference room for a whole day. Thus each one of us will be watched closely by his three colleagues and it will be impossible to get in touch with Adrienne Tott."

"An absurd proposal!" Ella Boon searched Bob Hendrick's green smoldering eyes. She could not imagine that the chairman of the Agency could take offense like any other ordinary person so she said sharply, "I did not expect your reaction would be so silly, Bob. You are being childish. Perhaps 'they' want all the four of us here exactly like that, in the soft twilight of the conference hall, doing nothing but waiting for Adrienne to make a move. 'They' would willingly accept our inaction!"

"What would you prefer, Boon?" Red Kyle asked. "Neurotic, panicky blunders ruining our investigation? Perhaps you want rapid thoughtless actions giving you an excuse to eliminate precious witnesses."

"Stop it, Kyle!" Ella Boon went on imperiously. "Could you do me a favor and listen to me at least once to the end. This is the last time I will participate in the investigation in my capacity as full member of the council. I can see you impeach my motives. Well. I'd like to share an idea with you. If we assume that each one of us is, to a certain extent, suspected of being 'their' agent, then we can formulate a hypothesis that our young colleague, Val Hughes, is 'their' guy. He might have informed Adrienne Tott in advance of the trap we plan to set for her. She'll know beforehand that we'll be giving her false information about the epidemic and it's only natural she'll declare she feels perfectly healthy. Adrienne will clear her name and fuel your suspicions that I am 'their' agent! So, if Val Hughes is really one of 'them.' Personally, I doubt that. I can hardly imagine Val is their agent, but if we assume he is, it makes no sense all the four of us to go on sitting here watching each other. Adrienne will be informed. That was my idea."

"The best we could do is take Adrienne from her home and bring her to Room 10 of the Agency," Bob Hendricks nodded his headed. "We should use Val's idea. It may prove valuable."

When Room 10 was mentioned everybody, even Ella Boon, laughed. Room 10 looked like a luxury honeymoon suite on the third floor of the Agency. One had everything in Room 10: choice drinks, cigarettes, delicious food five times a day. There was a TV set and a radio. There were even newspapers, erotic ones, but there were no daily newspapers. There was a posh small swimming pool and a sauna in Room 10. Lush green palm trees grew in one of its foyers. But none of the persons who stayed in Room 10 was quite happy with his sojourn in this tropical paradise. Usually, the stay in Room 10 was followed by a much longer in one of the four not too luxurious prisons in Northern Europe.

"Val, can I ask you a question before we go?" Red Kyle said still smiling, his eyes appearing almost violet. "Val, why did you make the blonde beauty, Adrienne Tott, describe two interesting incidents in her life? You've never done that before. As far as I remember, none of us has. Even godlike Ella Boon has not been inventive enough to use that trick on a prime suspect in one of our numerous cases."

Val's eyes dropped to the floor carefully avoiding Kyle's face.

"I believe it was a good way to get to know her thinking and her nature," his voice broke hesitantly at the end of the sentence.

"She is a very attractive woman, isn't she, Val?" Bob Hendricks said quietly. "One has to make every effort to take his eyes off her."

"Yes," the young inspector agreed turning his back on his colleagues.

"We can declare that the council is over, thank you," Bob Hendricks's tired voice was hardly strong enough to finish the last word of the phrase.

"You know what? I've noticed something very strange about our colleague Kyle," Ella stood up looking intently at her big, red-haired colleague. "As we discussed the Trail of Tears experiment Kyle very often pressed his hands against his chest. Perhaps he has some health problems? He is not a particular favorite of mine but I have to warn you what I saw impressed me."

"You'd better take care of your own health, Boon," Kyle retorted angrily. "I hate it when you watch me. I am all right and I want to go home."

However, something quite different happened. The personal cellular phones of the four inspectors beeped simultaneously in the quiet darkness of the conference hall. This remarkable fact would positively go down in the annals of the history of the Investigation Agency: the four supreme officers of the council were being summoned on the occasion of a murder case at one and the same time. The flat unemotional voice of the captain on duty in charge of the safety guards sounded muted and slurred by the four microphones in the hall.

"Urgent message! To the attention of the supreme Z class inspectors of the International Investigation Agency! Captain Williams speaking. Captain Williams speaking! Professor Rupert Bell's body, kept so far in Room 1 of the Agency, is missing. I repeat. Professor Rupert Bell's body has vanished from Room1. Till 7 PM, sergeant major Martin Posse guarded it. At 7 PM, after the supreme staff council began, sergeant Posse was dismissed. At a quarter past 7 PM, the security alarm system was activated. A rapid reaction squad checked Room 1 at 7:20 PM. Professor Rupert Bell's body was missing. I repeat"

A strained silence hung over the conference hall. Each inspector gazed steadily at the face of the person who sat next to him. The body of the murdered professor was no longer in Room 1. Room 1 was the mortuary. Only four people in the Agency had keys to it. The Chairman of the Agency, Bob Hendricks; Red Kyle, deputy chairman; Ella Boon; and Val Hughes, the youngest inspector from the supreme staff. Suddenly all eyes fell on Ella Boon's thin, tall figure. They had remembered Red Kyle's words. Only Ella was late, more than quarter of an hour at that! Can you imagine! She was late for the crucial session of the agency council!

Bob Hendricks, Kyle and Val Hughes appeared at 7 PM sharp just in time for the beginning of the session. Ella Boon was late. And she had a key to Room 1!

Chapter 7

Ella Boon sat perfectly still. She pressed her hands against the battered chair her eyes taking in every detail of the narrow space between the window and the small old table. She had never in her life thought she might land in the Black Hole. That was the nickname of the room adapted for a prison cell in the Agency. How many times had she checked the persons kept in the Black Hole? She knew every single object in it and could enumerate all items in alphabetical order if she was taken blindfolded to the improvised dungeon. Ella knew perfectly well that she could not escape from the Black Hole. There was an iron bedstead with broken rusty springs and an iron table, on which three of the most notorious criminals of the decade had scratched their names. She had unmasked and caught them all. There was no TV, of course. She could learn what the weather was looking through a tiny window with toughened bulletproof glass. A casual observer standing outside the building could not see inside the cell no matter how astute or inventive he was for the windowpane was disguised as a mirror.

There was no radio, no computer, no newspapers or books. The ceiling hung threateningly over the head of the prisoner swinging and swaying in all directions all the time. A devilish mechanical contrivance that, according to many famous psychologists, urged criminals quite successfully to think hard, be consumed with guilt and confess their crime, especially when the ceiling made rapid unexpected swoops. Even Ella, who had been in charge of the electronic system regulating the seemingly chaotic movements of the mechanism, could not get rid of panicky feeling that the whole enormous building would collapse crushing her to death. Apart from that, perhaps inspired by Ella's stay in the Black Hole, the leadership of the Agency had introduced rapidly movable walls.

Of course, she knew it was theoretically possible, but even at the time when Patricia Cox's murderer, the famous proprietress of Panama chain of fashion stores, was imprisoned in the Black Hole, Ella had objected to setting the mechanism in operation. It was only natural she could go for short walks between two sudden consecutive contractions of the walls for she knew the algorithm of their movements. But the very thought she was in the Black Hole was so depressing that she was aching all over.

"I didn't have a hand in the stealing of the corpse, I know that for sure Professor Bell Who should care to have a lifeless corpse? I am not involved in that. I am not! Let me think everything over again. All the rest were in the Agency at 7 PM for the beginning of the council. I was late. So what? I have people who can act as my witnesses." Ella had felt the poisonous web of suspicions strangle her. Somebody wanted to bring discredit on her, eliminate her, to keep her in the Black Hole forever!

"They" want it! Am I the key to something important? Ella asked herself. "But what is it? Could it be the mystery of that experiment? What is hidden in my mind? I don't think they are afraid of my exceptional intellectual abilities, she thought grudgingly. They leave so many clever people eliminating me! Attention! One of my three colleagues, members of the supreme council, is "their" agent! One of them is an enemy. I am not an enemy!

She suddenly had a terrible sinking feeling in the pit of her stomach. They might have used her while she had been under hypnosis! Was that possible? Could I have acted subconsciously? They might have erased the memories of that time! It is possible, yes! I don't remember anything a single detail of the two years I had spent in Walnut hospital. She breathed a sigh of relief. She could appeal for witnesses; she could summon so many people who had seen her, who had been around her. They would come forward with evidence! When the poisonous net of suspicions began to weigh her down she had made up her mind to provide witnesses who could testify for her. When at a quarter to 7 PM she saw somebody had punctures the tire of her Mazda, Ella called a policeman.

She had dropped in Mr. Hardy's food store before she arrived in the Agency. She left him a generous tip on purpose. She was sure the old man with his thin cunning face and watchful eyes would remember it. Actually, it was not so good that she had not talked to him; in fact she had never done that so far. She usually passed quickly through the store taking whatever she needed and giving him small tips. Ella pitied old Hardy; she could not explain why she had taken it to her head that he was a loner like herself and had to be thrifty and careful not to get into debt. The smile on his old face told her Hardy had noticed everything. Ella also thought that he attached a special, almost symbolic importance to her tips and her short but frequent visits to his discount store.

Her neighbors living in the apartment on the third floor had seen Ella hanging helplessly about the flat tire. In fact, they had called a mechanic whom Ella paid a fat fee for the service. No, they could not have used her as a stooge under hypnosis! Ella excluded the possibility of subconscious actions on her part. She could prove that. The damaged tire of hers was still in her garage. A strange clattering noise made Ella tremble. Somebody knocked at the door: an inadmissible course of action in the Agency. The door of the Black Hall where dangerous criminals were imprisoned should open without any preliminary signal. A thin, elongated shadow appeared in the bright square of light. Even the ceiling stopped swaying for a split second.

"Hi, Ella!"

She knew that voice very well. It was Red Kyle's. It all seemed quite strange, however. Not only because he didn't say "Good afternoon" as he should have; the very fact he had greeted her made her feel something was wrong. This time his voice sounded strange like fine sand thrown into warm spring see. Ella got scared. She had never heard Kyle speak as kindly as that.

"I don't think the leadership of the Agency hasn't selected the most appropriate man to question me," she managed to say maintaining her composure. "I don't want to talk to you Kyle. I warn you I won't tell you anything."

He gazed at her his eyes appearing distracted confused as if he did not see her face.

"You've grown old, Ella."

He's beating about the bush, Inspector Boon thought. That was not typical of Red Kyle. Or perhaps he was about to try a new approach? She had to be on the alert, anyway.

"Have you ever thought of your future life?" The red-haired inspector suddenly whispered. "You have no one to love, Ella. Old age will lock you up in your cheap flat. I know you enjoy your own company but perhaps then you'll long for someone to knock on your door. There will be no one. No one."

"I have not entered the mortuary where the body of the murdered professor was kept. I have nothing to do with the fact it disappeared," Ella cut off his effusive introduction. "It's not necessary to describe the tragic scenes I will be living through in my old age. They won't make me an accessory to murder. I didn't have a hand in the crime you are investigating. Go away, Kyle. Please, switch on again the wobbling ceiling and walls. I miss them."

"I can prove that you are one of 'them,' Ella," Kyle whispered. He stretched out his hand most unexpectedly touching Ella's shoulder. Then his fingers moved slowly to her throat.

"Are you going to strangle me?" she asked very calmly. "You cannot. They'll learn you did it right away. Everything that happens in the Black Hole is filmed. Everybody will know who killed me."

A trace of a smile played across Kyle's pale face.

"Why don't you assume I'd simply like to caress you?" he asked.

"To be honest with you, I think you'd rather liquidate me. Kyle, why do you try to make people believe I'm guilty of all crimes? Is it just because you want to keep me outside of the investigation?"

"Maybe because I am one of 'them,'" the Inspector said his eyes glued to her face.

"Maybe," Ella answered coldly. "Well, you were not brave enough to kill me. Go away."

Kyle did not answer. He took a step back and bent over the table where the complicated signatures of the ten most notorious criminals of the decade were still clearly visible. When he straightened up a tiny object flashed on the uneven surface of the table. Kyle's shadow prevented Ella from seeing it clearly.

"Think of the years when old age will keep you prisoner in your narrow apartment," Kyle whispered heading for the door.

"You forgot something on the table," Ella called out. "You know very well it is strictly forbidden to leave anything to the persons held in custody in the Black Hole."

"Maybe that was the reason why I had visited you. Maybe I wanted to leave a tiny thing to my detained colleague," Kyle went on in his strange voice. "There are cameras all around in there. Everything I did was filmed so there is no reason to panic. Nobody threatens you with a gun." Good bye, Ella."

She didn't answer. As soon as Kyle closed the door Ella rushed to the table. But she hadn't foreseen that the walls and the ceiling would start moving and rocking again. She hit her head against the sharp edge of the table and she took about a minute before she could think clearly. Finally, she managed to grab the objects that Kyle had brought.

At first she could not understand what the lusterless aluminum discs meant. There were two of them no bigger than a dime. Figures were inscribed on the circles: 11 on the first and 12 on the other. After a minute Ella knew what they were. When new inspectors started working for the Agency each one of them was given such an aluminum disc. She had received one on which 12 was inscribed. Kyle had taken the one with 11. She remembered very well the day when Bob Hendricks had handed over the little flat discs to them. It had happened a month after Bob became Chairman of the Agency. Vague memories came flooding back but Ella was unable to interpret them. Many years ago, as a child, she had seen gossamer hanging in the air in late autumn. Sometimes her outstretched had had become entangled in the thin transparent threads and an elusive shadow trembled on the yellow frozen grass. On such days Ella had always felt sad because she knew that the shadow would disappear without a trace. The thoughts of the past upset her.

But Ella knew what had thrown her off balance. After Bob Hendricks, an energetic middle-aged man at that time congratulated them on their first special assignments as inspectors something very strange had happened. Ella had kissed Kyle.

It turned out that time had spared that memory and she felt an overwhelming longing to be young again. In fact, Ella that day Ella had begun to suspect she'd have alone all her life. Alas, her premonition of disaster turned into reality. "Think of the years when old age will keep prisoner in your narrow apartment." It seemed to her she had heard those words long time ago and they had become her life-long refrain.

Again, the elusive shadow of the autumn gossamer made her heart sink. She didn't know how to name that feeling. "Old age will keep you prisoner." She could not remember when and where she had heard these words no matter how hard she tried. She had stopped noticing the jumping walls and the swaying ceiling. Actually, the Black Hole had contracted and she had the feeling that the crude plaster of the walls was rubbing on her body putting a straight jacket on her. The sensation was unbearable. She had to think about something else, for example about why Kyle talked to her and what he was driving at. And why, for God's sake, had she kissed him thirty years ago? There had always been open hostility between them for years and years on end. She seemed to be generally held in contempt by Kyle who never made efforts to conceal his animosity towards her. Wasn't that suspicious if one came to think about it?

Yes, this had happened earlier. When they had to work together on a certain case Kyle always reviled her theses, garnishing his logical statements with sneers and insults he hardly made efforts to conceal. He never took liberties with the other inspectors of the Agency

Ella shivered. Somebody had knocked at the door. It was the young Val Hughes. Ella smiled her eyes alight with excitement. She had hoped that the boy would visit her. Sometimes she called him the boy. Was it her desperate longing to talk to a son she never had? She liked young Val. His calm impenetrable face reassured her. She appreciated his straightforwardness, his courage to voice his opinions logically, coherently not fearing he might contradict persons higher up in the hierarchy of the Agency.

"Good morning, inspector Boon," said Val Hughes.

"Good morning, Val."

Look what you've done, she thought. You addressed him by his first name. Against her will, Ella sensed pleasant warmth at the thought she could have a son like him. The emptiness that engulfed her life seemed to dispel when she talked to Val but she always felt lonelier after he left her office.

"I will do something that is not allowed by the current regulations," the young man said quietly.

"Don't Hughes," this time she used his family name. "The cameras will record all your moves and wouldn't be surprised if you land up in the Black Hole after me. I could have recommended the place to you if you had not been so tall. You'll be constantly hitting your head on the low ceiling."

"There is no difference between the walls and the ceiling," the young inspector pointed out. He was right: the Black Hole had assumed the form of an enormous egg that could flatten them any minute. "I'd like to have a word with you, Inspector Boon."

"Let's not forget I am not an inspector working for the Agency any more," she answered.

"I'd like to tell you about an interrogation I had conducted. I examined and cross-examined the three young women, the ones who according to you had contracted leukemia because Larry Hoffburg had exposed them to radiation. After that Kyle found out that one of them was a pizza hut owner and the other two possessed a liquor store. It was a very strange interrogation, indeed."

"Why did you choose to tell me of all people about it, Inspector Hughes?" It was hard for her to address him in such a formal manner. At that moment she needed to call him Val trying hard to maintain the illusion that a son was by her side, a boy she was incapable of giving birth to. "Maybe I am one of 'them,' Val. Or maybe you have invented a mechanism to make me sit for a test the way you did with Adrienne Tott. Perhaps you are one of 'them,' Inspector Hughes?"

"I want you to know about that interrogation, Miss Boon. Even if you were one of 'them' you couldn't warn them, could you? As far as I know no one has ever succeeded in escaping from the Black Hole."

"So you come to have a word with me and your action is in flagrant breach of Agency's rules. Who sent you, Hughes? Was it old Bob or maybe Kyle?"

"You and I never really got on together and I am not particularly sorry that you are in the Black Hole. But well, I really appreciate your observations," his voice thinned. Something in Ella's expression made him lower his eyes but he soon pulled himself together. "So, let's come back to the three young women who have fully recuperated."

"I might have lied to you about their serious disease," Ella cut him short. "You should not trust me. At least that was what the Strategic Council recommended."

"I trust no one," the inspector said coldly, making Ella think of a sulking little boy intent on being angry forever.

"I have checked everything. The three young ladies did suffer from leukemia. I had their medical records meticulously delved into. They all had been treated in Walnut clinic and remember nothing about the treatment. But there were other issues that impressed me, Miss Boon."

Val Hughes paused, letting silence reign in the Black Hole. Ella watched him closely, quite grateful that the walls of the room had stopped jumping and kicking.

"Val, you said that nobody had sent you," Ella observed smiling. "Why should the ceiling stop rolling and shaking? Perhaps all the bricks know you personally and have made up their minds to do you a favor. Only the officer on duty has the right to terminate the movements of the walls. If my memory serves me well, today the officer of duty is Kyle."

"I already told you nobody had sent me here. I'd like to talk to you."

"It really annoys me when people tell barefaced lies," Ella said calmly. "It is well known how much Kyle loves me. I can just imagine him allowing friends to visit me in the Black Hole. It is quite clear you haven't come to the dungeon to help me out, have you?"

"I did ask Kyle to let me visit you. He agreed," Val said curtly.

"I like you, Val, and that is the only reason why I still haven't turned my back on you," Ella was still smiling. "I mean I like you as if you were my nephew," she suddenly sounded confused. "Well, tell me about the three young ladies. I am all ears."

"The name of the first one is Rosemary," the inspector said with a deep sigh. "She is very beautiful. She turns all heads if she enters a room with many people in it."

"But she is positively not as beautiful as Adrienne Tott?" Ella teased him.

"Rosemary McDermott, 25, single, had been Larry Hoffburg's secretary and mistress for about a year. During that time she had a boyfriend as well. A man called Henry Paulson. Paulson was a student majoring philosophy at the University of Jacksonville. After recuperating from the deathly disease and, subsequently, getting rid of Larry Hoffburg, Rosemary shacks up with Paulson who is head over ears in love with her. Rosemary spends Paulson's money very actively; she doesn't have a job and visits twice a week the owner of 'Soldiers of

Fortune' pizza hut informing Henry that she attends some complicated medical procedures at the local hospital. Henry pays the bills for the non-existent medical treatment, massages and health care. Rosemary makes up her mind to marry Mr. Soldiers of Fortune, organizes a secret and very discreet wedding after which she and her husband go on honeymoon to Jamaica. Henry is informed that his beloved Rosemary will stay at St. Laurence sanatorium for patients suffering from neurosis and all sorts of nervous breakdowns, so Henry pays again non-existent bills. Finally, discovering that Rosemary has been cheating on him, the poor student of philosophy declares that he will poison himself at the front door of the apartment where Rosemary and Mr. Soldiers of Fortune live. He is positive he won't commit suicide if only his beloved comes back to him and starts loving him again. Rosemary's answer is, "I'll buy you a virulent poison myself. It will kill you very quickly and you won't suffer."

The young lady told me later that she had laced Henry's wine with poison and told him what she had done. Several minutes after he drank it Henry died before her very eyes."

"I asked her," Val Hughes went on after a moment of silence. "'Didn't you feel sorry for your ex-boyfriend?' Her answer was, 'No, I don't. His death seems quite reasonable to me. Otherwise he'd be constantly pestering me with phone calls.'"

Ella watched him closely. The young inspector's face looked gray.

"Don't you think that Rosemary simply provided another very sick person to be treated in Walnut clinic? After all, Larry Hoffburg did the same with his secretaries. She just supplied 'them' with fresh victims expecting to gain a new pizza hut in return. If I were you, I'd check if there are seriously ill people among the guys and gals who frequent 'Soldiers of Fortune" eatery."

"You are wrong, Ella," the inspector said waving his hand. "Henry Paulson did not vanish without a trance like all the rest of them. He had been buried in the local cemetery. He had committed suicide on account of unrequited love. Rosemary thought his death was quite reasonable,"

"What about the second young lady?" Ella asked. She thought the tale about the philosophy student sounded slushy and pathetic. She still had no idea what Val was trying to tell her.

"Perhaps two young men committed suicide after they failed to win the second fair lady of ours?"

"Her name is Carla Pracht," Val said quietly. "She is 28 now. She had been married to Cyril Churchill before she contracted leukemia. Her seven pregnancies had ended in miscarriage at 11 or 12 weeks. Her mother told me that Carla and her husband had visited St. Catherine cathedral in New Orleans in France, and the monastery of St. Benedict in Germany praying to God to preserve their baby the next time. And their prayers were answered - this happened after Carla recuperated from deathly leukemia. She got pregnant and wanted a divorce. Several days after she gave birth to her son she placed the following advertisement in the local newspaper, "A young single mom offers her new-born white healthy baby son for adoption. She would like to have an automobile, Corvette XMC-12, equipped with automatic digital fuel saving appliance and an ejector seat."

"'This is quite reasonable,' Carla Pracht told me during interrogation. 'My ex-husband Cyril is a born loser. I could have never driven a Corvette XMC-12 if I had not divorced him. By the way, I'll marry Ted Edwards in a month. He owns a brewery where good beer is made. He promised me to build a new garage for my Corvette. It will be situated not far from the beach Well, Ted cannot stand children, you know'"

"And you got so upset that now you have anxiety neurosis," Ella scoffed. At that moment she felt sorry for her young colleague at the same time telling herself that if Val had that annoying love of melodrama he was quite unfit to assume any responsible position in the Agency.

"She sold her child," Val's eyes scorched her. It felt as if someone had cracked a whip over her face. The young man had divined what she was thinking just by looking at her. "I was perplexed by the fact that her ex-husband Cyril was the first to respond to her advertisement. He desperately wanted to buy her a Corvette XMC-12 in order to have the baby live with him, so he took out a massive loan, was unable to pay it back. Now he's doing time and his ex-wife has her Corvette XMC-12. 'This is perfectly reasonable,' she had declared as I interrogated her. 'Cyril is a sentimental snotty scumbag. He should stay in prison.'"

Ella had really nothing to add or comment. It was evident Val Hughes had developed another tricky little plan of his. She was unable to find out what he was driving at and why he was telling her about all that slushy romantic tales.

"The third young woman is called Bertha French. After she recuperated from her disease she started bringing beggars to Patrick Nicholson Hospital in her van. Bertha worked together with a guy called Gregory Simms. They offered to let the beggars sell them organs from their bodies, which later were used for transplantation in the hospital. It was sickening to listen to her speaking about how she haggled with the bums over the price of a kidney," Val Hughes said unexpectedly and at that moment, more than ever before, Ella felt the old nagging ache of loneliness inside her. She could never have a son like him.

"When I asked her why she mutilated people practically stealing their organs for a bottle of gin in return, Bertha said, 'It seems pretty reasonable to me. I don't make the wretches sell anything. They come running when I show up at the corner and entreat me to take a kidney, a retina, a liver Do you think their organs are worth speaking about? Trash! I give them what they ask for; they live shorter and suffer less. The town is rid of beggars, I make good money. Sometimes I can even save a worthy young man or woman's life. Is that bad? No. It is reasonable!' That was all she said."

"Why do you tell me all this," Ella asked quietly. "I have no idea what you want."

"I want nothing in particular," the inspector said almost inaudibly. "All the three young women used the words 'It seems reasonable.' I have always wanted to enjoy kindness, sympathy, tenderness in my life and that is not reasonable at all. The three ladies do only reasonable things. Don't they, Ella? They make money. But I was repulsed by them I was repulsed and very confused."

"You didn't come to the Black Hole to inform me how confused and repelled you were, Val Hughes," Ella took a step back. She realized she had been sitting too close to the young inspector and that made her feel uncomfortable. Well, speak up now. I suppose Kyle will soon make the walls jump and dance again."

Val fixed his gaze on her face.

"Ella, I've been working for the Agency seven years now," Ella - he had called her by her first name for the first time since she knew him. Ella could not remember anyone calling her like that with the exception of Bob Hendricks, the Chairman, and Kyle at times he wanted to sting her into fury. "I've been by your side for seven years."

Suddenly Val's voice broke with emotion.

"I have noticed that you very often use the phrase 'It sounds reasonable.' It's one of your favorite expressions, isn't it?"

"Yes, it is," Ella answered firmly. "So what?"

"You asked me why I'd asked Adrienne to describe two memorable events in her life. You received a very dusty answer, but now you'll have the full truth. I was impressed by the fact that Adrienne Tott used that phrase very frequently. 'It's reasonable,' 'it stands to reason that.' The events she has described reveal she is exactly the type of a young lady who acts very calmly and 'reasonably'!"

Ella was silent. She turned her back to the young man. He was right. There could be no doubts about that and she could not raise any objections to what he had just said. And yet, suddenly, like a stone someone had thrown while he lay in ambush, Val's question hit her.

"Aren't you afraid of loneliness, Ella?"

She didn't know what to answer him. Actually, what gave him the right to poke his nose into her affairs? Well, she was imprisoned in the Black Hole after all. Even so, Val Hughes should not he so tactless.

"Kyle asked me almost the same question half an hour ago," Ella said coldly. "The word order he chose was slightly different. He tried hard to describe how old age would keep me prisoner in my moldy cheap apartment. You seem to be deeply concerned about my loneliness, gentlemen."

"At times I think my future will be exactly like yours, Ella, and I am not overjoyed," Val whispered. Her eyes dilated with a feeling he could not read and perhaps that made him stop speaking abruptly staring at her. "But you all have so many things in common - the three young women, Adrienne and you, Miss Ella Boon. Professor Bell saved your lives in Walnut clinic. I hope Adrienne will be soon accused of murdering the professor and I suspect that you are one of 'them.'

It seemed Val was talking to himself for he had stopped looking at her.

"Nevertheless, I came to talk to you, Ella. I think sometimes you treat me like a son I cannot imagine I might have a mother like you. I don't like you."

"I am sorry about that," Ella said but he didn't stop speaking.

"In the beginning I didn't want to work together with you on the case. I don't want a mother like you, Ella Boon. I think that you betrayed our trust over and over again."

Ella was silent. Val Hughes slowly opened the door. At that moment the walls began to contract and expand, swelling out then shrinking abruptly as if they wanted to squash Ella. On leaving the Black Hole Val Hughes unexpectedly said to Ella, "Even your profiles look alike. Yours is almost exactly like Adrienne Tott's! Of course, she is much more beautiful than you."

The walls began again their fierce crushing waltz, but Ella had stopped paying attention to them. She was not thinking of anything. She could not imagine what would crop up at the end. "At the end of what?" she asked herself. She hated to admit it but Val's words had hurts her deeply.

"Can I have a word with you?"

Suddenly the whole surface of the four walls turned into an enormous microphone echoing with the Chairman's quiet, slightly hoarse voice. Ella knew very well that it was forbidden to use the system of microphones to make conversation in the Black Hole. The regulations wouldn't permit anything like that. Yet Bob Hendricks himself broke the rules after more that forty years in the Agency.

"Good afternoon, Bob," she said. Ella had grown accustomed to meeting Bob's gaze and sensing the notes of tension in his old voice. At the very beginning she felt embarrasses by her invisible interlocutor. "Bob, we've been working together for ages. You know that. Tell me what you all are up to. If you suspect that I am one of 'them,' let's not waste time on long discussions, please."

"Ella, we checked the witnesses whose names you'd given us: the mechanic who dealt with the flat tire of your Mazda, and Mr. Hardy the owner of the food store. I have to admit there was a small detail that fuelled my suspicions. You've been leaving him large tips of late and the old man feels quite confused. Perhaps you've been doing that on purpose so that you'd have a cast-iron alibi for the appropriate moment."

"I couldn't have given the old man a generous tip at the same time kidnapping the body of the murdered professor," Ella objected. "Bob, I'd like to ask you something. Did you make Kyle bring the aluminum discs with numbers inscribed on them? You gave my disc to me, Bob, a thin flat circular piece of aluminum with number 11 on it. There was another number, 12, on Kyle's."

"I didn't ask Kyle to bring any discs to you, Ella. I don't know why he did that," the Chairman's voice faded as strained silence hung over the Black Hole whose walls had momentarily calmed down. "So, he brought you the aluminum discs. I want to talk with you about Kyle. He's asked me to give you something. You'll have it at the end of our conversation."

"It would be much easier if you asked me directly about what you want to know," Ella said. "It's very unlike you to beat about the bush. I hope you haven't changed that quickly."

"Adrienne Tott was subjected to a very interesting experiment and I'm going to tell you about it," Bob Hendricks's voice faded again. That was not typical of the Chairman and Ella was suddenly worried about him.

"Ella, you knew what we intended to do with Adrienne Tott: we isolated her, she had no access to the Internet, to newspapers, to friends or acquaintances. In other words there wasn't virtually anything that might tell her what the situation outside her room was. There was a TV and a radio broadcast informing the citizens of a new, more acute attack of the epidemic. It was a false alarm, of course. There was no attack and no epidemic."

"I was in the Black Hole all the while so there was no one to tell Adrienne about your plan," Ella pointed out.

"Yes," Bob Hendricks answered. "But I have never said that you are one of 'them.' The three of us: Red Kyle, Val Hughes and I were together all the time. We were very careful watching each other suspiciously so 'their' agent had no chance of warning Adrienne whatsoever! Guess what happened. You couldn't imagine what"

Ella was surprised at the tension creeping up on Bob. She had not seen him so excited for ages.

"Bob, are you OK?" she asked. The Chairman had stopped speaking in the middle of his sentence breaking a forty year long habit. "Bob! Hey Bob!"

"I am OK, Ella. You can't imagine how pleasant it feels when somebody cares about you. It hasn't happened very often in my life, believe me. Let's come back to the experiment and Adrienne. The local TV and the radio stations circulated incorrect information that the town had been overwhelmed by a third explosion of the mysterious epidemic. We made sure Adrienne had watched TV and listened to the radio. The three of us: Kyle, Val Hughes and I visited her and asked her if she had felt anything. Do you know what the answer of the young woman was?"

Such rhetorical questions were very much unlike Bob Hendricks. Most probably the three inspectors had connived with the security forces to perform another experiment. She suspected she was to act as a guinea pig for them. She did not want to talk to the Chairman of the Agency. She closed her eyes trying hard to calm down.

"Adrienne Tott lied. She claimed that she had developed a splitting headache like al the rest in town," Bob Hendricks said, his breath coming in short gasps. "She had been lying to us all the time, Ella. There was no epidemic at all in Jacksonville. Therefore Adrienne is like you, Ella."

Ella's eyes remained closed. Adrienne Tott. What was the blond beauty's role in the great myth surrounding the Walnut clinic; in the unspecified experiment the Agency had most arbitrarily called Trail of Tears? Ella's name had again been related to that of Adrienne. What did the Chairman of the Agency want to fish out of Ella? What was so interesting for him? She could not give an answer to any of the questions. She tried to imagine what Bob Hendricks was doing at that moment. Perhaps he was watching her face closely thinking she was seized by panic or shaken by nervous tension. Well, he was quite wrong. She shouldn't let him think such silly misleading thoughts.

"I am listening to you, Bob," she said slowly looking calmly at the walls that had stopped kicking and jumping. "Would you like to tell me something else?"

"I fact, I didn't intend speaking about that with you, but" Bob Hendricks had not completed his sentence again and that was highly unusual. Ella opened her eyes shuddering with astonishment. Bob Hendricks's green penetrating eyes were staring at her for all the walls, the ceiling and the floor.

"I am glad I can see you now," Ella said. "It's reassuring to watch the expression on your face while we talk."

"I'll tell you all the same, Ella. You know very well one cannot escape from the Black Hall, so Kyle's reaction embarrassed me. When Adrienne lied she had had a splitting headache, Kyle fainted. I have checked his medical records in the Agency. Kyle is a man who has not consulted his doctor for ten years. But he most unexpectedly fainted."

Ella Boon had not seen the Chairman's face so tortured and gray. The thin skin of his wrinkled cheeks looked dead; his colorless, almost transparent eyelids trembled ever so slightly.

"You've grown strongly attached to Kyle, haven't you, Bob?" she whispered. "Don't worry. One single fainting fit is nothing to be afraid of. Kyle is a strong and healthy man."

"I am worried. He fainted directly after Adrienne said, 'Yes, my headache is worse than ever before. The pain is unbearable.' Kyle turned pale. Then we saw him fall as if somebody had shot him dead. Val Hughes could hardly hold his collapsing body. I'm afraid Kyle hit his head on the edge of the filing cabinet."

Ella could not comment on what she had just heard.

"Are you sure you are not lying to me, Bob?" was all she could think of. It seems hardly probable that our tough and hard-boiled Kyle might be so impressed by the lies of the perky minx Adrienne. Well, one never knows She's so pretty."

"I don't know what to say, Ella," at that moment she noticed the utmost exhaustion in his green eyes, on his face that watched her from the four walls and the ceiling.

"I really don't know. I don't believe that Kyle's fainting fit was an accidental thing. Why should he be astounded by Tott's lies? Did he lose consciousness on account of her lies? When Kyle came to, he excused himself and denied that there had been any relation between his fainting fit and Adrienne's lies. I don't know, Ella. I don't know."

"Kyle means so much to you, Bob," Ella said quietly. "Don't worry. One day we'll know everything."

"Have you ever thought of loneliness? The old man whispered. His face seemed to have lost the determined, impenetrable expression of the Chairman of the Agency. Old age had ruined his strength. "I am afraid I'll meet my death all by myself in the evening. One day I simply won't show up in my office in the morning, Ella. That will be all."

The inspector shuddered. It was for the third time today that her colleagues had spoken about loneliness to her. She didn't like that, didn't like that at all.

"I'm afraid I was of no help to you, Bob," she muttered lowering her eyes. She had no wish to meet the old man's eye and she could not understand why she felt so embarrassed and unwilling to speak. Maybe because she knew that the Chairman of the Agency had lived alone all his life.

"Thank you, Ella," Bob's last words sounded weak and emotionless. Then the walls of the Black Hole became gray and almost at the same moment the ceiling above her head began to plunge down and hop above her head. She had the feeling she was about to scream when Bob's voice sounded again, "Listen, I almost forgot. Please, forgive me, girl."

How long was it that he hadn't called her like that? She tried to remember. The case related to the Trail of Tears experiment seemed to have made a different man of him, insecure, old, and distant.

"Look here, Ella," the Chairman said. "Kyle asked me to give you this. He wanted you to study it very carefully. Excuse me once again. I disturbed you. Take care."

One panel of the ceiling started descending smoothly towards her the gray plastic assuming the shape of a hand that set a brown envelope on the table. It was a most ordinary bag made of brown paper like the ones the shop assistants put the things you bought in a food store. Ella took it and opened it carefully. There was a photograph in the bag. It looked old, faded and brittle but it was quite evident that the person on the photograph was Ella Boon.

Ella Boon was very young. Nothing in the photograph could surprise her, nothing till the moment when her eyes fell on a very strange detail. A wedding ring glittered on the finger of the young photographed Ella Boon. The wedding ring didn't look stylish and expensive like the ones you could buy at La Pierre Precieuse but it did glitter quite brightly. One could definitely say it was a gold ring.

Ella had never married. She hated to spend money on jewelry, rings, gems, necklaces and the like; she hated gold. She had fallen in love only once as a schoolgirl. He had been the brightest student in Joseph Conrad High School and she was convinced he was a genius. Ella had even overcome her paralyzing shyness and just before Christmas had put in the pocket of his overcoat a greeting card. She wished him success everywhere he went. She had written she admired him.

Of course, that young man was not a genius. He became a lawyer rich enough to afford splendid villas on the south coast of France and Italy and the most famous private colleges for his only son. Well, in fact that was all he had achieved in his life. Ella had met him a decade later and he told her he had felt immensely flattered on account of her greeting card. After all, Ella had been his most serious competitor, the student who won the physics contests and she had always beaten him. He was even afraid that Ella had tried to make fun of him using another of her insidious methods: sending a greeting card to her opponents. He had not even start guessing how wildly she had loved him.

Ella was the only child of an elderly provincial couple. Both her mother and father were doctors who died when she was very young. Ella Boon had no children. But why had she put the goddamned wedding ring on her finger?

Chapter 8

Inspector Val Hughes had pulled back the curtains in his narrow dark office; that was against the rules he had established for himself at that time of the day. He had never broken them before and felt nervous on account of sunlight streaming in and galloping everywhere in his small realm. Of course, he could sit in the dark with the curtains drawn waiting for the dusk to gather in the corners of his office. But then he wouldn't be able to see the delicate profile of the young woman who had settled on the only uncomfortable chair in front of him.

Val Hughes wanted to look at her, trying hard to believe that he, in his capacity of a conscientious professional, actually did his best to gauge the fleeting expressions on her beautiful face. He repeated to himself his only aim was to catch her out in a lie and expose the contradiction in her words. Yet deep in his heart, Val Hughes knew he enjoyed watching the tender outlines of her chin, the graceful curves of her body. He tried not to think about how attractive she was.

The woman sitting before him was Adrienne Tott. The unshakable confidence had left her eyes; she had not used any make-up and instead of an expensive dress she had put on a gray uniform, the only attire the persons detained for questioning at the Agency were allowed to wear. But the truth was the gray uniform really became her. Adrienne looked even prettier as helpless as a little girl that had lost her way at a busy crossroads.

Val Hughes hated the thought of having to do what he had carefully planned and prepared: the late Larry Hoffburg's wife swathed diligently in mourning weeds, Mrs. Jennifer Cost - Hoffburg, was waiting in the office next-door. She looked forward to meeting Adrienne Tott face to face. Adrienne had not yet been informed of the forthcoming meeting. Not once had she turned her eyes to the inspector; her hands rested in her laps and Val could not drive away the feeling he had to talk to a schoolgirl who had studied very diligently for a stiff entrance examination. At that very moment, Adrienne reminded him of a sweet girl in the high school who invariably occupied the seat in front of the teacher and always had the correct answer in her notebook. Val seemed to harbor some resentment against grinds all his life. But Adrienne Tott was pretty.

He had already waited for a long time and was convinced that Adrienne would start talking first, but she remained silent, her eyes dreamy and quiet, her hands perfectly calm and motionless.

"Miss Tott, we proved in an unequivocal manner you had lied again," the Inspector said. "You were perfectly healthy during the two outbreaks of the epidemic. You lied to me when I first interrogated you."

"Interrogated me?" the woman cut him short. Her energetic tone of voce had nothing to do with the image of the little girl who had lost her way at a busy crossroads. "Then you called our meeting 'a dialogue,' Inspector Hughes. And I would like to underscore the importance of the fact that you and your Agency held me captive and I had been subjected to a degrading experiment. That is against the law, Inspector. Was it you who invented the humiliating trick the Agency pulled on me?"

"Yes, it was my idea," the inspector admitted. "But I didn't expect you were lying, Miss Tott. I"

"You will have to pay for the pleasure you took in using me as a guinea pig, Inspector," Adrienne's eyes searched his for the first time and he did not feel malice or hostility. Well, in fact he was not sure. He could never know what the decision of that woman would be. "My lawyers are informed and I will sue you and the Agency," she said perfectly motionless on her hard uncomfortable chair.

"You have the right to do whatever you wish only after you have proved there is no relation between you and Professor bell's murder."

Val watched her. Composure and distant chill seemed to envelop her face challenging him.

"Miss Tott, first you have to give me an answer why you lied that you had a splitting headache while at the time the epidemic struck the town you were well. I hope that your explanation will be plausible otherwise the Agency would be within its right to continue interrogating you. So, why did you lie?

"I think you should find that by yourself," she objected. "That's what you are paid for." She thought for a while and added, "Why on earth should you accuse me of lying. I remember perfectly well what I told your unpleasant colleague, Inspector Ella Boon. I informed her that I felt fine while all the rest in town groaned and moaned with pain. I even shared my experience with her -- I told her I got rid of a chronic disease I had been suffering from for years. The unpleasant colleague of yours had all necessary facts at her disposal."

"You told me a different story," Val Hughes interrupted her. "As far as I remember, you said you had a splitting headache."

"Why don't you assume I was attracted to you, Inspector Hughes? I was so impressed by, let's say, your sense of humor. I don't remember exactly what I was impressed by. I had probably made up my mind to show you how much I suffered hoping I might deserve your compassion and your love."

"What did you do to deserve the love and compassion of the sixteen guys on Larry Hoffburg's list who in his opinion were your intimate friends? How come you became his mistress after he learnt about them?"

"I don't think that these sixteen guys were lesser men than you," Adrienne Tott remarked. "In fact each man on the list outdoes you when it comes to good manners and prowess. Be advised that Larry Hoffburg's information in this respect was far from being comprehensive. I assure you I choose my sexual partners very carefully, Sir."

"Don Highsmith was one of your sexual partners, wasn't he?" Val Hughes said feeling his throat constrict with hatred for that pretty woman. He could not explain why his hatred was mixed with admiration.

"Yes. Don Highsmith was one of them," she admitted. "But he never excelled in anything so I can hardly remember any details about him."

"He never excelled in anything apart from killing Professor Bell."

"Yes, Inspector Hughes. He killed Professor Bell, but let's not forget he used to be Mrs. Jennifer Cost's fiancé before that fat lady threw him out of her heart and became engaged to the ambitious Larry Hoffburg. That was exactly the reason why Don attracted me: I wanted so much to learn what the lady of the British aristocracy had felt as she talked to him and lived with him."

"Maybe sleeping with the ditched fiancé of an aristocrat made you feel an aristocrat yourself?" Val Hughes said. Irritation had already crept into his voice and he tried hard to conceal it.

"You hate me," the young woman whispered unexpectedly her face once again like that of the little girl in the fairy tale frightened to death by the ogre. "I annoy you. You forgot your question why I lied about having a splitting headache. You only thought about the sixteen guys on Larry Hoffburg's list."

"Why did you lie you had suffered from headaches?" Val Hughes asked shuddering involuntarily. That strange woman could read his thoughts and was so beautiful.

"Many people met their death in our town," Adrienne said. "Professor Bell and Larry Hoffburg were killed. What did they have in common? What was typical of them? Please, answer me."

Val Hughes looked at her curiously. What was she up to again?

"Neither Professor Bell nor Larry Hoffburg had any medical complaints at the time the epidemic swept the town, my dear Inspector."

Val Hughes had pressed his palms against the polished surface of his desk that the boards creaked.

"Of course, dear my inspector, you knew very well both Professor Bell and Larry had no medical complaints whatsoever. What happened in the long run? For one reason or another they were both killed. I didn't have any medical complaints either so I very rightfully expected the worst - an attempt on my life. Not that I'd mind if somebody did it, but" Adrienne's eyes met Val's for the first time and a wan smile touched her lips. "I met you and you are a young and attractive man. Perhaps tomorrow I'll meet another attractive man and I am very rich, so it's no good dying so young."

"How come you know that Professor Bell was a 'reverse effect' guy?" Val said slowly hardly able to breathe.

"What do you mean by a 'reverse effect guy'?"

Adrienne laughed. "If you think the Professor was gay, you are quite wrong. He wasn't and you can take my word for it."

"The phrase 'reverse effect' means that the individual under question does not suffer from headaches, weakness, fits etc., while the epidemic spreads. On the contrary, he or she gets rid of some severe chronic disease that has turned his or her life into a caravan of unbearable days and nights," the inspector explained then he stood up and paced up and down the narrow passage in front of the window. He moved much more quickly than his usual rolling gait would suggest. On the whole, his colleagues in the Agency could hardly boast they had seen Val walk so edgily.

Very quietly, as if he didn't want to shatter the peace and quiet in the room, he asked, "Are you really sure Professor Bell was not gay?"

"I know that your hatred for me will flare up, but, as I mentioned before, Larry Hoffburg's list of my boyfriends was incomplete. Professor Bell was not included in it, and I feel sorry about that because he was the only man I really loved. In fact I still love him."

"Then it turns out that you all the time cheated on the famous Larry Hoffburg who let you manage his company Toys International," Val Hughes nodded his head gloomily.

"Yes, strange things will always happen," Adrienne remarked. "Professor Bell was an exceptional man. He could have been a billionaire but he squandered his money on charity and night shelters for the homeless He was so lonely. He allowed no one to become really close to him. If I had not visited him from time to time he would have committed suicide much earlier."

"It sounds strange," Val said. "I've heard people speak other things about the professor. Rumor has it that he could make his patients laugh although often their days were numbered."

"Yes, he could change completely if his work demanded it," Adrienne's admiration for the professor was tingled with sadness and her face looked even prettier. Val Hughes waited for her to brace up. There was another surprise for him: Adrienne changed the subject looking him straight in the eye. "I knew both Professor Bell and Larry Hoffburg very well. I can assure you they were perfectly healthy while the whole population of the town writhed like worms as the epidemic raged and struck young and old. Both of them were murdered. Inspector Hughes, I am sure that somebody is after the persons who remain unaffected by the scourge of the epidemic. I think that he'll kill them all."

Val was surprised, greatly surprised. The light, rushing into the room from the window, touched the young woman's perfectly calm face. Outside the agency, spring had already erased the clouds from the sky, the sun shone brightly and inspector Hughes imagined for a moment what it would be like if he was near his favorite mountain lakes. This time he was unable to feel the cool breeze and the imperceptible smell of pine trees and water. The image of a pretty young woman was on his mind, the distant mountaintops gleaming behind her long hair loose on her shoulders.

"You don't seem to scare easily," the inspector said. "The threat had no effect on you. As far as I remember Don Highsmith threatened you'd be the next corpse."

"Don was not in the habit of threatening anybody," Adrienne answered unperturbed. "I have never taken his words seriously and I do not think he could kill me."

"Why?" Val Hughes asked, astonished.

"An old flame of mine wouldn't do me any harm" she started but didn't finish the sentence to the end, leaving it hanging in the air. She looked the inspector in the eye, swayed her hips gently and spoke slowly smiling, "Inspector Hughes, you haven't asked me a very important question. It is related to Ella Boon, your unpleasant colleague."

Val could not resist the temptation to let his eyes settle on her smiling face. He was smiling, too, although he did not feel like beaming with joy. In fact, few people could boast they had seen Val Hughes smile.

"In fact it's not a question but an approach to checking the facts. You know what, Adrienne?" he called her by her first name and paused to see if that would have any effect on her, but she didn't seem to notice. "Adrienne Tott, your profile resembles hers so much I mean Inspector Boon's profile. The high forehead, the nose, the lips."

The young woman stood up and put her hands on the smooth polished surface of his desk. If the inspector edged his own hands an inch forward he might touch her fingers.

"You are talking nonsense!" was all Adrienne said before she sat down on her hard uncomfortable chair.

"I have taken photographs of your profile, Miss Tott, "Val said. "You can have a look at this one," the inspector produced two postcard-sized color pictures out of a desk drawer. "This one is a photograph of Inspector Ella Boon's profile. You can see the close resemblance."

The young woman took the pictures, studied them for a while and muttered, "It's amazing. I could hardly believe it. It would be disgusting if I look like this cold, haughty woman when I grow old. "Adrienne left the photographs on the desk and whispered, "Inspector Hughes, I bet you were thrilled while you had my picture taken. It is not necessary to refuse to admit the truth. I can see it on your face Inspector, you had to ask me why I had not lied to your colleague that I didn't suffer like all the rest in the course of the epidemic."

Adrienne's eyes gleamed, her fingers trembled slightly and seemed to caress the desk. "I was sure that someone would try to kill Ella Boon. I was convinced that would happen because I knew she was one of the 'reverse effect' folks. Don Highsmith had mentioned her name in a note he had left for me. And that was a sure sign Ella Boon would be his victim I can see you stare at me intently, Inspector Hughes. Don't. I knew Don Highsmith well. He never spoke directly about what he intended to do. For example, if he wanted to have sex with me, he didn't say a word about that. He simply went and bought a jar of honey - one of the little jars that cost ten dollars apiece. After we finished he mixed honey with water and drank it to fortify himself. That's why I was convinced that Ella Boon would be the next corpse, not I. I knew, or rather I suspected that Inspector Boon was one of the 'reverse effect' people based on

86

observations I had made: I knew Ella Boon suffered from eczema. As chance would have it, she and I received medical treatment in Professor Bell's clinic at the same time. When Inspector Boon examined me, her eczema was not there. You understand that I had to warn her although I didn't like her at all."

Val was silent. Suddenly Val rose to his feet approached Adrienne, leant over her and asked quietly, "Have you heard anything about the Trail of Tears experiment?"

It seemed to Val that he waited for ages before Adrienne Tott answered his question.

"Yes," the young woman swallowed nervously as she tried to find her voice. "I think the purpose of the experiment was to select the five persons from our town who were not affected by the epidemic. After that a fine guy would kill them all. That was it."

"You said that five persons were not affected by diseases!" Val almost shouted. "How do you know they are five?"

"Inspector Hughes, it is clear that you have not lived with a woman long enough to learn some useful things, at least not with a pretty one. You are not married, are you?"

Val did not answer and averted his eyes from her face. He suspected she was making fun of him and felt deeply humiliated.

"I have not lived with women like you, Miss Tott," he grumbled without looking at her smiling face that for no apparent reason made him think of ancient secrets and beauty. Val hated lies but this time he stretched the truth, "I would never allow a woman like you to enter my house."

"Somehow, I doubt the sincerity of your statement, young man," Adrienne remarked. "Anyway, if you had ever lived with a lady long, you would have known that most of your secrets wouldn't be secrets to your lady. I assure you - Professor Bell warned me many times that the five "reverse effect" persons participating in the Trail of Tears experiment would be murdered. He knew I was one of them and desperately hoped I wouldn't be sent to the world beyond too soon. He thought I'd be last to be killed, if at all."

That strange woman, who spoke about death, was smiling at him! It seemed to Val that she had very carefully planned the way to spring a surprise by telling him the truth bit by bit. Or was she telling him the truth? Adrienne kept up the conversation and steered it away from the topics she didn't like. She chose the fragments of information she disclosed and selected the time to put out the bait for him. It was evident she was having a good time.

"Professor Bell told you that there were five "reverse effect" persons," the inspector said curtly. "Had he mentioned their manes to you?"

"He didn't mention any names but my own," the woman answered her voice suddenly cold and flat. "Inspector, don't you think we talked for too long today? I don't know how you feel, but I am absolutely exhausted."

"Don't be in a hurry to go home, Miss Tott," Inspector Hughes said approaching Adrienne's chair his arms outstretched in an apologetic gesture. "I have arranged a very interesting meeting for you." He did not wait for any questions on her part and issued his announcement in a brisk, matter of fact tone. "Miss Tott, you'll meet Mrs. Jennifer Cost-Hoffburg. I hope you know that remarkable lady very well."

After a short silence, the young woman uttered a few words, in which all discontent and contempt she had allowed to fester in her mind, showed through.

"What do you expect from Mrs. Jennifer Cost in the course of the meeting? Would you prefer it if the obese lady came down on me like a ton of bricks to beat me black and blue?"

Val Hughes did not answer. He approached the window and glanced unwillingly at the deserted narrow alleys in the Agency's park. All the time, he felt Adrienne's eyes on his back and turned abruptly to look at her, but found that the fair-haired woman contemplated the opposite wall, her face inscrutable and so distant as if Inspector Hughes had never talked to her and was not present in the room. It was unnaturally hot outside, the wind touching gently the cypress trees, making them appear much younger and naughtier. The grass was of a rich green color and for a moment Val Hughes compared it to the dark green shades he had noticed in Adrienne's eyes. He tried to imagine his favorite mountain lakes and the picture of pine trees and mountaintops lingered in his mind. He thought he saw streams of darker water that came from a thawing glacier, but this time on the shores of the lake a solitary figure of a woman waited - a lonely pretty woman isolated from the rest of the world. The inspector knew that woman and was sure he would never forget her name - Adrienne Tott. Adrienne Tott

He had never believed that the cypress trees could sway so gently in the breeze. He had not noticed the beauty of the old metal fence along the asphalt paths in the park although he had been working for the Agency for such a long time and had always thought he was a highly observant man. He wished he could turn around and look at Adrienne although he doubted he'd be able to take his eyes off her.

It felt awkward, so awkward. He had made almost no progress in the task he had taken upon himself; he had not cleared up the mysteries surrounding the Trail of Tears experiment. Far from it! He knew that in the evening when he'd try to analyze the information that he had collected in the course of the day, he'd ask dozens of tricky questions he had no answers to. In spite of that, there was something in the way that woman spoke and in the peculiar green color of her eyes that riveted his attention. It all didn't make sense!

Yet the two of them had many things in common: both Adrienne and he were 'reverse effect' persons, they both were threatened with murder, if one believed what Adrienne had just said. That was interesting. Professor Bell had mentioned that Adrienne would be last to be killed, if at all. She had been detained for questioning in the Agency and that was a perfectly safe place for her. Being under interrogation was infinitely preferable to having five knives plunged into your back. It seemed somebody had taken good care to withdraw Adrienne from the dangerous race against death. Wait a minute! Inspector Ella

Boon was detained for questioning as well! Ella's arrest could be interpreted as securing a safe place for her as well.

Val concentrated to sum up the situation.

Both Ella Boon and Adrienne were in the Agency and the Agency was the safest possible place. They both were 'reverse effect' women and only they among the five of the group could be sure, at least for the time being that they wouldn't be killed. Larry Hoffburg had been murdered and he, according Adrienne Tott's statement, was a 'reverse effect' man. Professor Bell, another reverse effect guy, had been killed.

It was so easy to make a conclusion as to who'd be the next victim. That had to be Val Hughes! Yes, Val Hughes, of course, because he was a 'reverse effect' guy and no one had secured a safe place for him. That theory did not shock or frighten him. Whoever planned to make an attempt on Val Hughes's life had to work on that very hard, indeed. The young inspector could promise him that.

"Why is our dear Mrs. Jennifer Cost-Hoffburg so late for our meeting?"

Val didn't answer her right away. He needed a couple of seconds to realize that Adrienne had asked him a question and was expecting an answer. In fact the verb 'expect' was not the precise word Val should use since the young lady had abandoned her hard uncomfortable chair and was pacing up and down the narrow space in front of the window. It was evident she was not in the least concerned with the fact she had a spring in her step, which didn't look too graceful. "I have no intention of waiting for her till kingdom come. Or perhaps her absence is a part of your strategy aimed at getting on your enemy's nerves, Inspector Hughes?

"I'll ask her to come in without delay," Val Hughes said. "Please, excuse my strategy, Miss Tott."

"There must be something wrong with the list of the five 'reverse effect' persons. I cannot make out who they are." Unpleasant thoughts raced through Val's mind. He felt like going out for a long walk in the busiest streets of Jacksonville. Yes, that might be a good idea, the noise, the cars, the traffic lights and hurrying people had always helped him to concentrate and think rationally. The faces of the strangers, distant, nonchalant, flitting reassured him. But now he couldn't go out for a walk. Adrienne Tott was in his office standing with her back to him and he had to ignore her presence.

"I know the following "reverse effect" persons," the inspector thought. "One - that is me, Val Hughes; two - Adrienne Tott; three - Ella Boon; four - Professor Rupert Bell (murdered); five - Larry Hoffburg (murdered); six - Don Highsmith, missing at present, Professor's Bell alleged murder; seven - Inspector Red Kyle. So what is the conclusion? Two of the persons on the list are not 'reverse effect' folks, they have simply pretended that they are all the time. But why? Who are these two persons and what is their role in the Trail of Tears experiment? Very simple questions, there could not be doubt about that!'

But he had made his hypothesis on the basis of Adrienne Tott's statement - she had heard Professor Bell say that the "reverse effect" guys were five. Did she really hear that or had she made up that story, which was not easy to check? Did she pursue her own interests? Yes, so many fives had been scribbled on the note they found by Professor Bell's body. Everywhere these strange fives

Someone knocked loudly at the door and, enormous like a man of war, intent on taking Val Hughes's office by storm, a lady was admitted into the room. She did not greet anybody as she turned her head in all directions in the cramped office apparently searching for something to sit on.

"Good afternoon, Mrs. Hoffburg," Val Hughes met her at the door and politely offered her his own chair. The lady treated his gesture as an affront to her sensibilities for she needed at least three chairs to settle comfortably behind the small desk.

"Good afternoon, dear Jennifer!"

Val Hughes choked, amazed. Adrienne had a radiant angelic smile on her face as if she finally found her beloved friend she had not seen for ages.

"Come off it, Rosita, you know I hate you. I detest your smiles, your face, your dresses and everything related to you!" the lady spoke quietly, hardly capable of suppressing her anger. Her cheeks wobbled in time with her wrathful pronouncement, her blushes becoming warmer.

"Let us not forget, my dear, that Larry, your late husband, called me Adrienne and I am known by that name in town, or should I say in the whole country," the young woman remarked calmly then jumped to her feet and shook Jennifer Cost's hand prolonging the contact interminably.

"Take your filthy hands off me, Rosita!" the enormous aristocrat said in a booming voice producing a series of frighteningly sonorous words. "Yes, you are Rosita, the cheap slut who could do nothing but crawl into bed with lewd third-rate men"

"And it is an art form, which requires skills, that you can never master, my dear," the stunning young woman added the smile on her face happier than ever. "The gentlemen were lewd, I grant you, but don't describe them as third-rate. The truth is quite different, you know. Don Highsmith was your fiancé, and Larry Hoffburg - your husband, God bless their souls. Would you call them 'third-rate men'?"

"Inspector Hughes," Jennifer turned to him making visible efforts. "I was given the dubious honor of attending that meeting and I said yes if the Agency's Chairman, Mr. Robert Hendricks, took part in it. I can see that the respected gentleman is not here. So I flatly refuse to talk to that scumbag" she raised her heavy hand and pointed to Adrienne Tott. "In my opinion, Inspector, you do not perform your duties the way you should. You stand here quite inertly admiring her arrogance! She deliberately misled you about the nature of her numerous relationships right from the beginning. Firstly, her name is not Adrienne she is Rosita. Let me inform you, Inspector what was your name? Let me inform you, Inspector Hughes, that Don Highsmith hated her guts! She threw him out of her house when his convulsive fits became frequent.

He used to cry, Inspector! He sobbed like a helpless child outside her front door. He didn't want her filthy money, mind you, he pleaded with her not to leave him. All he wanted was that slut's love! And what did she do? What do you think she did? She didn't give a damn! She hid in the house, which Don Highsmith had bought her with his own money! He wept uncontrollably while she had sex with another of her numerous lovers! That's what she did! Poor Don He was seriously sick. His liver was enlarged and damaged: his heart was failing. But she threw him out, Inspector Hughes, I assure you, she kicked him out most mercilessly. Don told me about that. He tried to speak to her about his diseases and she promised to take care of him, that appalling parasite, that poisonous mushroom! But when his fits became frequent and he had to be operated on, she threw him out"

"Mrs. Hoffburg, please, calm down. Have a glass of water. It might help you," Inspector Hughes carefully placed the glass in front of the agitated woman who carefully studied the transparent liquid in it and in one gulp drained the glass "Mrs. Hoffburg, are you sure that Don suffered from so many diseases?"

"Of course I am sure, Inspector. He had liver cirrhosis, his kidneys and gall bladder were no good, and he had problems with his heart. Poor Don, he had frequent convulsive fits," Jennifer's cheeks wobbled again and she gesticulated nervously at Val. "Oh, Don was seriously ill. But it would have been immeasurably better if I had married him. Unfortunately I chose Larry Hoffburg, the treacherous midget! To walk out on me after five years - what a rat! Don Highsmith would have been at least grateful for the money that I'd give him. Larry Hoffburg sneered at me. Can you imagine the humiliation I suffered, Inspector Hughes? It was on Wednesdays, only once a week, when he dragged himself to my 18-th century country mansion to have lunch with me, half an hour after he climbed out of that that slut's bed! I am so happy they killed him! I would have killed him with my bare hands, Inspector! Yes, I would have! Would you like to know why I didn't do it? Because she was going to inherit all his property! Everything would go into this slut's hands! The lousy hypocrite bequeathed his entire estate to her. And he came to have lunch with me on Wednesdays and all my relatives saw us together chatting away like old friends. I stuck it out! Can you imagine that? Now I am happy. He is dead in his grave and the worms eat his ashes. Isn't that wonderful?"

"Mrs. Hoffburg, calm down, please."

"Do not call me Mrs. Hoffburg, Inspector. I hate it!"

"I will not, Ma'am," Val Hughes assured her. "Perhaps you need a drink. Whisky? Here you are. Please, calm down." Then he turned to the younger woman. "Adrienne Tott, can you vouch for the fact that Don Highsmith suffered from the serious diseases Mrs. Jennifer Cost has just spoken about?"

"Yes, I can," Adrienne answered, unperturbed. "However, I am sure nothing depends on what I say or do not say in relation to Don's health. You can simply check his medical records and you can see if Jennifer tells you the truth. I"

"Don't you dare to call me by my first name!" Larry Hoffburg's widow shouted trying to get up from her chair. "You ruined my fiancé's life! You stole my husband! I wish I could tear you limb from limb with my own hands!"

"Why should you be so angry with me, my dear?" Adrienne said as gently as if she was crooning a lullaby. "I made both your fiancé and your husband genuinely happy. You know very well that I gave the house back to Don Highsmith. I gave him back all the presents he had bought me - the golden necklaces, the earrings, the bracelets and bangles. I still keep the receipts, bearing his signature, and I can show them all to you. I even sent him money"

"Do you know how he spent that money?" Jennifer Hoffburg fumed. "You bitch! He made one million copies of your photograph and pasted them on the walls of his dingy hotel room!"

"Isn't that a proof that he still loves me?" Adrienne asked dampening the aristocrat's enthusiasm.

"He hates your guts! He hates all the photographs of your naked whorish body! He stuck a razor blade into each nasty picture of you - into your belly, into your mouth, between your tits, between your legs!" Jennifer laughed and her enormous heavy body rippled and shook contentedly like a pool of glutinous liquid. "I helped him to stick the razor blades and it did my heart good! It is a pleasure for me to inform you, Rosita, that he came back to me. Yes, he came back to my bed! I took him to Professor Bell to receive medical treatment. I helped him recover his health! I kissed him, I caressed him, and I had sex with him hundreds of times. I took care of him and I"

"Could I ask you a question, Ma'am?" Inspector Val Hughes interposed. "Do you know that that the police suspect Don Highsmith might have committed a vicious crime? They think that he killed Professor Bell in a particularly cruel manner by sticking five knives into the victim's body."

"No! It is impossible!" Jennifer Hoffburg cried out. "Don Highsmith adored the professor! He knew he owed Professor Bell his life. Don visited him once every three months and had a thorough medical examination. I can assure you, Inspector Hughes - every time he walked back home a free and healthy man. It seemed Professor Bell wiped out all his diseases by a magic wand.

Well, Don was a maniac in a way. I'd say Adrienne had become an obsession with him. He used to write down her name on white sheets of paper then he cut the sheet into narrow pieces, and swallowed the ones that had her name on them. In the evenings, he usually drank himself stone drunk, took off all his clothes and wallowed naked in the heap of paper clippings he had not swallowed yet. It was only natural that his unhealthy lifestyle brought him back to Professor Rupert Bell.

"Of late, Don had started telling tall stories about a big bug allegedly intent on murdering Adrienne, the bitch! The accident, in which Don lost his power of speech, occurred at about that time. I saw him sneak around the bitch's house at least three times a day! Later he told me he had wanted to protect her he boasted that he was ready to place his body between her and the bullets. He ranted and raved he'd die for her! Oh, my God! She called the police and the paramedics drove him to a mental home where I went to see him several times. Yes, Inspector Hughes, I did visit him! And I am proud I paid a generous sum as a result of which Don was transferred to a private clinic. He bragged to the doctors there that even if Adrienne was killed he could regenerate her. But Don didn't stop there: he crowed he could resuscitate dead people! Wait a minute, I got mixed up. Don told me he didn't want to die because he hoped that one day he might save Adrienne's life"

"So you think that it was impossible for Don Highsmith to kill Professor Bell?" Inspector Hughes asked calmly and his measured tone seemed to suppress the aristocratic lady's fierce excitement.

"Don Highsmith wouldn't kill Professor Bell! No power on earth can make him do it," Jennifer Cost declared.

"Could you tell me in details what Don Highsmith had said about regenerating dead individuals?" the young inspector's voice sounded soft and pleading. "I think that my request may sound eccentric to you, but I'd very much like to know your opinion on the subject."

"Of course, Inspector Hughes," she flashed him a dazzling smile. "I might have made a mistake sometimes it is difficult to make a realistic assessment of a person who questions you, although I am shrewd in my personal assessments... It appears that you pay attention to the remarks of a worthy and well-meaning lady."

"Your positive attitude towards the inquest is greatly appreciated, Ma'am," Val Hughes said and made a stiff bow to her.

"Don promised me, too," Jennifer went on seriously. "He had repeated many times that Professor Bell was able to regenerate human tissues so that the injured or dysfunctional organs became healthy again. 'My dearest Jenny,' he used to turn to me He really called me 'my dearest Jenny', believe me, Inspector Hughes! 'My dearest Jenny, I am the most impressive example of how successful the regeneration process is. Professor Bell is a smart one, indeed! My liver, my gall bladder, my spleen and my stomach were absolutely no good. My glands were swollen. But you know, my dearest, how well I do in your bed after I visit Professor Bell!" He performed perfectly in my bed, Inspector Hughes, and you can count on that! This scumbag here," she pointed impetuously to Adrienne. "This scumbag is not the only woman capable of satisfying a decent man's sexual desires! I am capable of doing that, too, and"

"What did Don promise you, Ma'am?" Inspector Hughes asked insistently although his voice sounded soft and pleasant.

"He said he could convince Professor Bell to regenerate me. You know what, Inspector Hughes, I have always dreamed of having a good figure - if not a lovely one then at least a slender and neat one, "Jennifer Cost-Hoffburg smiled charmingly. "Don thought Professor Bell could easily do that. Don told me something else, too - he said he had a mistress once, a very nice and intelligent woman. The doctors told her she had leukemia - you know what doctors are, Inspector Hughes, they'd do anything to wring money out of you, just anything! But Don's mistress was really in trouble, she had leukemia and her family, both her close and distant relatives, started hinting at imminence of death and spoke about the necessity of arranging her funeral. But Professor Bell regenerated the girl and today she is alive and kicking, and as far as I know owns a pizza restaurant. Don visited her from time to time and she sold him food at a discount. That is what I call kindness and understanding unlike the pretensions of that heartless bitch Adrienne Tott! You arrested her and I warmly welcome this decision of yours! I hope you've made an excellent job of her interrogation, but you'd better throw her into jail without delay. I'd jail her for life, if I were you, Inspector Hughes! Thus she will not be able to corrupt innocent men's souls So, if Professor Bell was alive, he'd help me deal with my excess weight and Don could hope I could give birth to his legitimate heir! Why should Don kill Professor Bell! It doesn't make sense!"

Val Hughes listened carefully on while Adrienne Tott's face displayed icy contempt, her lips pursed in a derisive grimace.

"At a later stage of Jennifer's dramatic soliloquy her guardian angel flies out of paradise, perches on her enormous shoulder, and breathes angelic fumes all over her. Jenny's excess weight turns into lumps of cheese, which fall onto the floor by her feet." Adrienne burst into laughter. "Then all men I have thrown out of my bed will rush to Jennifer and she will satisfy their urgent sexual desires. It sounds logical, doesn't it?"

"She envies me! She's green with envy!" Jennifer waved her ringed hands her voice thundering again like a roaring ocean. "She'd give anything to be in my shoes! Yes, you slut! You know very well that the professor couldn't regenerate you! Don knew that, too, and that was the reason he tried to commit suicide several times. After he stayed in that mental home and Professor Bell restored his ability to speak, Don stopped driveling and talking nonsense. The professor simply told him that Adrienne was one of the five freaks in town that could not be regenerated. She was one of the five monsters! Don was not all there at that time. He whimpered and whined, once he stuck five rusty razor blades into his chest and lay prostrate on the floor watching his wounds bleed

Then I took him to my bed. Yes, Inspector, I did and I told him it made no sense to kill Professor Bell. Why should the poor surgeon get the blame for everything that went wrong? He had nothing to do with the fact that Adrienne was a freak. He could regenerate all citizens in town with the exception of the five freaks. And this bitch was one of them! I shouted with joy when I learnt this.

Would you be so kind to pass me a glass of water, Inspector Hughes? Oh, thank you so much. I suspect that Larry Hoffburg, my errant, mean husband, is one of the monsters, too, and will explain to you, Inspector, why I think so. It was Wednesday you know that the rascal visited me on Wednesday to have breakfast with me -- he was doing his best to keep up appearances. On that particular I was very angry and I paid his bodyguards to go and have a drink in a posh pub. So when Larry started gorging himself on pancakes, none of them were around. I grabbed my big kitchen knife and tried to slit his throat with it Adrienne, do you remember that your lover bled almost to death? I could have collected a whole pale of blood if I had had half a mind to do so. But I wouldn't do such a thing! Inspector Hughes, I have many cuddly toys in my house and I long to have children. An ambulance came and took my perverse husband to Professor Bell's clinic. I was informed he had received medical treatment in the course of six months and he felt dizzy and unwell two years after he left the clinic. Who was in your bed at that time, Adrienne?"

"I always had someone," the blonde woman answered casually.

"Do not pay attention to her, Inspector!" Jennifer Cost shouted imperiously. "Let me explain something else. You can see that I am open with you - I admitted to you that I had committed a crime. Only Adrienne and I knew about it because my perverse husband Larry refused to tell the police I had attacked him with a knife. If he could have been regenerated, he'd have been safe and sound after five days the way it always happened to Don. But no! Larry, the worm, stewed in his own juice and was racked with agonizing pain. Inspector, could you give me another glass of water? Thank you."

"Adrienne Tott," Val Hughes spoke loudly and clearly approaching the blonde's chair. "Did you know about Jennifer Cost's attempt on her husband's life?"

"Yes, I am familiar with her determined effort to cut his throat."

"Why didn't you tell the police about it? The inspector asked.

"I was not required by law to do that," the pretty woman answered a mocking smile lurking in the corners of her chiseled mouth. "Perhaps I simply wanted to cover for Jenny."

"Adrienne kept her mouth shut because if she had spoken the police would have learned Larry was different from al the normal people and could not be regenerated!" Jennifer's alto voice boomed out.

"Who wanted to know if Larry Hoffburg could be regenerated or not?" Val Hughes questioned echoed like a distant shot of a gun.

"I don't know," the lady of the aristocratic family shrugged her huge shoulders but almost immediately her eyes gleamed sharply again. "However, I have constructed a plausible hypothesis, Inspector Hughes. To put it plainly and more directly, Don Highsmith told me that well, it is true that happened only a couple of days after he came out of the mental home and about a week after Professor Bell restored his ability to speak"

"What did Don Highsmith tell you, Mrs. Cost?" the inspector asked and prudently offered the lady another glass of water.

She gulped it down, wiped her mouth with a napkin she produced from her handbag, and declared, "It is a pleasure for me to talk to you, Inspector Hughes! I will write a letter of grateful acknowledgement to your boss about you. Your colleague I had spoken to earlier, a red-haired man with a colorless haughty face, simply made me feel as though I was trampled underfoot, if you can see what I mean. It was obvious he thought I had a screw loose."

"Who had questioned Jennifer?" Val tried to remember and the answer was immediately there: it was Red Kyle. How typical of him - he couldn't stand pampered babbling ladies like Mrs. Cost-Hoffburg. It appeared she had been too much for him. Val smiled and his voice came loud and clear, "Dear Mrs. Cost, what did Don Highsmith tell you after he came out of the mental home?"

"Oh, yes!" Jennifer exclaimed triumphantly. "The late Professor Bell had mentioned the following in Don's presence: if the five monsters - I mean the people who cannot be regenerated, of course If the five monsters got together in the same area, I don't remember within how many radii of Professor Bell's clinic, all persons who had been subjected at least once in their lives to regeneration, would be racked with an excruciating pain, spitting headaches, weakness and the like In other words, the five monsters would take their revenge on the normal people and make them suffer because they could be regenerated and cured and thus they could live forever."

Val Hughes listened to her in amazement, suddenly unable to move.

"Now you can see, Inspector! Adrienne, Larry and all the rest of them get together maybe because they want to avenge themselves on me on account of the fact that dear Don came back to my bed. Don't you think I'm right, Inspector Hughes?

Inspector Hughes shrugged his shoulders silently.

"Inspector," Jennifer went on excitedly, her breath coming in short gasps. "A mysterious epidemic swept our town a week ago. I myself had a splitting headache; my knee and elbow joints were inflamed, swollen and unbearably painful. Don't you think that the five freaks got together because they had a plan to ruin our health and homes? So why don't we execute Adrienne Tott? We can hold a referendum on that issue and I am convinced that each normal person will prefer to maintain his physical and mental health. We all will vote against that scumbag, Adrienne Tott!"

Perhaps the enormous lady felt she was going too far, or maybe she noticed the inspector's set face.

"You can simply put her in jail," she offered then thought about it and decided that the punishment she was thinking of was not severe enough. "Throw her into the dungeons! Let her spend some years in solitary confinement so she won't be able to deprave young and decent men. Inspector, can I have some mineral water, please?"

Mrs. Jennifer Cost-Hoffburg quickly drained half of the glass and splashed the rest of the water on her face.

"I'll let you into my secret, Inspector Hughes," she said nodding vigorously. "I wrote a letter to Professor Bell some time ago and confided my suspicions to him. I wrote openly that my errant, mean husband in all probability was one of the five freaks that could not be regenerated! Do you know what, Inspector - the professor followed my advice." Jennifer had an amused expression on her face, which very soon became grim.

"In fact, he followed my advice partially" she added. "The professor recommended my husband go and live in a mountain town far away from Jacksonville where he could enjoy mild winters and pleasant springs. Larry took his advice and went to a place in Austria where one of his horrible toy factories had been recently built. Inspector, I adore simple toys made of wood, but I hate the mechanical and electronic and clockwork monstrosities that Larry produced! I am very happy that his factories are going bankrupt one after the other! So Adrienne will inherit nothing but Larry's old moth-eaten chair!"

"Mrs. Cost, why did you say that Professor Bell followed your advice partially? What do you mean by 'partially'?" Inspector Hughes asked most respectfully during the short interval of time, which Jennifer had used to breathe a sigh of satisfaction.

"Because Adrienne Tott was not removed from our native town! The professor did not make her leave Jacksonville," Jennifer answered angrily. "Professor Bell was a bad egg, if you ask me, Inspector. I never really liked him. Believe me - I still shudder at the thought of how he ogled Adrienne! I know about men's eyes, Inspector, you can count on that, and I am positive that a man, who leers at her sweating buckets, has slept with her! The bitch! So, Inspector Hughes, I accuse Professor Bell of causing the epidemic that struck Jacksonville. It might sound very far-fetched to you, but it is true! He let Adrienne remain in town thus allowing the five monsters to get together and torture us all, honest, law-abiding citizens and tax-payers!"

Jennifer Cost's effusion came to an abrupt end as she paused to look at Inspector Hughes. Something must have caught her attention for she suddenly yelled, "Inspector! You are like them all! You stare at this slut in exactly the same way! I thought you were a decent man, I told you everything, and now I hate myself for that!"

Chapter 9

The walls of the black hole, the Agency's notorious maximum-security jail where Ella Boon was kept, suddenly became immobile. With a great effort of will Ella had forced herself not to pay attention to them. But, when the space that surrounded her assumed the form of a funnel she had to prostrate herself on the floor her stomach sticking firmly to its ice-cold metal surface. Stinging edges and razors protruded from the funnel and prodded her in the back, legs, and neck cutting her skin if she tried to make the slightest movement. Someone had turned off the lights and the Black Hole was plunged into total darkness.

"I'd like to have a word with you. Could you spare me a minute?" an almost inaudible whisper reached her ears. "It's me, Red Kyle."

"Make yourself at home, Kyle," she answered in a loud voice as she attempted to raise her head. A thin cutting edge jutted out of the black metal walls and slashed her naked neck. It was pitch dark and nothing but a rattling noise of heavy steps came from the condensed impenetrable space. "Could you turn on the lights, Kyle? I'd like to watch the expression on your face while we talk."

"No, Ella. Darkness refreshes memory and I am here to make you remember a thing or two."

"I have an excellent memory," Ella said firmly. "So far, it has never let me down. In my capacity of an inspector working for the Agency"

"An ex-inspector," Red Kyle corrected her.

"I kept a diary in the course of the years I have been working for the Agency," Ella went on, unperturbed, although she lay prostrate on the cold metal floor. "The information in it is classified and the diary itself is kept in the Agency's Documentation Department. So, it is not necessary to make me remember a thing or two, Kyle. You can simply read my diary - you are the person in charge of the Documentation Department."

"What did you do with Professor Bell's body, Ella? Why did you want his dead body, damn it!"

"I have nothing to do with Professor Bell's body or with his murder," Ella said as tried to sit up, but a row of iron spikes descended on her back forcing her to change her mind. "Kyle, I would appreciate it if you didn't call me by my first name. My family name is Boon and I hope you won't forget that."

The rattling noise of heavy steps faded away, the darkness lifted slowly, the funnel of the walls disintegrated and the Black Hole was once again an ordinary prison cell. Suddenly Ella felt an earth tremor, first the ceiling and the floor then all the four walls shook. The ceiling became blue, then purple then scarlet and without warning the air in the room was dazzlingly red, all the four walls were scarlet and the prison cell felt like turning into a bathtub full of blood.

"Have you ever been married, Ella?"

The walls unexpectedly vanished, dissolved into the stifling crimson air and the Black Hole most illogically looked like a spotless tiny kitchen -- Ella Boon's kitchen in her comfortable third -floor apartment. "You can take a seat now and relax," Red Kyle offered as he waited for Ella's answer. Ella thought for a moment, the silence lengthening. "Have you ever been married, Boon?" Red Kyle repeated.

"No, I have not," she said refusing to move, lying stubbornly prostrate on the floor.

"Please, stand up," he said his hand touching her shoulder. "The hairs on the back of your neck look beautiful your shoulders are beautiful, too," Inspector Kyle whispered. "I don't doubt other men have told you that many times."

Red Kyle touched her shoulder again.

"What's eating you, Kyle?" Ella asked coldly. "It appalls me if the Agency could simply force you to make open advances to me. There is no use doing that. You'd better ask me what you'd like to know and I will tell you."

"Have you taken lovers?" Kyle asked unexpectedly. Ella studied his face: it appeared distant, rapt in thought, or even lost in ludicrous reverie, but she could detect not the slightest sign of hostility, mockery or ridicule. Interesting

"I had two lovers," Ella answered calmly as she rose to her feet. "Kyle, you know perfectly well who they are. Their photographs, their recorded phone calls, their CVs are in the dossier the Agency has on me. So I advise you to read my dossier instead of asking me nonsensical questions."

"I checked your dossier quite thoroughly, you can count on that, Ella. Both your lovers ditched you," Kyle whispered. "Both of them said many pleasant things about you. In their opinion, you are a gorgeous woman very skilful in bed, too. But you didn't care a damn about your men, Ella Boon."

"If you are really interested in my lovers, I could give you the telephone number and the Email address of psychologist they both used to see once a week. He could explain to you what sort of persons they were like," Ella turned her back to her red-haired colleague then added, "Go away, Kyle!"

Red Kyle pulled up his chair and leant over her.

"Do you remember when you and I started working for the Agency - our first year?" he asked. "We were both young. I liked you quite a lot, but you tended to treat me as nerdy and dull. You were so nasty to me, so nasty! I felt depressed I tried hard to take you to my bed, but"

Ella was silent. Her face looked cold, inscrutable, as if it had appeared on a big TV screen while she was one thousand miles away from the Black Hole, immobile, reserved, cold, having every confidence in her own abilities.

"Ella, I'll tell you why I came to your dingy padded cell," the inspector spoke in low, measured tones. "Listen to me carefully. I gave you a photograph of yourself, which I found in your dossier. Do you remember it?"

"Yes, I do," Ella answered coldly.

"And you knew right away I didn't give it to you just to compliment you on your pretty face when you were thirty years younger. The picture shows you as a stunning young woman but I don't feel like discussing that now."

The inspector rose to his feet and paced the floor energetically, but the Black Hope was too narrow and he had to sit down again.

"Ella, I noticed a wedding ring on the third finger of your left hand. Yes, a wedding ring! I examined it carefully under a magnification of 10 times the actual size. I think I noticed some initials on the wedding ring. But you told me you had never been married."

"I have never married anybody," Ella said.

"Perhaps you put on that wedding ring because you wanted to look like all the other normal women, at least for a moment," Red Kyle said flashing her a wry smile.

"I am a normal woman. You can take my word for that."

"I have never seen you wear jewelry and we have been working together for thirty years now," Kyle pointed out. "Neither has Bob Hendricks. He thinks you've never put on rings, bracelets, necklaces or other trinkets. So you should know where the wedding ring on your third finger came from.

Tell me where you keep it. You'd agree - it would be absurd if a woman threw out her wedding ring, wouldn't it?"

"Yes," Ella muttered under her breath. "I noticed the wedding ring when you gave me the photograph. I asked myself when and why I had put it on and I have no explanation for my strange behavior. I don't know anything. I don't know where the wedding ring is now."

"And you don't know how Professor Bell's body vanished without trace from the mortuary," the inspector gave her a meaningful look. "You don't anything about the wedding ring too many things you don't anything about, Ella Boon. You deny all knowledge of the affair and your odd behavior invites suspicion. Do you hear me, Ella?"

It was very quiet in the Black Hole. Inspector Ella Boon sat immobile her distant, inscrutable face seeming unaware of the man's presence in narrow cell.

"Ella!" Red Kyle called out. "Ella!"

"I can hear you very well, Kyle," she said meeting his gaze. Rumors had it that many women were attracted by his rugged good looks, but Ella could hardly stand his arrogant, aggressive manner. "Inspector Kyle, listen to me attentively, please. I have been checking my dossier once every two months, updating it in accordance with the Agency's latest requirements. I'd like to emphasize the fact that my duties included introducing the necessary additional information on the tasks assigned to me. I am absolutely certain that the photograph you had spoken about - the one with the wedding ring on my finger - was not in my dossier. You did not take it from my classified index and now you must tell me who gave it to you."

"I took the photograph from your dossier, Ella Boon. Both Bob Hendricks and Val Hughes were in the Repository when that happened and they can confirm what I've just said."

Ella Boon stood up, arranged her grizzled hair and spoke her voice flat and matter-of-fact as if she was making casual comments on the April weather forecast.

"Kyle, I suspect your work undermines the Agency's position. In fact, I don't trust any of the inspectors, but you are my prime suspect. Firstly, because I've never had such a photograph in my dossier and you know that, but you invested a great deal of time and effort in bringing Val Hughes and Bob Hendricks to the Repository, where they 'found' a picture of me with the wedding ring. You made old Bob climb the steep flight of stairs leading to the Repository -- storage of documents outside it is strictly forbidden and no one, not even the Chairman of the Agency, can take, or work, or check a document outside the Repository. But you made Bob climb the steep stairs. I know you love Bob Hendricks, Kyle. Why should you torture the old man if the general intention behind your plan was an honest one? What were you driving at? What did you want? To discredit me? Highly improbable! I am jailed and I could hardly hinder the inquest. You want me imprisoned in the Black Hole, Kyle. You"

"Haven't you ever been struck by the sudden thought that the Black Hole is a very safe place, indeed? In fact, you are much better protected here than most of the full citizens of the country who stride along the streets in Jacksonville Nobody can kill you in the Black Hole, Ella. Maybe I don't want anybody to kill you and that's all to it."

Ella Boon was silent as she sat down again.

"Ella, do you love Adrienne Tott?" Red Kyle's voice suddenly sounded big and energetic.

"I am not attracted by homosexual acts," Ella Boon answered coldly. "Kyle, I tried to be courteous but I hope I didn't encourage conversation."

"You misunderstood me, Ella. In fact, you were invited to give your opinion of Adrienne Tott. What do you think of her as a personality, as a human being, do you like her? Or are you put off Adrienne on account her manners?"

"I see no point in continuing this conversation, Kyle."

"I asked you serious questions that constitute an important part of the official investigation," the inspector warned her. "What's your opinion of Adrienne Tott? For example, would you like to have a daughter like her?"

"If I had wanted a daughter, I'd have had one," she lowered her voice more than usual. Perhaps Ella Boon regretted that she didn't have a child. "I don't have a very high opinion of Adrienne Tott," Ella said flatly. "Firstly, she has a cool head. She is cold and calculating, capable of using information so that it is of benefit to her while keeping her opponents at bay. Secondly, she is very pretty and knows that very well, so she manages to get a good price for what she is. Thirdly, even if she were my daughter, I'd do my best to avoid meeting her. That is all I have to say about Adrienne Tott."

Unexpectedly, without any warning, Red Kyle rose to his feet and rushed to the wall. It was no surprise to Ella that the metal surface parted in front of him and he left the Black Hole in a flash. The wall reappeared immediately behind his back blocking the view from the short-lived crevice. Ella did not seem astonished that Kyle left her cell so quickly. Having worked with the inspector for thirty years she thought she could provide a plausible explanation for every move he made.

It was evident Kyle was displeased with something; perhaps she had offended him as soon as she had opened her mouth, unfortunately, she didn't know what exactly had enraged him. The strange questions, which he had asked her, his hand that had touched her shoulder, her photograph Yes, his behavior had been highly suspicious. Ella had a wedding ring on her finger in that photo, but she had no idea how it had got there, she could not remember anything. But wait a minute Of course!

There was a period in her life about which she remembered virtually nothing. Well, memory could play tricks on you the years after the traffic accident when Professor Bell had saved her life. Professor Bell again! Somebody had murdered him and now no man on earth could tell Ella what had happened to her back then. Did Red Kyle know anything about that or about the crime shrouded in a series of minor appalling mysteries? She hated the very sound of the words 'mystery and crime'. Perhaps the inspector had given her the photograph because he wanted to drop a hint to her that he had valuable information at hand?

Anyway, something had offended Kyle gravely or he had been too unpleasantly surprised for the inspector had slipped out of the Black Hole without the usual minor quibbles so typical of him. Ella remembered something: two or three years ago Bob Hendricks made a suggestion to the Agency's executive council. Old Bob wanted Ella Boon to become his successor and work as assistant chairman and his first legal advisor. On hearing that, Red had had stood up, silent and grim, and left the session of the council. Ella had refused to become Bob's successor and his first legal advisor Yes, of course, the walls of the Black Hole had started dancing again, but now their waltz was much more graceful and their rhythm much more regular than before.

The Black Hole seemed more spacious and airy and even the hard chair she had sat on had turned into a comfortable cushioned thing resembling a small sofa. She found with gratitude she could recline on it enjoying the gentle touch of the soft cool fabric under her fingers. She felt like relaxing and hopefully drifting into sleep. Yes, she had to snatch a few hours' sleep - she desperately needed it. Ella had got accustomed to the humiliating thought that she had been isolated from the investigation.

"So what?" she had often repeated to herself and it was a relief to be able to say it out loud. But at heart-stopping moments when the walls of the Black Hole did not shake and wobble but stood firmly in place like all normal walls of a building, she sank to the depths of despair.

She could not live without her work, without the Agency. She could not imagine the hours, the days, the evenings she had to spend in her apartment. Maybe she had to learn to knit cardigans, to cook, to start practicing crafts, such as embroidery and tapestry. No, it was impossible! Ella Boon hated the thought of it! She preferred to be kept in jail, in that nasty dingy cell, the Black Hole, where she could breathe the air redolent with the smell of secrets and dark crimes that challenged her will, her imagination, her ability to think. Otherwise life would not be worth her while.

Unexpectedly the walls started assuming different shapes before her eyes, the cutting edges she knew too well appeared first, after a short while some startling mushrooms and cones grew in between then the ceiling and floor coalesced into a gooey mess, which closed in on all sides around her. After what seemed ages to her the walls turned into three enormous microphones out of which a tired deep man's voice crept out. The sound of it sent shivers down her spine. Bob Hendricks was speaking to her! He usually had important things to say.

"Ella, we'll come to the Black Hole in an hour, my girl. We'll conduct something like a mini-session of the executive council and I invite you to participate in it. Your chair in my office looks so portentously empty that the three of us lose out tongues if we have to stay there for a long time. We'll speak in your presence. Even if you are one of our 'enemies' you can't get out of the Black hole. Details of our discussion will not leak out, I am sure."

"I can always think up a way," Ella muttered. "Be careful, Bob. I feel that experimenting on Ella Boon may cause unnecessary failures. I am a very treacherous person, you know."

Inwardly, Ella felt like jumping for joy and that found expression in an almost invisible wry smile on her face if at all one could interpret a grimace like that as jumping for joy.

"I know you are a treacherous person, my girl," the walls of the Black Hole answered sounding like Bob Hendricks. "Take it easy. We will conduct an experiment, but it will not be a sore trial only to you. We all will take part in it: you, Red Kyle, Val Hughes and I."

"Are okay, Bob? I mean have you thought things over?" Ella asked, concerned. "You shouldn't participate in any experiments, you can hardly climb the short flight of steps leading up to the Agency's front door."

"It is going to be an exquisite experiment!" laughter crept into Old Bob's voice. "Dozens of citizens would envy us if they knew what the experiment was about. So, Ella, wait for us in an hour!"

"How nice of you," Ella managed to murmur before she fell asleep. It seemed to her she had never been so happy before. She hoped she was going to learn the news of the investigation and was looking forward to asking a few questions. She was positive they'd allow her to speak and she would, damn it! Ella Boon adored facing challenges to her mind, will and imagination and could hardly wait to rise to them. Yet an hour's sleep would have a stimulating effect on her now that the walls of the Black Hole had stopped reeling kicking. It was magnificently quiet and she thought she could fall in love with her prison cell.

***

"Let me size up the situation," Bob Hendricks said as an introduction. "In fact, I will read the analysis I have made including the information on Jennifer Cost-Hoffburg's interrogation and Adrienne Tott's cross-examination - the latter had been cross-examined for over two hours."

The Chairman of the Agency spoke too quietly but perhaps that was not the reason because of which Val Hughes's and Red Kyle's eyes were drawn to Ella Boon, the only woman in the Black Hole at that moment. They had found her sleeping and while Val had expressed his admiration for her equanimity, Kyle had called down fire and brimstone on all nutty crones to whom Ella Boon undoubtedly belonged. In his opinion, the more cracked the old hags became, the longer they slept during the day. Yet none of the three inspectors could ever imagine that Ella Boon was an old hag, a crone, or simply an old woman. It was true she was graying at the temples, but her voice not too cheerful, awkwardly cool and steady, forcing them to accept that she was a woman one had to be particularly careful with.

"Let's concentrate on Jennifer Cost's interrogation," Bob Hendricks cleared his throat attracting everybody's attention. "Firstly, according to Jennifer Cost's statement, Don Highsmith has been seriously ill, he has suffered from cirrhosis of the liver and gall bladder dysfunction. Adrienne Tott confirmed this information.

"Secondly, there are five "reverse effect" persons who have not been affected by the epidemic. Jennifer Cost declared she knew that for sure, Adrienne Tot said in so many words that she had heard it as well. Adrienne thinks that someone is intent on killing the five "reverse effect" guys.

"Thirdly, Jennifer Cost is sure that if the "five monsters" get together and remain in a certain area sticking to each other for a short time, they will trigger a widespread epidemic characterized by splitting headaches, swollen joints, skin complaints etc. Jennifer does not remember how far from one another the 'monsters" have to be in order to cause outbreaks of serious diseases. Jennifer Cost continues to assert that Don Highsmith told her everything about the 'cruel freaks' after he was released from hospital, two or three days after Professor Bell restored his ability to speak.

"Fourthly, Jennifer Cost is convinced that Don Highsmith couldn't have killed Professor Bell, since only the professor could cure Don's degenerative diseases. In Jennifer's opinion, Don Highsmith is not one of the five "reverse effect" guys because the Professor " has already regenerated him" i.e., the professor has helped him get rid of all his suffering immediately or at least for a very, very short time. Then Jennifer compared him to Larry Hoffburg who unlike Don, had been recuperating from his operation for years after Jennifer tried to slit his throat.

"Number five, which is particularly important - Jennifer Cost speaks about Professor Bell's ability TO REGENERATE TERMINALLY ILL PATIENTS, OR PATIENTS WHO HAVE DIED SHORTLY BERORE THE REGENERATION PROCESS! Jennifer mentions that Professor Bell regenerated a young woman suffering from leukemia; after that she felt perfectly healthy, so she became a pizza restaurant owner. As far as I remember, Ella Boon found and questioned that young woman."

Beads of perspiration trickled down old Bob's forehead, he looked much paler after he uttered so many words, yet he continued to read.

"The regeneration of terminally sick patients may turn out to be the core of Trail of Tears experiment. How is this regeneration process conducted? What role do the five 'reverse effect' persons play in it? Were they used as an instrument leading to large outbreaks of disease? Is there someone, an unknown Mr. X, who wants to physically destroy them?

As you see, there are many questions that we cannot answer, but let us concentrate on the straightforward, undeniable facts."

Old Bob took a deep breath as he stretched out his bony freckled hand to pick up a glass of water. His colorless lips trembled slightly, his frail body seemed powerless, but his voice hardened, firm, unemotional.

"I think we need to check our facts once again. Larry Hoffburg was murdered. Both Jennifer Cost and Adrienne Tott claimed that he was one of the 'reverse effect' guys. Professor Rupert Bell was murdered and he, too, was one of the five strange persons. Ella Boon, Adrienne Tott, Val Hughes and Red Kyle declared that they had not been affected by the outbreaks of the epidemic, therefore they all are "reverse effect" individuals. If we add Don Highsmith, as elusive as ever, who is nowhere to be found we will inevitably come to the conclusion that there are SEVEN "reverse effect" persons instead of five! "Jennifer Cost is convinced that Don Highsmith is not 'one of the five monsters.' She was sure Professor Bell had regenerated Don several times. SIX persons have stated they are invulnerable to diseases when the town was struck by the epidemic. In my opinion, one of them was lying all the time. One of the persons we know very well: Ella Boon, Adrienne Tott, Red Kyle and Val Hughes lies that he or she is a "reverse effect" individual.

Larry Hoffburg and Professor Bell are dead. Let us suppose that one of the four persons I have just enumerated -- the one who lies -- is exactly the criminal who wants to eliminate all his true "reverse effect" colleagues. Otherwise, he wouldn't have pretended to their small community that he was one of them."

"This time you've gone too far, Bob! It does take much imagination to embroider the story you've just told us," Ella said louder than usual a touch of sarcasm in her voice. "It would be pointless to engage in ungrounded hypothesis before we have the facts. Apart from that, you drift away from the goal the Agency has set itself - to establish what the Trail of Tears experiment is about."

"I don't drift away from it, girl," Old Bob said quietly as he laid his hands on the small table. "Perhaps the five 'reverse effect' individuals are the most important part of the Trail of Tears experiment. Yes, you are right. It would be pointless to engage in hypothesis. I have never done that, or if you prefer, I have never dreamt about unusual places and things. Please, forgive your old boss Robert Hendricks. Perhaps he watches the garden come into bloom for the last time in his life."

Ella and Val Hughes exchanged glances. What was the matter with Bob? He lived alone in his old age. Somehow the phrase 'old age' did not become him; Bob would never be an old man on the verge of senility and the dangerous glint in his eyes told them he was again up to some mischief.

"So, please allow Old Bob to put each one of you through a little test before he meets his maker. We all - Ella Boon, Adrienne, Val Hughes, Red Kyle and I will stay together here, in the Black Hole, for two days. It is only natural that we will change the furniture so that the prison cell will look like a conference suite in a luxury hotel famous throughout Europe. We will live on superb food, we'll have everything we need: swimming pools, wonderful restaurants, books etc. The only thing we won't have is information from the outside world! We won't know what happens there. Throughout our time in the Black Hole we will have no contact with other people.

"But at a certain time the medical committee to our Agency will inform us that an outbreak of a dangerous epidemic is again expected in the area - splitting headaches, swollen joints, etc. We'll see then who of us will be taken ill and who is invulnerable to diseases. I think that it will be easy to catch the liar who claims that he or she is a "reverse effect" individual."

"Bob, you want to make us do a test like the one Adrienne Tott took?" red Kyle asked, shocked. "That's absurd. Two of the 'reverse effect' guys have already been killed. Let us assume that Jennifer Cost has told us the truth - then our town will be threatened by another outbreak of the dangerous epidemic if the five 'reverse effect' individuals gather together. But that is impossible."

"Our little test won't do anyone any harm," the Chairman smiled a slow, small smile. The others stared at him unbelieving for Old Bob smiled rarely, indeed. "At least we can be sure that another 'reverse effect' individual won't get killed while we all do the test."

"Bob, why on earth will you participate in this ludicrous experiment?" Kyle asked sharply. Probably the inspector felt insulted by the fact that Bob Hendricks had not discussed the idea with him. Kyle was notorious for harboring resentment against people who took him by surprise and had declared many times he hated surprising things of any kind - especially when the Agency's Chairman sprung absurd surprises on him.

"I'd like to prove I am clean," he flashed Kyle a broad, untypical smile. "Colleagues, don't forget I am your boss and I every now and then should exercise control over your activities."

"Let's not forget, Bob, that you are one of us so you, too, fall under suspicion of being a 'reverse effect' man," Kyle said. Maybe you are 'their' agent.

We all know that one of us works for our enemies, the guys who conducted the fiendish experiment."

"We still have no right to say the experiment is a 'fiendish' one," remarked Ella. "We don't know what 'they' wanted to achieve."

"We don't know who murdered Professor Bell," Kyle said the rising tone of his voice revealing his exasperation. "What happened to the professor's dead body? Perhaps Ella could tell us something about it."

Ella Boon did not answer. She remained calm, quiet, and immobile on her high-backed chair. Nobody said anything.

An awkward silence fell over the room. The inspectors who had been working for years together did not trust one another. No one seemed to notice what the others were doing. Unexpectedly Val Hughes asked a direct question, which sounded harsh and unpleasant.

"Red Kyle, are you on medication? I saw you take some pills in the morning. Are you ill?"

"I am okay, my friend," the red-haired inspector answered forcing a wry smile.

"What exactly was the medicine you took?" Val Hughes insisted.

"Energy Forte", Red Kyle replied tersely. "I didn't think that you might be interested to know about my medicine, Val. I told you -- I'm fine and I only approve of herbal medicines, which boost one's immunity to common illnesses."

"'Energy Forte' is available on prescription," Val Hughes went on stubbornly. "Kyle, could you tell us the name of the doctor who prescribed you that medication?"

"What do you want from me, Val?" Kyle asked blushing scarlet. It was a sure sign that Inspector Red Kyle was angry. He dealt with such arrogant behavior on a case-by-case basis and as a person of principles, he got even with his subordinate who took the liberty of infringing on his private affairs. It seemed, however, that Val Hughes was not suitably impressed with the grim fate that was in store for him in the immediate future.

"Which doctor prescribed you 'Energy Forte'? The young inspector asked once again.

"Tell him, Kyle," said Ella Boon. "Perhaps he is afraid the doctor could poison you. You declared that you were one of the 'reverse effect' guys, didn't you, Inspector Kyle?"

"I would appreciate it if you minded your own business, Miss Boon!" Red Kyle said seething at this challenge to his authority. "You'd better concentrate on your deep emotional distress."

"What was the name of the doctor who had prescribed you the medication?" Val Hughes repeated quietly but firmly. His face was expressionless as his eyes glowed strangely.

"I think it was Doctor what was his name, let me see. I think it was Doctor Silverstone. Yes he prescribed me 'Energy Forte," Red Kyle said calmly. "Wait, I am not completely sure. I cannot remember the name."

"Could I see your prescription?" Val Hughes asked.

The Chairman of the Agency and Ella listened very carefully to the conversation. Something quite unnatural was happening before their eyes. Both Bob Hendricks and Ella knew about the tremendous admiration the young inspector had for Red Kyle. Val Hughes had never spoken about it, but on Red's birthdays the two of them went to the cafe in the big City Park to have a vodka and lime. They didn't talk, just drank quietly celebrating Red's birthday and parted an hour later in front of the shallow lake, Red still unwilling to go home, Val eager to return to his cramped office in the Agency.

"I am sure you'll say you've lost your prescription, Inspector Kyle," Val Hughes said staring intently at the red-haired man's face.

"I haven't lost it," Red Kyle answered coldly. "I left it at a local pharmacy."

"Which pharmacy?" the young inspector asked quickly.

"The one at the corner of Schiller Street and Park Street."

"You did not leave your prescription at that pharmacy, Inspector Kyle," Val Hughes muttered sadly. "After I noticed you take your medicines I checked both St. Frederick's Hospital and Southeast King's Hospital. No one of the doctors in the two hospitals had examined you. No one of the doctors in our town! Then I checked all the eight pharmacies in Jacksonville including the one at the corner of Schiller Street and Park Street. You bought your medicine from "Cortex" drugstore. Do you remember the pharmacist who worked there, Inspector Kyle?"

"I cannot say I remember the names of the drugstores and the faces of pharmacists I happen to meet in them, my friend," Kyle's flushed cheeks resembled the red-hot plates of a burning cooking stove. "I bought 'Energy Forte', an innocuous combination of vitamins, not cocaine!"

"You don't remember the pharmacist's face, but he remembers yours very well," the young inspector said quietly. "He remembered your name because you gave him a very strange prescription - a prescription that was really signed by Doctor Silverstone, an internist, living in the town of Rainflow, but there is something very peculiar about it, Kyle. The pharmacist declared that he had recognized Professor Bells' handwriting. He suspected that Professor Bell had written your prescription himself, but the professor, as we know, was killed long time ago.

Kyle, I talked to Doctor Silverstone. He remembered he had examined you, but he thought he had not given you any prescription. How can you explain these facts? I checked on Doctor Silverstone - he is an internist of repute in North Rhine region and his clinic is in Rainflow, a town situated two hundred miles away from Jacksonville. Kyle, can you explain why traveled so far to have a routine medical examination?"

"My health is my own business!" Red Kyle answered quietly. "I am not responsible for the pharmacist's nonsensical arguments. He could say I brought him a prescription written out by the President of the USA! Young man, are you sure Doctor Silverstone hadn't given me a prescription? I can tell you he did prescribe me 'Energy Forte', which I bought from 'Cortex" drugstore."

"Doctor Silverstone was not completely sure if he had given you a prescription," Val Hughes answered slowly. "He thought he most probably had not prescribed you anything for in his opinion you were perfectly healthy. The pharmacist working at 'Cortex' drugstore, however, was positive your prescription was written in Professor Bell's handwriting. He said he could have sworn he saw Professor Bell's handwriting."

"Wouldn't it be easier if the pharmacist looked for the prescription in his own office instead of swearing to God?" the red-haired inspector asked with heavy irony. "I left my prescription in his drugstore hoping he could find some medicinal herbs for me."

"The pharmacist searched for your prescription," Val Hughes admitted. "But he could not find it. He thinks he might have given it back to you. He said he was convinced he couldn't prepare the infusion of herbs you wanted for such a short time."

"Young man, you've checked only half of the hard facts and I think that is not enough to cause sensation among us," Red Kyle paused deep in thought. "What are you trying to prove? Put the blame for all crimes on me? You are most welcome. Why? What are you driving at? There is probably information that casts suspicion on you and you are anxious to suppress it. I can see no other answer to the questions I've just asked."

Val Hughes was silent for a long while after he looked the red-haired inspector straight in the eye.

"I am glad you dispelled my worst suspicions, Red," he said.

"He could not dispel mine," Ella Boon said coolly. She had not spoken so far and her voice sounded sharp and cracked. "An interesting thought has just struck me. A man leaves his prescription in a drugstore to have some sort of herbal tea prepared for him, but later he does not remember the address of the drugstore. Then he says he bought his vitamins from another drugstore.

"One more thing that appears strange: Inspector Kyle saw an internist who had a clinic situated two hundred miles away from Jacksonville. It strikes me that Kyle doesn't remember the doctor's name after he selected that internist among so many others, and went to a lot of trouble to travel to his clinic."

There was a moment of silence before Bob Hendricks, The Agency's Chairman, spoke firmly, "Let us not forget that Red Kyle has hardly been ill in his life and has rarely consulted any medical specialists. The contradictions in his statement are so flagrant that even a child would be outraged. A criminal does not act like that. Red Kyle has been working for the Agency thirty years now and he is to become its Chairman after I retire."

"But Kyle could not answer the questions Val asked him!" Ella objected.

Nobody said anything. The four inspectors in the Black Hole almost simultaneously looked out of the window. There was nothing of interest outside the prison cell, which had been transformed into a luxury hotel room. A brilliant sun shone through the trees, a gentle breeze rustled the long grass, the air was pure and everything around the building was green. The Chairman of the Agency was doubled over with exhaustion, his eyes glinting, his hands relaxed on the small table.

Red Kyle lounged back in his chair while Ella watched the treetops sway gently in the breeze, showing no sign she enjoyed what she saw, her right hand scribbling illegible figures all over the table top. It seemed young inspector Val Hughes was in a no-win situation. Beads of perspiration stood out on his forehead as he rubbed his throbbing temples.

"I'd like to know one more thing, Red," the young inspector said. "In the morning, you talked to Ella Boon and asked her a series of embarrassing questions about Adrienne Tott. You, Bob Hendricks, and I had agreed not to tell Ella anything about Adrienne. Why didn't you keep to our agreement?"

"I was curious to find out what our ex colleague thought about the pretty young woman," Kyle answered thoughtfully. "I remembered something quite interesting: Adrienne warned Ella Boon that somebody might kill her in the immediate future. It was quite evident the young woman could not stand Inspector Boon, yet she advised her to be on the alert. I wanted to see how Ella would react, that's all."

"I have one more question," Val Hughes spoke quietly, gently, as if he was talking to a bunch of little haughty children. "When I gave you the recording of Adrienne Tott's interrogation, which I conducted a week ago, you selected only a very small part it - the two brief descriptions Adrienne gave me of the two most important events in her life. The first was when she killed her friend's fish with a safety pin, and the second told the story of how Adrienne fell in love with her adoptive father. Red, why did you choose these two meaningless descriptions, which apparently have nothing to do with the Trail of Tears experiment?"

"Because," Red Kyle's voice rose in angry protest. "Because Adrienne Tott is so pretty! She is lonely and has suffered so much! She's spent her life tortured by the memories of her childhood. All her selfish lovers "

"You love Adrienne Tott, don't you," Val Hughes asked softly averting his eyes from the older man's face.

"Yes, I do," Red Kyle answered.

"I see," Ella Boon said after a long awkward pause, her voice sailing the sea of anxiety like a lifeboat, which they all needed. "Inspector Kyle," she went on. "I want you to tell me something. I had asked you the same question today when we talked in the Black Hole, and I'll repeat it now again. You gave me a photograph in which I had a wedding ring on my third left finger. I have never been married or engaged to anybody so I wondered where the wedding ring came from. Kyle, where did you find that photograph? You lied to me you had taken it from my dossier. I am absolutely sure it has never been there."

"I'll answer your question, Ella," Val Hughes said unexpectedly. "I asked permission and Professor Bell allowed me to check the archives of his clinic. I was collecting information on the two consecutive outbreaks of the epidemic, its victims, and the "reverse effect" individuals when I found your photograph in an album. There were dozens and dozens of other pictures of men and women whose lives the professor had saved. I think the album was dedicated to the 35th anniversary of the clinic Ella, I noticed you had a wedding ring on your finger, unfortunately I couldn't ask Professor Bell to explain to me when your photograph was taken. He was murdered before I could talk to him."

"Thank you, Inspector Hughes," Ella said dryly as she looked up her eyes intent on his face. Years ago, she had wished secretly to have a son like Val. This young man managed to be everywhere and check everything. Perhaps it was better she didn't have a son.

She'd feel as if somebody constantly watched and spied on her, if an astute observer, as clever and shrewd as Val, lived in her apartment with her. And she had to be alert to the slightest sound, to the possibility of danger, to the expression on his face. Yes, it was much better she didn't have a son. For a moment, Ella thought what Val's mother could be like. Perhaps she was a cold and overbearing woman, but of course she might be quite different. Ella had been working with Val Hughes for eight years now and knew nothing about him and his family.

"It's my turn now, my friend," Red Kyle threw his head back suppressing a mirthless smile. "I'd like to ask you a question or two if you don't mind."

The young man nodded at Kyle to begin speaking.

"Val, Professor Bell was murdered on 2 April, wasn't he?" Kyle began as he ran his fingers through his thick reddish hair. "I studied very carefully the personal schedules of the non-commissioned officers and junior security officers who were on duty in the Agency on 2 April. Sergeant Martin Posse was one of them. Do you know him?"

"Yes, I do," answered Val Hughes.

"What can you tell me about him - marital status, medical records, likes and dislikes, etc.?"

"Martin Posse is fifty years old. In fact, all of you know him very well. He's been working for the Agency twenty-three or twenty-four years now. He is single, in perfect health. It is not necessary to speak at length, let me point to the fact that sergeant Posse is famous for"

"What?" Red Kyle whispered narrowing his eyes.

"Some people say that Martin Posse and Professor Bell look very much alike," Val Hughes said. "You know that, too, Red. It was impossible to substitute Professor Bell's dead body for Martin Posse's, and it was impossible for Professor Bell to run away. The agency has set up a medical commission, which certified that Professor Bell was murdered, not somebody else!"

"The conclusions the medical commission reached are beyond any doubt," Red Kyle said nodding his head. "Martin Posse bears an uncanny resemblance to the late professor, but this nothing to do with my question. Listen, Professor Bell was murdered on 2 April. The professor's corpse disappeared from the mortuary on 4 April. On 5 April, Martin Posse took his annual leave and his leave certificate bears your signature, Val. You didn't make a report on that although you should have. Why didn't you report that Sergeant Posse went on annual leave? Perhaps you wanted to conceal not only that, but also other important facts from us."

"I didn't conceal anything from you, Kyle. I wrote a report that read, 'Sergeant Martin Posse is entitled to twenty day annual leave, which he will take from 5 to 24 April, 2041. I, Inspector Val Hughes, registered Sergeant Posse's leave application with the medical commission to the Agency on 28 March. I signed Martin Posse's leave certificate on 30 March." The young inspector's face was set and hard.

"Let us all see your report," Red Kyle said. "Val, could you dial its code so we can have it in our computers?"

"Yes, of course," Val quickly dialed a complex combination of numbers on the additional keyboard attached to his computer monitor, and one of the walls of the room immediately turned into a large flickering screen. All waited in silence their eyes drawn to Val. The screen remained blank. Inspector Hughes redialed the code. The screen flashed briefly and went blank again.

"Will you give it another try?" the red-haired inspector asked then nodded his head meaningfully. "Young man, why don't you admit to us all that you have never made that report? You probably wanted to conceal some facts from us, but you failed. So what? We all will have to pass a test that will reveal the criminal among us, the monster that is not a 'reverse effect' individual. We'll make the evildoer explain why he wants to murder all the other 'reverse effect' persons, after that we'll force him to tell us more about the Trail of Tears experiment. Val, why don't you simply declare you haven't written the report? It is evident you are lying about it. The report is not in the computer of the medical commission. If it was there we could read it on the screen."

"Perhaps someone has deleted Inspector Hughes's report?" Ella Boon asked looking at no one in particular. "Yes, Sergeant Martin Posse bore a strong resemblance to Professor Bell who was killed. I remember that when Martin was on duty in the clinic, the hospital attendants mistook him for Professor Bell. The reports I received indicated that had happened quite regularly. However, I keep on asking myself something else. Was it pure coincidence that when the murdered professor's body was stolen from the mortuary, Sergeant Martin Pose was on duty? A day after that, Inspector Hughes let Sergeant Posse go on leave. I think that looks rather suspicious," Ella Boon paused briefly, looked at Val Hughes and went on, "I wonder who drew up the work schedule that rostered Sergeant Posse for Wednesday, 5 April when Professor Bell's body disappeared?"

"Don't you remember, Ella? You drew up the duty roster!" Red Kyle said and rose from his chair. "You did!"

"I signed the duty roster and checked the names of the sergeants who had to be on duty in the clinic," Ella said calmly as she fixed Bob Hendricks, the Chairman of the Agency, with a penetrating stare. "Bob, you drew up the duty roster, didn't you? You asked me to sign it and I did."

The inspectors were silent, their eyes fixed on the Chairman's old tired face. He got shakily to his feet, closed his eyes and she nodded at Ella.

"Yes. Yes."

"Somebody must have taken great pains to make sure that remarkable coincidence happened - Sergeant Martin Posse and Professor Bell looked strikingly alike and Sergeant Posse guarded the professor's dead body. It all is so strange." Red Kyle spoke very quietly and perhaps no one paid much attention to what he said. Everybody watched the Chairman of the Agency standing still and upright behind the small table. His eyes moved slowly from face to face drifting over to Red Kyle's chair. The old man rested his hands on the tabletop for support and started speaking, very, very slowly, as if each word he uttered made him feel pain.

"Kyle, I have no relatives. I have no son. I have always thought and believed that you will accomplish successfully the difficult tasks I failed to complete. You were more than a son to me, Red, because your mind is beautiful and brilliant. Red, you can't have forgotten that I asked you to draw up the duty rota, and I was so grateful after you did that for me."

Ella and Val Hughes turned their eyes to inspector Kyle's face. He was perfectly calm and did not try to look away.

"Yes, now I remember I drew up the duty rota," Kyle said. "But if there was anything dishonest or suspicious about it why should I speak about Sergeant Martin Posse? Why should I bring up that matter - to dig my own grave or what?"

Bob Hendricks's tired voice sounded very quiet.

"I would have brought that matter up if you hadn't, Red Sometimes I feel happy that is the last spring in my life, kids"

Chapter 10

This year, spring was cold and wet in Jacksonville. The tall poplar trees caressed the sky, the wind blew persistently; cars and vans hurtled along the highway and many couples strolled along the Main Street. The factories of Toys International were about to close down and the locals commented that the town would soon see the end of a business that had been quite lucrative. Val Hughes thought about the neat houses with steep red roofs in the Main Street, imagining he could feel the moist gentle breeze on his face. There was the river too, whispering in his ears, but what it wanted to tell him was not so important. What really mattered was that a very attractive blonde woman walked by his side.

She did not say anything, she just smiled at the wind and the sky and Val Hughes could not dream of anything more. He knew that her gentle smile was meant for him. What a pity he did not intend to take the beautiful lady for a leisurely walk. In fact, he had to hold a serious and unpleasant conversation with her. What a pity that the facts incriminated her, what a pity he was almost fully convinced she had committed a heinous crime.

"Miss Tott," Inspector Hughes started firmly losing irrevocably the illusion about the leisurely walk by the river and about the blonde woman's smile. "Miss Tott, during one of our previous discussions you declared you were very rich. Can you explain to me why you had said that? Your statement defies logic. The factories you inherited after Larry Hoffburg was killed would go bankrupt any day now. This is simply a matter of time. You, too, must be losing much money, even if you haven't turned into a beggar."

"I don't understand why you care so much about my financial stability, Inspector. Perhaps you have made up your mind to ask me to marry you but you have already started hesitating on account of my bankruptcy. Is that it?"

The smile on Adrienne's beautiful lips had nothing to do with the one Val Hughes that had seen in his dreams. The woman was sneering at him, making no effort at all to hide her contempt for his words. That was more than he could endure.

"Well," the inspector said tersely. "We wasted much time trying to analyze your comedies. Listen to me now. I'll reveal to you the source of your affluence!" He stood up, rubbed gently his temples, and waited a minute, staring through the window behind which the sun had already made efforts to shine the way it should in spring. Adrienne was watching him, the smile on her lips becoming broader as she tied to remove an invisible speck of dust from her sleeve.

"You can have a look at this," the inspector said leaving a sheet of paper on the table before her. "It is a list consisting of eight women's names. Now you will tell me what you have offered these ladies."

"It seems to me you are quite good at pulling out various lists from your breast pocket, Inspector Hughes," the woman said as she nodded her head. "In the beginning you unearthed the disturbing collection of my male lovers. This new list perhaps enumerates my female ones arranged in an alphabetical order. If this is the case, I can assure you the list is quite incomplete."

"You paid all these eight women to get medical treatment since they suffered from various gynecological diseases. They received the treatment at Walnut clinic," the inspector said.

"So you think I got rich quick because I paid the bills for the medical treatment of the eight ladies?" Adrienne Tott laughed. "You have strange ideas of getting rich, Inspector Hughes. I would think about making an appointment to see a psychiatrist if I were you. You do need it."

"You know very well that the eight ladies did not need any medical treatment. I've checked both their medical records and the registry of the hospital where the lists of all its patients are kept. Their names are not on the lists and I will tell you what you did," Val Hughes approached Adrienne Tott and peered into her calm eyes. "Miss Tott, you exposed these women to radiation in order to make them contract some terminal disease and"

"Very clever, Inspector Hughes," the blond woman agreed, suddenly appearing humble and submissive. "I'd like to point out however that you leave out a very important fact: as far as I know all the eight ladies on your list run very successfully their own businesses and are perfectly healthy. I have not heard any of them complain of any problems pertaining to health. There has been no whimpering on their part as you very well"

"Yes, they are perfectly healthy because in Walnut clinic they were most probably subjected to regeneration," Val Hughes interrupted her. Your opulence is the result of your efforts to find innocent victims who at a later stage are subjected to regeneration. I think I am right. You were not only Larry Hoffburg's mistress, you were his most worthy business partner who attracted the new guinea pigs to the experiment. Larry Hoffburg got a toy factory for each girl, a secretary of his, whom he subjected to radiation causing lethal leukemia. It is interesting to see what you got for the eight young women on the list."

"You can go and talk to each one of them in person," the young woman said, unperturbed. "Ask them what they think of me. Try to find out if I have subjected them to anything whatsoever related to contracting terminal diseases. In my view, their answers should be the most reliable information on the issue."

"I have talked to Larry Hoffburg's three secretaries, Miss Tott. Yes, they feel like million dollars, they are in exuberant health, and they have big booming businesses." Val Hughes looked the young woman in the eye and she stared back, perfectly composed and calm. "But these three girls are no longer human beings! The first one exchanged her child for an automobile; the second poisoned her boyfriend because he interfered with her plans to marry another, much wealthier guy. Look. Miss Tott, I have talked to the eight women on your list. They all seem to be prospering since they met you. But they are not human beings. None of them has children. All are sexually promiscuous and seem to take great pride in their lifestyles. These ladies are not afraid of any diseases, they all told me, 'Adrienne Tott will let us pass through the apparatus again.' They even said the sessions gave them great pleasure and they felt much refreshed after them."

"So, what do you accuse me of?" Adrienne Tott stood up and took a step towards the inspector. "Shall I take it you charge me with bringing wealth, prosperity and good health to the girls? Who are you to accuse me of extricating them from the crippling drudgery by the screeching and droning machines? I treated them like human beings worthy of respect. They are women who refuse to fawn over or flatter their rotten bosses for fear they might lose their foul jobs. I have not resorted to any regeneration, machinations or whatever you said I had done."

"When I interrogated them they all admitted you made them use some peculiar piece of apparatus," the inspector said firmly. "And they had to pay two grand for that. I have their sworn statements with their signatures."

"I also have perfect legal documentation with respect to the procedures the ladies have been subjected to," Adrienne Tott announced flatly. "The so called procedures constitute exposure to ultraviolet lamps used to provide a special type of heat, especially as a treatment of flu. As a head of the Personnel Directorate of a multinational company I must be involved in social activities aimed at improving my employees' general health. Inspector Hughes, you could, if of course you are willing to delve deeply enough into this issue you could find amidst the dusty files a list of more than eight thousand women who would like to follow the same medical procedures. All of them would gladly pay two grand for that. Each lady has signed her application form on the principle that her participation is perfectly voluntary and I can assure you the women are looking forward to it."

"I've already seen these lists accompanied by application forms," Val Hughes whispered. "So you work on a grand scale O, my God if the population of the whole town passes through your equipment! Miss Tott, are you aware of the monstrous experiment you are taking part in?"

"What experiment are you talking about?" the blonde lady smiled quietly. Her knees hidden under the thick fabric of her dress, her eyes lowered, she reminded him of a schoolgirl trying hard not to hoot with glee at the absurd thing the teacher had just blurted out.

"I am sure you understand I have in mind the Trail of Tears experiment," the inspector said quietly. "People are subjected to some procedures. You tell me it is exposure to ultraviolet lamps I think it is not. They go out of the regeneration rooms perfectly healthy, overflowing with energy, prepared for a major financial breakthrough. But they are not human beings, they have no children, they irretrievably lose their ability to love, to feel for other people's misfortunes. To tell it simply and more directly, they just cannot be normal good people. Death does not mean anything to them, your equipment cam always bring them back to life."

"You are ill, Inspector Hughes!" the blonde woman cried out. "I'd better send for a doctor."

"Human beings are subjected to regeneration as if they were tin cans. They emerge from the procedures clean and brand new boys and girls, healthy, young, and itching to have sex, craving new, more skilful intimate partners. The thing that interests them most of all however is money," the inspector paused, took a step to the chair of the young woman, bent towards her, and touching for a split second her white exquisite hand, said, "I bet you 100 dollars, Miss Tott, that you still have not passed through the regeneration rooms. I set a trap for you and you were imprudent enough to fall into it. I exposed you as a liar and a cheat. You a 'reverse effect' person! You cannot feel pain when the whole town shake and groans in agony. But there is a very important point that your very good friend Jennifer Cost made: the 'reverse effect' guys cannot be regenerated. Poor Adrienne Tott, the only thing you can do is to find new and new victims for the experiment. That is your only chance of making much money."

He could see the tops of the cypress trees fresh and golden in the sun. His office was gloomy and chilly bringing to mind dark memories of dead pharaohs; never before had his office resembled a clammy tomb so much. The air, all the objects inside it, even the people, were completely isolated from the cool April day, from the sun and the grass, from the branches of the golden cypress trees swaying gently in the breeze. One single movement of the young blonde woman made the room alive again.

Adrienne Tott stood up, her graceful body tense and impatient, as she reached out her hand to pick up the receiver, her voice sounding quiet, soothing as if she were talking to a sick child, "You really need to see your doctor, dear Inspector Hughes. Don't you worry; I'll take care of that. The ambulance will come in no time. Your nerves are in tatters but well, I've heard there are good pills that can help you"

"I can prove what I've just stated, Adrienne," the inspector said. "I can be a very cunning and treacherous opponent, but I'd rather not treat you like dirt. I'd like to spare you the humiliation of having to live through another interrogation, of being held in detention after that. Adrienne, tell me everything. I'll give you a second chance, I really will. If you turn it down tonight everything will be over for you. I will show your true face and there will be no way out for you."

"You want me, don't you, Inspector Hughes? I knew it the minute you set eyes on me." A hesitant rivulet of tenderness seeped into her voice. "All men I know react exactly like you. But you are much lonelier than the rest of them, Inspector Hughes, so it is much more conspicuous with you. Your face tells me how painfully you need me. Perhaps that is the reason why I feel absurd pity for you. I wish your doctor was here now. You remind me of poor Don Highsmith when you look at me like that. I speak from bitter experience. I've lived with him and I've developed a feeling for other people's misery. I know exactly when it is necessary to send for the doctor. You need one now, believe me."

"Do you think Inspector Red Kyle wants you as well?"

Val Hughes's question was an unexpected one; it made the young woman tremble. Although she had been two weeks under interrogation, this was the first time such a thing had happened to her. She had trembled! So Val Hughes wondered: that woman who so far had not exhibited any symptoms of embarrassment or confusion had shuddered when he mentioned Red Kyle's name. Why? On the other hand, when it was proved that Adrienne Tott was a 'reverse effect' individual and remained unaffected by the epidemic, Red Kyle had fainted. Remarkable!

"You shuddered, Adrienne. I mentioned a phrase or two about Red Kyle and you almost jumped as if some one had touched you wit a red-hot iron rod."

"Now you insult me, Inspector. Well, I admit I am a 'reverse effect' person. But as my dear Jennifer Cost has pointed out it is simply impossible to regenerate the 'reverse effect' folks. Then why should I have all appalling futures typical of the regenerated freaks? My sexual behavior is promiscuous all right, I am anything but good-natured or amicable, and I wouldn't even look at you if I don't get the full benefit of the efforts I've made," Adrienne Tott nodded her head and smiled. "The theory you subscribe to, Inspector, seems to be no good."

"I ask you once again," Val Hughes said calmly. "Do you think Inspector Kyle is attracted by you to a degree that makes him want you?"

"If he is not gay, you could be sure that the answer to your question would be positive. Yes, he wants me or rather he'd experience that odd tingling sensation the first minute he gets down to interrogating me. So far, he hasn't worked on that but I promise you that I'll make him dote on me no more than ten minutes after the beginning of the interrogation."

"You know what?" Val Hughes said thoughtfully. "My colleague, Inspector Red Kyle, took very seriously your two shorts tales about the most interesting events in your life. You positively remember them, the ones about your friend's little fishes, which you killed, and about your father's suicide... It was only Red Kyle among all the inspectors of the Agency who made special personal copies of them. I wonder why he did that. And there is something more to it. He passed out when I proved that you are one of the 'reverse effect' individuals."

The blonde woman's exquisite body trembled again. This happened within a split second, so rapidly that Val Hughes even thought he might have imagined it. Then Adrienne Tot was waiting for him to go on, imperturbable, distantly beautiful like an ancient mysterious statue.

"I gave you a chance, Adrienne," the inspector said feeling tired. "You wasted it and it is a pity. Now all the other inspectors will come: Ella Boon whom you absolutely worship, Red Kyle, the one you think you can so easily enchant, and Bob Hendricks. You have seen him as well. They'd like to talk to you."

"I'd love to see them again," the young lady declared her voce sounding so sincere that for a moment Val Hughes hesitated-- this woman could hardly have anything to do with the Trail of Tears experiment. She was watching him with amusement her eyes smiling gently, enticingly, tenderly, exactly the way he had seen in his dreams. Adrienne Tott, the woman he had taken for long walks in his thoughts so many times a little bit afraid she might be hurt or embarrassed, or uneasy if he told her what she meant to him. "The absurdity of it all, I am going crazy," the inspector thought yet he did not want to get rid of his thoughts about her.

This year, April was cold in Jacksonville. The poplar trees caressed the sky in the wind. Couples holding hands strolled along the Main Street laughing and joking. From time to time they stopped at florist shops, talked, smiled at each other even kissed. The people lived with the memory of the two consecutive outbreaks of the epidemic, but they avoided speaking about them. Men and women went to work, tradesmen went about their business, young mothers pushed baby carriages, schoolboys and schoolgirls had again started buying ice-cream from the pastry shops, some venturing to choose a cafe table in the open. Val Hughes could only dream of the steady monotonous heartbeat of the clean calm town.

It was cold and gloomy in his office and the blond lady, the one who by a strange twist of fate had made him feel absurdly young and naive, the only woman in his life whom he'd love to go for a stroll with down the Main Street, was involved in a dirty game dubbed, for convenience, the Trail of Tears experiment. Val Hughes was sure the Agency's hypothesis was perfectly right. He had laid another trap for the blond lady and was quite sure she was about to walk straight into it. He was going to prove beyond suspicion he was right. He didn't want to do that. If only he could be in a remote border town far away from his gloomy office... He wished he could sit at a small table reading his newspaper absent-mindedly at Sunday mornings, or better yet, climb the hills where his beloved mountain lakes lay hidden under the dazzling July sun.

But did it all make sense if he could not hear the whisper of Adrienne's blonde hair, if her shadow could not touch his and he could not see her smile. It was the first time in his life that he had regretted ever having become an inspector.

A loud knock at the door diverted young Hughes's attention from his dark thoughts. The knock could mean only one thing: Bob Hendricks, Red Kyle and Ella Boon had already arrived. In less than a minute, their conversation with one single interlocutor was to begin and Adrienne Tott would have to answer all their questions. Val stole a look at her and she looked more defiant and mysterious than ever.

The inspectors entered Val Hughes's office. Bob Hendricks staggered in his eyes glued to the floor as if the tiles on it concealed many threats and invisible traps; Red Kyle walked slowly by his side holding his arm, trying to help him move on or at lest prevent him from collapsing. Ella Boon looked emaciated. For an instant her eyes fell on Adrienne Tott's face the spark of anger growing into a flame of resentment in them.

Val Hughes noticed it and concluded how incompatible Inspector Boon and Adrienne were isolated from one another by the mote of abhorrence. As far as he could remember Ella Boon's features had been inscrutable as a piece of faded plastic. Val had intercepted that nervous spark in her eyes only once, seven years ago. Then, Ella had interrogated a woman who had killed her second husband's two children in a fit of jealousy.

"Good morning, Miss Boon. Welcome, gentlemen!" Adrienne Tott greeted cheerfully the newcomers, leant her back against the wall and said smiling broadly, "I am ready to answer all your questions and I hope that the mystery shrouding the Trail of Tears experiment will be unraveled as soon as possible."

"Perhaps the guilty party will no longer be a mystery to us before the day is over," the Chairman of the Agency said and a wry grimace bearing only a superficial resemblance to a smile distorted his mouth. He refused to sit down, his green eyes fixed on Adrienne. A minute or two elapsed; the old man looked the blonde woman straight in the eye, unblinking, immobile, but she stared stonily back. "You are an exceptional person, Miss Tott and I am not exactly sure if that makes me happy or miserable What do you think of the young lady, Kyle?"

"She is quite pretty," the red-haired inspector pointed out. "And she is too young for old men like me."

"Why?" the Chairman of the Agency murmured. "Larry Hoffburg was not much younger than you, Kyle. By the way, are you satisfied with the remuneration you receive from the Agency?"

"I don't understand why you ask me that question now," Red Kyle spoke indignantly. "What are you driving at, my friend?"

"It was simply a question," Bob Hendricks let out a small weary sigh as his face twisted into some semblance of a smile. "You rent the apartment where you live, so if you have been saving your salaries now you should have four or five million"

"Most of my money went to charity, I am a generous person," the inspector answered then opened his mouth to say something else, thought better of it apparently making up his mind to avoid such a controversial topic. His high cheekbones trembled slightly. Red Kyle was notorious for his proverbial intolerance of people who poked their noses into his private affairs. He wouldn't forgive even Bob Hendricks for his undue curiosity.

Val Hughes followed the discussion with amazement. Ella Boon sat staring into space, distant, reserved, isolated from everyone around her, as cold as an iceberg.

"Let us sum up the information we have on the case dubbed the Trail of Tears Experiment," the Chairman of the Agency suggested and since nobody expressed a wish to take the floor he took on the thankless task himself. "Have in mind I suggest a hypothesis that no one has yet proved. Still, I am optimistic that we'll have our surmise confirmed.

"So firstly, no people die in our town for several consecutive years. This appears a strange having in mind the fact that Jacksonville is a settlement boasting sadly of the highest number of terminally ill patients suffering from diseases related to malignant tumors. We can only surmise that somebody deliberately makes the citizens of Jacksonville ill with the aim of subjecting them at a later stage to recuperation procedures we have named 'regeneration'.

"Among the thirty-five thousand citizens of our town there are five persons whom we called 'reverse effect' folks. There is another important thing associated with them: according to Jennifer Cost - Hoffburg's evidence whenever the five 'reverse effect' persons get together or to put it plainly and more directly, when they are close enough to one another, an epidemic breaks out in town, large number of cases of a disease characterized by horrible headaches, bone degeneration, etc.

In our opinion, Professor Rupert Bell had been involved with the regeneration procedures. Several weeks ago the Professor emailed Inspector Ella Boon asking her to meet him in order to discuss issues of considerable importance. We can only guess what he had wanted to tell her. It might seem too farfetched to conjecture that he wished to disclose information related to the Trail of Tears experiment, yet we cannot exclude that possibility. On the very same day, Adrienne Tott also sent Inspector Boon an email in which she wrote she'd very much like to meet with the inspector. That evening, Professor Bell was killed.

The only outsider the law enforcement agents intercepted in the vicinity of Walnut hospital was Adrienne Tott. Our colleague, Inspector Red Kyle, was the first to arrive at the scene of the crime. He informed us that an anonymous person rang him up while he was in his apartment and told him about the incident as a result of which Inspector Kyle started for the hospital."

Bob Hendricks was silent giving the red-haired inspector a long hard stare. For a minute it seemed the old man had forgotten where he was as his eyes suddenly faded becoming bleary and lusterless. He muttered something there appearing no relation between what he had just said and the words he was articulating slowly and painfully after that.

"Red, I have always treated you as an equal as a man who will continue what I have begun and had no time to finish. When my confidence was at low ebb and I had lost all hope, I thought of you to summon up my courage. And I faced the hardships. You know that, don't you, Red?"

"Yes, I do," the inspector answered tonelessly.

"However a strange thing happened, or perhaps I should name it a totally confusing event," metal clanged in Bob Hendricks's voice sounding as if the old man had squeezed the trigger of a gun. "A pharmacist in Jacksonville recognized the handwriting of the then already dead Professor Bell on a prescription. There is a very peculiar thing to that document. It turned out that prescription had been written later date than the date when the professor was killed - but words and medicines in his own handwriting were on it! It sounds incredible, doesn't it? It was our colleague Red Kyle who gave the prescription to the pharmacist. Red Kyle."

The old man's green eyes were intent on Red's face.

"Could there be any explanation?" Bob Hendricks went slowly on. "It might really appear loony to you, but I'll speculate about it. Someone had regenerated the professor who by that time had already been murdered. Let us remember what Adrienne Tott had told us when we interrogated her: she stated that Professor Bell was a 'reverse effect' guy; therefore he belonged to the group of the five freaks who could not be regenerated. But there is a hard fact we must not overlook - the prescription was written in his handwriting after his death. What should be our conclusion then? I think that Adrienne Tott, for reasons best known to herself, had lied to us.

"Professor Bell was not a 'reverse effect' guy! He had been regenerated. There is another hard fact: thanks to Val Hughes's trap he has set for Adrienne Tott we learnt that she is a 'reverse effect' lady. When our colleague Red Kyle came to know that he fainted.

"So, judging by the facts we have at our disposal I'd say that there is a secret relation between Adrienne Tott and our colleague Kyle. They both make best efforts to conceal it but if one takes his time to study the series of tiny facts he'd positively stumble upon some inconsistencies, which give the game away. Now will you let me take a seat?" the Chairman of the Agency asked weakly. He sat down without waiting for the approval of his colleagues. He looked absolutely worn out.

"Mr. Hendricks, your methods of investigation have made you a living legend," Adrienne Tott spoke quietly from her seat in the corner listening very carefully to the old man. "I thank the quirk of fate that has allowed me to make your acquaintance no matter I saw you for the first time under circumstances rather unpleasant for me. I think few could boast of having talked to a person like you.

"I listened to you with great interest and I think that someone must have misled you. I do not have the honor of knowing Mr. Red Kyle personally although I have heard many people talk about him awestruck. Unfortunately I do not have and I have never had a relationship with him. I hope that when the Trail of Tears case is over the inspector would not mind talking to me in private. We could make our minds to do many interesting things together."

"You are an exceptional young woman," the Chairman of the Agency whispered raising his head. "And I am not sure if I feel happy or miserable about that Well, I started speaking again and I'd better not stop now. I'd like to inform you that yesterday I received an amazing letter from Mrs. Jennifer Cost - Hoffburg, which I am going to read to you:

Dear Robert Hendricks

I took the liberty of writing to you while in all probability you are quite busy, but I think I am within my rights to demand your attention. You do not now me in person but I am sure you have heard my name. I am Jennifer Cost, Larry Hoffburg's widow, the lady who has put up with his arrogance, pandering to all his hellish whims and vagaries for ages, an honest and loving wife whose name he did not even bother to mention in his will! Adrienne Tott, my appalling husband's venal mistress, had totally possessed him during his lifetime and he had the cheek to bequeath his entire estate to her. I shall contest his will in court, of course. I most sincerely and hope that you, Mr. Hendricks, will prove Adrienne Tott's (never in my life will I use the dignified appellation 'Miss" in relation to that fiendish vixen!) sinister role in the crimes that have given rise to the blood-curdling epidemic striking our beautiful town. I pray to our beloved maker every day that Adrienne, the evil demon, would land as soon as possible in prison where she belongs!

I am a lady of great fortitude, Mr. Hendricks, but I write this letter to you because I am deeply apprehensive that something might go wrong! I saw something very interesting on the TV the other day: the broadcaster informed the public that Theodore, my abominable husband's butler had committed suicide. I have to admit that after I learnt about his sad demise I wept bitter tears of grief. Poor Theodore! Yes, he did faithfully serve that idiot, my husband Larry, but nevertheless Theodore was an honest soul! He was the only one among the domestics who dared to call Adrienne "bitch" although everybody else thought she was one! Theodore never failed to warn my husband what little snake Adrienne was, but Larry wouldn't listen. No wonder he did that: he and Adrienne were tarred with the same brush!

But I loved Larry's butler! I swear to God, I gave him a $100 bonus every week although in the very beginning I detested him on account of something very mean he did. I still shudder at the thought of that rainy depressing evening when I threw a party and Theodore brought Adrienne, I hope she chokes on her own blood in the nearest future. I can assure you she well deserves that. Theodore introduced her to Larry Sometimes I even suspected that Theodore might be pretending; he most probably called her 'bitch' only when I came within earshot of them both.

I suspected that Theodore made best efforts to cement the appalling sexual relationship between my estranged husband and that slut (forgive me for using that very offensive word, but I am positive she deserves no better. However Theodore killed Larry, so doesn't that mean that the butler respected me sincerely? I hope to God he did.

After I described how I felt for Theodore let me explain to you the reason because of which I am so nervous and worried: it seems to me that several consecutive days I see a strange man hanging about my estate. He looks old, scraggy, round-shouldered, walking with a stoop. If he is not Theodore himself then he must be the spitting image of my late butler.

I personally am not afraid of that man But Mr. Hendricks, I'd like to make a clean breast of something and you are the only person I trust. I admit that I've done something wrong - I voluntarily hid my beloved Don Highsmith from the police, from the inspectors of the Agency. In fact I, Mr. Hendricks, might have been making love to him while you were looking for him, leaving no stone unturned in Jacksonville.

I know very well I may be prosecuted under the Health and Safety Act but am not afraid of justice and law. I make a full confession not because I feel scared or because I want to get off with a relatively light sentence. No, Mr. Hendricks! I do not care what sentence I will receive.

I love Don Highsmith. You said he suffered from acute psychotic disorders, that he was schizophrenic, maniacal, what not. What a load of bunk! He loves me. He has assured me many times that I do better in bed than that slut Adrienne (please, forgive me again for using that word!) You couldn't possible imagine how much these words mean to me. I treasure them more than my life. I love Don more then I love myself, a dozen million times more!

That strange man who looks like Theodore so much, the one who hangs about my estate, shot at Don twice. I am positive he wants to kill him. I decided against calling the police. I know how rude they all are, how unrefined and uncivilized. They will arrest my poor Don in connection with that note. You know, Mr. Hendricks, he has written the note in which he admits to having murdered Professor Bell. That is not true, Mr. Hendricks! Please, believe me! Don adores the professor. I hope that you will help a noble suffering lady in distress. I would be very grateful if you could hide Don and keep him at a safe place until the police find and catch Professor Bell's murderer. I ask you to be sagacious. A noble woman who is truly in love for the first time relies on your understanding and acumen. God bless you!

Sincerely

Jennifer   Cost

After Bob Hendricks read the letter he looked Adrienne Tott in the eye but the young woman did not say anything at first. Silence as thick as blood reigned in the room making the five human beings invisible, immobile, non-existent.

"Mr. Hendricks, if you have not concocted that story all by yourself, a task that is not too arduous after all - one simply has to swear at me and use foul language - so if you have not fabricated dear Jennifer's tale, you most probably have already caught Don Highsmith, the hen that lays golden eggs," Adrienne Tott concluded amicably smiling her face none the worse for the lack of any visible sign of embarrassment. "If you have really apprehended Don Highsmith then he should have already told you I have nothing to do with Professor Bell's murder. Sir, you could interrogate Don instead of me, meanwhile I could get some sleep or grab a sandwich."

"Yes, we have arrested Don Highsmith, "Val Hughes said. "He's still hopelessly in love with you. You know him well, Miss Tott, that is why you are so sure he has not betrayed you."

"There is simply nothing to betray," the blonde woman chimed in.

"You know Don Highsmith very well," Val Hughes went on ignoring her remark. "Don Highsmith spent eight months in your bed telling you his most closely-guarded secrets. Why don't you assume he might tell his secrets in other woman's bed as well?"

"And that woman is of course Jennifer Cost," Adrienne Tott said ironically. "Your hypothesis, gentlemen, relies too much on the evidence that the enormous lady of noble blood provided you with. Well, I would think twice before I took her seriously. As she admits in her letter, she dreams of seeing me choke on my own blood. That lady is capable of devouring a gallon of sulfuric acid if that could guarantee her you'll put me in jail. She lies through teeth to drag my name through the mire."

No one took the floor after Adrienne Tott stopped speaking. Val Hughes stared at her, Bob Hendricks's green tired eyes sparkled lingering on her face. Cold, dispassionate, threatening, Ella Boon looked straight through the young woman.

"Bring Jennifer Cost!" the Chairman's voice sounded unexpectedly sharp, his eyes locked on Adrienne's face, a pretty, cheerful face that remained perfectly unperturbed. The blonde's blue eyes laughed alight with excitement as if they enjoyed a colorful pageant invisible to the rest of them.

As soon as Jennifer Cost entered the room her huge mass blocking out most of the sunlight, it dimmed briefly just like before the moment of a true solar eclipse. Uncontrollable and blind like an avalanche, Mrs. Cost looked around the place searching for a suitable chair to relax in. There were no empty seats except for a greenish plastic-covered pouf appearing insufficiently solid for her imposing size. The lady studied it for a while preferring to stand in the long run, her blazing eyes focused on Adrienne Tott.

"I am at your disposal, gentlemen," she declared in a booming voice turning her back angrily on them all as Adrienne Tott blew her a kiss.

"Dear Mrs. Cost," the Chairman of the Agency spoke to her with utmost respect. "Could you remember what Don Highsmith told you about Professor Bell's murder?"

"Don went off his head again," the lady of noble blood heaved a deep sigh and was beginning to break a sweat. "He has promised me, the moron! He agreed to testify against that bi but now he refuses to accompany me. He refuses to give evidence Oh, my God! She's taken possession of his soul. She is a demon sucking up the last bit of his blood, addling his wits, ruining his life! He promised me he'd speak the truth about against the mean snake but O, God! This morning he said he'd withdraw his allegations. He refuses to admit she killed the professor. He refuses point-blank! He forgot too quickly that a week ago he wept in my bed like a baby. I brushed his tears like this" she waved her hands to show how she consoled her dearly beloved. "Could I have some mineral water, please?"

After the lady drained her glass in one gulp she spoke to the point.

"This one," Jennifer Cost pointed a finger of blame at Adrienne Tott, "The mean snake has not let him touch her for almost three years. Most unexpectedly - lo and behold - she changed her behavior incredibly. The rag asked Don over for a drink. Could you believe where she took him? To the luxurious apartment where a year ago she had committed adultery with my husband every single night! Yes, gentlemen, wrapped in her debauchery she got poor Don into bed, my own king-size bed into which she and Larry crept together every night while I was married to that moral wretch!

Poor Don was so happy. Seeing her again warmed the cockles of his heart and he, the naïve soul, believed she'd be nice to him again. Nice my foot! That rag has no heart at all. I know that if I stick a knife into her chest, slops will spurt from her wound. She is so mean that Yes, yes Mr. Hendricks, I'll speak to the point

"Adrienne told Don, 'My bed will be yours for a whole month if you write down a short note that I'll dictate to you.' A whole month! That was more he had ever hoped for. He'd betray the world for that bitch's tits, the moron! He'd die for her, the dunce! He'd do virtually anything if she but shot him a casual glance! That was how Don Highsmith wrote the damn silly note which made him a man on his way to the gallows. How could he admit to having killed Professor Bell? That is a blatant lie!

"Don had not even seen the professor that day, he swore he didn't! He told me he wrote another note that the little snake Adrienne dictated to him, but he could not remember what it was about She had promised him the professor would be perfectly safe and sound and nothing would endanger his life It was only natural the slut kept her promise with respect to seducing Don into lechery for a whole month! So, Adrienne," Mrs. Jennifer Cost turned to her chief rival for Don Highsmith's love. "I hope that my testimony will be crucial to the prosecution's case and I believe you will soon face death by the electric chair in a state prison. Or at least, if worst comes to the worst, you will serve a life sentence for murder."

That was the end of the noble lady's evidence who, sighing and coughing in turn, left the room as she sucked out the all the air around her and left the others gasping for breath.

Now even Ella Boon's eyes were intent on Adrienne's face. The young woman's features, delicate, redolent of ancient pagan temples, beauty and grace, remained perfectly calm. In the depths of her blue eyes bold defiant sparks flew. Finally Adrienne Tott spoke.

"Inspector Boon, it is the first time you have deigned to look at me today. Do you find me attractive? Do you think I am worthy of your ubiquitous colleague's love? When I used the phrase "your colleague" I meant Inspector Val Hughes, or why not even Inspector Red Kyle."

"I don't like you," Ella boon answered coldly.

"Don't you?" the blonde woman murmured smiling. "Inspector Val Hughes told me once that I was very like you. To be honest with you I am prettier. But let me speak to the point," Adrienne Tott said hurriedly waving her hand. "The comprehensive statement Jennifer Cost made is false from the beginning to the end. She has made it up in order to deceive you. Don Highsmith will not support her allegations against me. They are untrue, totally unsubstantiated and useless. Let us assume Professor Bell was really murdered.

At the beginning of the session today however Mr. Hendricks, the famous Chairman of the Agency, declared that the professor had been regenerated and had even given Inspector Red Kyle some prescription. I wonder why you make every effort to punish the murderer while the victim is still alive and kicking."

"I can see you put yourself in the murderer's shoes and you are doing the right thing. It is quite provident of you. I'd strongly advise you to start searching for mitigating circumstances," Ella Boon said abruptly. Her gray eyes had lost their usual abstracted concentration and flashed taking on the challenge that the blonde beauty had hurled in the air, flaunting her ability to behave disruptively.

"I have never pleaded guilty to a murder charge and I never will," Adrienne Tott said cheerfully. "I succeeded in wrenching you out of your apathy, Inspector Boon. It does my heart good to see you enraged. Contrary to popular myth, your equanimity is not unshakable. I coped with the task of disrupting it and I think I my effort should receive high praise. I'd like to ask you a question: what happened to the guy who looked very much like Theodore, I mean the stranger who wanted to eliminate Don Highsmith, dear Jennifer's great sexual consolation? I bet you, gentlemen, will make him out to be a regenerated freak as well. Theodore, the loyal butler, has been successfully subjected to regeneration, now he is alive and kicking, fairly well-off, but he is absolutely inhuman and callous That was your theory on how regeneration worked, wasn't it, Inspector Hughes?"

"Now I will describe how the brutal murder of the famous professor took place," the young inspector said. "I will give you another chance to state that what I say is definitely true and correct. Hopefully, you will be partially exculpated when all the facts are known. You convinced Don Highsmith to write the note, in which he said he had committed the murder. Professor Bell, by your own admission, was on the list of your lovers. You could easily visit him while all the people in Jacksonville groaned in the face of the epidemic. You went to the professor's office on the pretext of asking him to help relieve the symptoms of your suffering.

"You killed him. Perhaps you poisoned his tea or offered him a drink having a soporific effect. You'll tell us later what you did. Then you plunged the five knives deep into his back. You knew that the professor was not a 'reverse effect' guy therefore you could regenerate him after the murder took place.

"That is why his dead body was kidnapped from Agency's mortuary. While the abduction of professor's corpse took place, you, Miss Tott, were being held in custody in the Agency's central building. It is clear you did not abduct the body, your accomplice did. You killed the professor at the crucial moment when he was about to supply Ella Boon with information on the Trail of Tears Experiment. Your accomplice and you, Miss Tott, wanted Ella Boon eliminated from the investigation.

"So you made Don Highsmith write another note which you "found" on your bedside table. The note cast suspicion on Inspector Boon and she landed herself in big trouble: she was imprisoned in the Black Hole, the cooler from which no one has as yet escaped. Even if Professor Bell had been regenerated to resume his work on the experiment, Ella Boon would have been neutralized.

"You, Miss Tott, and your accomplice could control the professor: you knew how to regenerate human beings. I am convinced that your list of eight thousand women who applied so eagerly for your 'recuperation procedures' was of critical importance to your career! You quite rightfully believed you would attain a god-like stature: you would be the deity bestowing upon the common mortals good health, glamour and prosperity. First, you will reign over Jacksonville then over Northern Europe, a dozen of years later over the whole continent, over the whole world!"

"Inspector Hughes, an hour ago I asked you to make an appointment to see your doctor," Adrienne Tott spoke slowly sounding really concerned. "Now I plead with you. You need medical advice; you seem to be suffering seriously from a psychiatric disturbance. As far as I know there are rehabilitation centers for men of all ages where you can recover from your illness. You are talking utter nonsense. Soon you will tell me that I am an insect and we all are on the small red planet Mars."

"Stop that, Adrienne," Ella Boon said her hollow voice trailing off as if she spoke to an entranced audience in an ancient temple of the dead. "We have a witness. One you could not have possibly expected to see here now. Inspector Kyle, I repeat specially for you: a witness you know very well, who has come here to talk to you"

"It is very unpleasant you should choose to address me of all people, Ella," the red-haired inspector said, displeased.

"Adrienne Tott, I will describe for you how the abduction of Professor Bell's dead body took place," Ella Boon said. "You killed the professor, you knew he was not a 'reverse effect" person and therefore he could be regenerated. But his corpse was in the mortuary. How could you steal it from there? You already had a brilliant idea: you thought of Sergeant Martin Posse who bore a striking resemblance to Professor Bell. Sergeant Posse was on duty guarding the mortuary on the day when the professor's dead body vanished into thin air! In my opinion, it was not pure coincidence.

"Let us again remember who had designed the work schedule assigning that interesting task to Sergeant Posse. After long and tedious investigation we proved that our colleague, Inspector Red Kyle, had drawn up the duty rota. Now I will explain to you in details what happened to Professor Bell's 'dead' body. I was late for the session of the Executive Council of the Agency, the only members of which were the inspectors attending our meeting today. Somebody had slashed one of the tires of my car. I had the key to the mortuary, so I had been identified as the prime suspect. However, the truth was quite different.

"We all noticed that in the course of the session Red Kyle often reached out his hand to his heart. That made us all think he felt ill. I don't know if you remember: he left the discussion of the Council for a while. Perhaps at that time Inspector Kyle had regenerated Professor Bell."

"What is she jabbering about now? It's absurd!" the red-haired inspector shouted. "That woman would be better off in a mental hospital."

"After the regeneration, Professor Bell became stronger and more energetic," Ella Boon went on unperturbed looking at no one in particular. "The professor simply got out of the building and the staff members thought it was not their boss, but Sergeant Martin Posse on his way back home. After all, the two of them looked so much alike, didn't they? The public had already been informed that the professor was dead.

The question is what happened to the real Martin Posse. He was not on duty that day. You remember: several days ago Val Hughes and Red Kyle were engaged in a fierce dispute. Val Hughes maintained he had submitted a report as to when Sergeant Martin Posse was to go on leave. Kyle was positive that no such report had ever been filed. Val Hughes's report was not saved in the computer. Perhaps somebody must have made a special effort to delete it. Martin Posse had been simply eliminated; I suppose he had been regenerated as well. This is pure surmise on my part but I don't doubt I will soon have it confirmed."

"She's talking nonsense! Somebody make her shut up!" Red Kyle shouted jumping up from his chair.

"I will not let you insult me, Red," Ella Boon said firmly. "I've already told you that an eye witness will come forward with evidence, a witness you wouldn't imagine I could produce. To cut a long story short, let me now explain the reason why there were five knives stuck into Professor Bell's body. The very thought of Adrienne's delicate hand plunging the blades into the cold dead flesh makes me sick."

"I have never stuck any knives into the professor's body," Adrienne Tott declared, perfectly calm. "I have nothing to do with the murder and I am positive I will sue you for slander, Miss Boon."

"All right," Ella Boon agreed. "Perhaps you did not plunge the knives into Professor Bell's body. Most probably our colleague Red Kyle did it. He was the one who wanted the five 'reverse effect' guys browbeaten into panic and obedience. He didn't know who they were. Larry Hoffburg had mentioned before Theodore killed him that the five 'reverse effect' freaks were the embarrassing error in the experiment. Jennifer Cost said that when they were close enough to one another the epidemic struck our town and all the 'normal' people were racked with agonizing pain. The conclusion is that the 'reverse effect' guys caused serious problems. In fact, after the second peak of the epidemic the young woman who swapped her newborn son for an expensive automobile, came back to look for her child. I have a theory that might sound absurd to you: the five 'reverse effect' persons, or those of them who are still alive, have a peculiar effect on the rest of the regenerated patients making them again capable of feeling compassion and love, of being human. The physical expression of that was excruciating pain. The 'reverse effect' patients could not be regenerated and therefore they had to be eliminated one after the other. It must have come as a shock to Red Kyle when he learnt that his accessory

Adrienne Tott, the woman he was in love with, was a 'reverse effect' individual. I think that was why he fainted."

"Nonsense! Shut up, Ella!" Red Kyle growled.

She did not look at him.

"Kyle, as I have already mentioned, we have a witness to the killing. Would you be kind enough to pay close attention to what I have to say? Thank you. Let us concentrate on the five knives stuck into Professor Bell's body. There were five 'reverse effect' individuals in Jacksonville, the town where the experiment began. Red Kyle had to eliminate all of them, but first he had to intimidate these people into giving themselves away. He learnt that Adrienne Tott was a 'reverse effect' freak as well. It was not a coincidence that one of the notes said she was to be the next corpse! All this happened for the simple reason that Miss Tott was the woman Red Kyle was in love with. Who were the other "reverse effect" personas? Initially, the list was suspiciously long: 1. Adrienne Tott; 2. Larry Hoffburg; 3. Val Hughes; 4.Ella Boon; 5. Professor Rupert Bell; 6. Don Highsmith; 7. Red Kyle.

The Professor should not be included in the list because he had been regenerated; ergo he was excluded from the club of the 'reverse effect' monsters. The same was true of Don Highsmith. Red Kyle is not a 'reverse effect' guy and he knows that very well. I suspected him at a very early stage: I called him on the day when Professor Bell was killed, the day of the horrible second peak of the epidemic. Red Kyle's voice sounded strange - strangulated and slurred. To sum up, there remain only four 'reverse effect' enemies in Jacksonville. Kyle does not know one of them, but the crucial point here is that the inspector has no idea how he could find out the unknown freak. There will always be one stalking 'reverse effect' threat, one error in the experiment that could thwart all his plans and ambitions. One obstacle that has been placed in his path could ruin everything damn it!

"Red Kyle never doubted that the 'reverse effect' guys were no more and no less than five. Adrienne Tott learnt that from Professor Bell, so Red Kyle had to think carefully before he struck again. Furthermore, the inspectors working for the Agency knew that one of them had turned traitor acting entirely in his or her own interests. Poor, poor Larry Hoffburg! He must have blabbed something very important to the sleuths before he got killed.

Kyle, I wonder if you would be interested to hear my views on the issue of 'reverse effect' guy number five?"

"It requires strong effort of fevered imagination to concoct that nonsensical theory, Ella Boon." Red Kyle said. "I thought you'd never stop gassing. There is not a shred if evidence that"

"You have worked with me for decades, Inspector Kyle. You should know I do not formally write or say something if I am unable to prove it."

Ella Boon spoke quietly her words cold freezing the twilit air in the room. She remained perfectly composed her tall thin figure immobile, her eyes glowing dully, puzzling frigid eyes showing no emotion, no response, nothing.

"There are two questions, to which I have no answer," Ella Boon went on her voice clear and slow. "On the one hand, I have received medical treatment in Walnut clinic and I have no memories of the time have spent there. On the other hand, Val Hughes has also undergone medical treatment; Professor Bell saved his life as he had saved mine. But Inspector Hughes can remember everything about the procedures, the medicines, the injections, and even about the nurses who took care of him. My first question is: why some of the patients completely forget about the treatment that they have had while others remember even insignificant details?"

Ella Boon was suddenly quiet a moment's stunned silence making them all look up.

"Will you answer my question, Red Kyle?" Ella Boon asked as her red-haired colleague rose from his chair shouting angrily.

"What are your grounds for asking me? You are crazy, Boon. I have nothing to do with the experiment"

"Very soon you'll say something quite different," the tall thin woman interrupted him her distant eyes staring into space. Cold and calm, at that moment she looked very little like a human being. "The second question I'd like you to answer me is related to Theodore, Larry Hoffburg's butler. In my opinion, Theodore was a man playing an important role in the Trail of Tears experiment. He managed to eliminate Mr. Hoffburg, one of the 'reverse effect' guys, the minute when the president of Toys International was about to disclose valuable information concerning the experiment. Theodore looked strangely familiar to me. I thought and thought trying to remember where I had seen him. Unfortunately, nothing cropped up. In my view, the medical treatment I had received in Walnut clinic and the subsequent loss of memory could be related to the total lack of information about Theodore in my mind, a man I feel I had known. I hope Kyle tell us something about him."

"All you said is pure guesswork and I don't intend to confirm your absurd conjectures," the red-haired inspector declared as he turned to the Chairman of the Agency, his muscular back to Ella. "Bob, with your permission, I'd like to leave the session of the Council. My colleague's views tend to the extreme. Her theories are arrogant nonsense, which makes me mad. I have never boasted of my skill in putting up with the whims of our prima donna, Ella Boon. This time she went too far."

"Inspector Boon," Val Hughes said nodding at his high-ranking colleague. "You were the first among the inspectors who had received medical treatment in Walnut clinic and you remember nothing whatsoever about the procedures. My abiding memory of my stay in Walnut was of precision and perfect order, all the more vivid and clear in my mind today. I think that you were the first case in the very beginning when Professor Bell's method had not been fully developed yet. The subsequent cases, like me, suffered no loss of memory, which might logically mean that the method had simply been corrected. The professor improved it eliminating the side effects including loss of memory."

The young inspector paced up and down the room deliberately turning his back on Adrienne Tott.

"As for Theodore, let us concentrate on the hard facts of which we are sure," Val Hughes went on looking at Ella Boon. "Theodore introduced Adrienne to Larry Hoffburg. As Mrs. Jennifer Cost had suspected all along, he might have supported the relationship between Adrienne and Larry, facilitating their dates and life together although he called Adrienne names when Mrs. Cost was nearby. It was Theodore who brought Miss Tott to Toys International and therefore he gave her a chance to become Larry Hoffburg's business partner, the charming lady who found the easy victims, the candidates for regeneration in the future. Let us leave our colleague Inspector Kyle to say a few words on that issue."

"Val, you were the only person in the Agency I went to have a drink with on my birthday," the red-haired inspector said quietly. "I trusted you. I hated the evening of my birthday to be as empty as all the rest in my life. We usually had a beer. Now, Val, you are with them. They got you and they are all lying to you. They are trying to make me a scapegoat for somebody else's incompetence. Ella cooked up a story doing her best to involve me in a dirty affair I know nothing about."

"I promise you that you will take back what you've just said, Kyle," Ella breathed her eyes glinting.

"I admired your indomitable will to win, Red it was there at the very beginning of your career in the Agency, "old Bob Hendricks said quietly, standing again, looking thin, frail, his face a drab cold patch in the darkened room. "You were a stern, dogged boy working hard to be always number one, the strongest, the cleverest, the best. I liked you so much, Red. You could make a brilliant Chairman of the Agency coping with stresses and strains of the job like no one else. To my eye, you were the one to be in the limelight, the leader, the center of public attention enjoying ladies' adoration, provoking men's envy. Deep in your heart you knew how much that idea attracted you."

Bob Hendricks's suddenly hardened sounding metallic. "Just imagine you are the only man who can control the mechanism of regeneration. Thousands pleading eyes follow every your gesture and you decide if people will get rid of a horrible disease or writhe in agonizing pain. You can restore terminally sick patients to life; you will give them health and prosperity if you choose to. Who will live on, who will die shrieking in a squalid hospital? It's up to you. You will possess the power of a god! A cruel god thirsty for human sacrifices who must be persuaded all the time how loyal his worshippers are. An idiotic deity whose aim is to corrupt humankind, an ogre who leaves, after each regeneration, calculating healthy monsters capable of surviving no matter what opposition they trample underfoot. Freaks of nature controlling immortality that after each subsequent death are to be born hardier, better calculating killers, richer and more appalling criminals!"

"Stop it!" Kyle shrieked. " The whole story is nothing but a pack of lies, Bob! They deliberately mislead you. You are too frail and they've used that!"

"There are, however, a few 'reverse effect' individuals in the ocean of the immortal, powerful regenerated semi-gods. When the "reverse effect" nonentities get together" Old Bob's voice suddenly thickened with emotion. "Oh, then, Red, the regenerated human beings start groaning with pain.

"After the agonizing seizure is over they remember the children they have abandoned, the friends they have put to death, their beloved ones they have betrayed. The pain makes them human again. The 'reverse effect' guys are the glaring error in the experiment, Red, these miserable and weak 'reverse effect' freaks. They should be regarded as a last resort of nature to preserve humanity when all other means have failed. Nature would not allow complete degeneration of values like love, trust, and sympathy, Red!

"Didn't you think about that? You were desperately looking for the 'reverse effect' enemies because you wanted to destroy them. But Adrienne Tott, the woman you love, is a 'reverse effect' monster as well."

"Adrienne Tott is not the woman I love and everything you said is nonsense! I don't care about any 'reverse effect' idiots. You must be crazy to speak like that, Bob!" Red Kyle had risen from his chair and took a step towards the Chairman. "Don't say anything more!"

"Adrienne was afraid of you, Kyle," Ella Boon said calmly her flat voice tying Red Kyle's muscles in its icy invisible knot.

His face darkened as he clenched his fists.

"Adrienne Tott had concealed from you the fact that she was a 'reverse effect' individual. She had been scared all the time; she had tried to turn to me for advice because she had been sure I was a 'reverse effect' woman like her. So she admitted to me and to no one else that she did not feel pain while all the people around her collapsed in agony, suffering. Am I right, Miss Tott?"

"You are talking nonsense, Miss Boon," Adrienne said but Ella Boon chose to ignore her remark. "I think it is high time we told Inspector Kyle who the fifth 'reverse effect' freak is," the blonde beauty suggested.

"I don't give a damn for him," Red Kyle shouted his voice trailing off, dead like a broken bough, stony silence falling over the twilit room.

The Chairman of the Agency stood up, ran his colorless fingers through his thin white hair, and spoke slowly as if he was afraid his words would hurt the air.

"Red Kyle, you learnt, perhaps by accident, about Professor Bell's experiment and his success. You quickly saw the enormous benefit you could derive from the scientist's achievements. At the moment when he declared he wanted to reveal the startling research results to the public you, or perhaps your accomplice Adrienne Tott, killed him in order to eliminate him temporarily until people calmed down. Then you organized the kidnapping of Professor Bell's dead body.

You had to regenerate him, of course, and perhaps you did, but you knew that was a package of temporary measures. There was an error in the experiment: there were the 'reverse effect' guys, so you needed the professor desperately. He could correct the mistakes in the future regeneration procedures and he and only he could destroy the would-be 'reverse effect' freaks who might result from the experiment in the years to come.

Your major task was to kill the five 'reverse effect' enemies in Jacksonville. You could continue the Trail of Tears experiment on one condition: that you destroyed all the 'reverse effect' threats. All of them!"

"A complete fabrication from start to finish! You cannot provide any proof," Inspector Kyle's voice echoed like a shot of a gun in the far corner of the room. "A pack of lies!"

"Red Kyle knows who the four 'reverse effect' individuals are," the Chairman went on sounding unexplainably sad. "He will find a way to eliminate them one after the other. Adrienne Tott will be the last corpse because she was his beloved one."

"I already said I had never known Inspector Kyle," the blonde beauty declared, perfectly calm. "I will state as much in any court you may choose to take me."

"But Red Kyle doesn't know who the fifth "reverse effect" freak is," Bob Hendricks's voice cracked hiding in the dark like a little insulted child. "Red has to find that man by all means. He, or perhaps Adrienne, stuck five knives into Professor Bell's body hoping that the fifth, the last one of the monsters, will give himself away."

"A barefaced lie!" the red-haired inspector thundered.

Outside, the wind was blowing from the twilight and the all the windows were closed. No noise and no signs of life in town could penetrate the Agency. The Main Street, the couples in love, the young mothers pushing baby carriages, and the students from the local high school on their way home had nothing to do with the gray building. No ordinary citizen had ever seen the narrow asphalt alleys and the cypress trees, the corridors and their special plastic floors, which absorbed the noise produced by the steps of the living beings in the Agency.

"I'd like to tell Red Kyle, "Bob Hendricks's voice broke and died and when the man spoke again Ella Boon shuddered. It was tinged with an unusual touch of grief and doom, his old weak voice. "Red, I want you to know that I am the last 'reverse effect' freak" the Chairman of the Agency raised his head, strained his muscles to straighten his shoulders and his whole body convulsed. "You had to kill me first, Red!"

Red Kyle trembled slightly, grabbed the coffee table with both hands his head hanging low. He seemed scarcely to breathe, as he remained immobile, frozen, impenetrable for a whole minute and when he finally spoke his face appeared grave and impassive.

"I have nothing to do with the Trail of Tears experiment, Bob. I suspected that you were one of them well, one of the "reverse effect" individuals as early as the very first outbreak of the epidemic. The pain had been so desperately severe that an old man like you could hardly live through it. Do you remember how many times I asked you about your headache?"

"Yes, I do," the Chairman whispered. "But I thought you cared about me, Red."

"I did I still care about you," the inspector muttered without raising his eyes.

Strained silence reigned weighing the people down. The Chairman, feeling utterly exhausted, slumped into his chair. Val Hughes appeared tense as he screwed up his eyes, his whole body leaning towards Kyle. Dispassionate and calm, Ella Boon searched Adrienne's beautiful face fixing it with a penetrating stare.

"You won't turn into a god, Red," the Chairman of the Agency said unexpectedly. He was breathless from the exertion of standing up, but his voice gradually deepened cutting through the silence. "I am happy I stopped you. Mankind does not need murderous gods who have no mercy on the sick and dying men, on the outstretched hands pleading for one more day, one more hour. I am sorry for you, Red. I asked you once if your salary was good enough for you. I wonder what you did with your money. You might have saved up millions"

"Shut up, Bob!" Inspector Kyle shouted as his hands dropped hitting hard the coffee table.

"Inspector Kyle, I accuse you of incitement to Larry Hoffburg's murder," the Chairman of the Agency continued firmly." I accuse you of conducting experiments ruining the health of thousands of people. I accuse you of betraying the institution you have been working for and of slandering our colleague Inspector Ella Boon. I accuse you of causing the two horrible outbreaks of the epidemic, of the unbearable pain racking the whole town!"

"Nonsense, Bob! Nonsense!" Kyle's face looked thin and sallow.

"All right then. I thought you wouldn't admit to it of your own free will," the Chairman of the Agency paused then his voice sounded hollow yet powerful. "Bring in Professor Rupert Bell! Now we all will listen to what he has to say."

Kyle's face clouded, his skin stretched taut across the cheekbones appearing as though it had been patched together from several different gaunt pieces. The twilight in the room thickened closing in as a tall stoutly built figure of a middle-aged man appeared in the rectangle of light behind the open door.

"Bell?" Red Kyle whispered. "Bell!" His red-haired head made a rapid move, his colorless lips twitched as he bit the collar of his shirt. A muffled crunching sound was heard then Kyle's arms hung loose, his cheeks sagged, a grimace of pain distorting his strong handsome features.

"Red!" Adrienne Tott shrilled. "They cheated you! He's not Professor Bell he's that sergeant Doctor! Call the doctor immediately! For God's sake!"

"You have summoned Sergeant Martin Posse, old Martin" Red Kyle drawled his speech slurred. "Clever, very clever I'll bet you young Val concocted this foul smelling scheme He's good at that. Clever, clever."

"Call the doctor!" Adrienne Tott jumped up from her chair rushing to the telephone.

"Don't do that, honey," the red-haired man said his lips pouting in a strange joyous sulk. "Doctor or no doctor, I'll die in three minutes They still

135

haven't found the professor, so they can't regenerate me The poison will damage my brain for good. Adrienne, I wouldn't advise you to regenerate me. Who'd care about a litter - lout in good shape with a hopeless swelling in his brain People don't need a bloodthirsty god like me."

"You shouldn't have done that, Red!" Adrienne Tott whispered.

"I will never rule the world, not even Jacksonville," Red Kyle smiled. "I won't be the next Chairman of the Agency Hum, a bleak future in prison with well meaning guards has never tempted me."

"Adrienne Tott, I think you are guilty of complicity in Larry Hoffburg's murder and in Professor Bell's murder. I accuse you of illegally conducting experiments ruining the health of unsuspecting people!" Ella Boon said staring at the young beautiful woman. Again, Val Hughes noticed in her eyes the sharp, murderous gleam that had frightened him some days ago. "Adrienne Tott, I accuse you of blackmailing and extortion, of giving false evidence, of"

"Wait a minute, Ella!" Red Kyle whispered gasping for air, choking. "Come up to me, please I'll tell you something and it's interesting, I can assure you. Ella, do you remember that photograph do you remember the wedding ring on your finger, Ella Do you remember? Do you remember what Larry Hoffburg said when you interrogated him he mentioned something about a little fair-haired girl Ella that girl was our daughter yours and mine, Ella. You married me it happened at the time when you were at Walnut clinic The two years you have completely forgotten Adrienne Tott grew up decent people adopted her. Theodore found them Theodore kept an eye on our daughter all the time, Ella Adrienne Tott is our daughter your daughter, Ella. Ha! Ha! She doesn't know she's my daughter She must have wondered why I chose her why I disclosed the method of regeneration to her Ella!"

The two women, the blonde pretty one, and the middle aged inspector with the cold expressionless eyes and bony shoulders bent over Red Kyle as violent shivers convulsed him. His eyelids looked discolored, half closed, his lips were suddenly covered with white froth as his fingers trembled crooking then extending, bloodless, fearfully transparent.

"You, Adrienne" Kyle's words were hardly audible. "You asked me if I didn't like you. Why I didn't want to sleep with you but you are my daughter, Adrienne I remember you as a small, thin, thin girl Val! Val! You cooked up that scheme good for you! You sent Posse instead of the Professor I guessed right I knew it but it makes no sense to go on"

"Yes, I devised that plan," the young inspector said quietly. "I hoped you had nothing to do with the experiment. I hoped against hope, Red!" he whispered. "I loved your birthdays when we drank together. You were my only friend."

But the red-haired man could not hear him. He was dead.

Adrienne Tott and Ella Boon did not dare to touch him. Neither of them cried. Val Hughes bent and closed his eyes. It was quiet in the dark room. The light of the sunset tried to creep in through the window but the murky corners absorbed it transforming the last bright sun's rays into tense oppressive twilight.

God of Traitors

"Ella!" Bob Hendricks said in a weak, hollow voice. It seemed to Val it was for the first time that he had heard the Chairman sound so indecisive as if another man, a stranger, was talking in the dark. "Ella, I've heard that Adrienne's treated her mother with respect and consideration I mean her adoptive mother Adrienne's covered all her expenses: living, household, medical etc. I'm sorry, Ella. But I have to tell you all that."

Inspector Boon did not say anything. Her eyes fastened on Adrienne dilating with surprise, fear, disappointment, and expectation. Her face did not look like a piece of plastic for the first time since Val Hughes met her.

"Ella!" Bob Hendricks finally broke the long silence. "You know what? You look very pretty. I am not lying to you. Well, Adrienne is familiar with the processes of regeneration. Perhaps, one day in the future, people will be able to fight and cure diseases but can remain human beings. What do you say, Ella? You know what? I've heard that Adrienne's treated her adoptive mother quite kindly and sympathetically. All the neighbors were said to envy the old woman."

Inspector Boon was silent. She felt a warm blush creep up to her cheeks and raised her hands to conceal it. Suddenly she thought it was not typical of her to give vent to her feelings. She had never done that, so she turned her back on Adrienne, Bob Hendricks and Val Hughes. No one interrupted the embarrassed silence.

"Red was an odd man," Ella said quietly.

This time, her voice did not sound cold and flat like the surface of a frozen lake.

THE END